I0746220

Supernatural

Beatriz Clemence

Copyright © 2024 by Beatriz Clemence

All rights reserved.

No portion of this book may be reproduced in any form without written permission from the publisher or author, except as permitted by U.S. copyright law.

Contents

Prologue

F ive years earlier...

"What about a little dog? Like a golden retriever or--"

My mother interrupted me by her loud, hearty laugh surrounding our car. "Is that what you classify as small, Taylor?"

I looked at her amused expression from the rear view mirror and gave her a sheepish smile. "I mean, it's smaller than me."

My mom laughed again but it quickly turned into a scream. Looking away from her, I saw a car that was driving on the wrong side of the road, coming straight for us. It didn't even truly register to me what was happening until I saw my mother's hands begin to hesitate on the wheel...

And then everything slowed. Suddenly it was like I was watching a 3D movie in slow motion with the best graphics ever made. The scream I had been holding in escaped my mouth and without thinking, I put my hands out in front of me and I focused on our car.

We were forcefully jolted to the right at the same moment time went back to normal, throwing me in the corner furthest from the oncoming vehicle.

Now, the car was coming at an angle. I had only a split second to catch my mom's eye before the car sped forward and hit us. I didn't feel any pain as the screaming stopped and everything went black.

I woke up at the hospital later that day. The doctors told me it was a miracle I had survived, and even more so that I made it out with little to no injuries. The witness report said that they hadn't even noticed we had moved slightly out of the way until they saw where the opposite car hit us. What was supposed to be a head-on, completely fatal collision turned into only one casualty, the driver's side to be completely caved in, and the back right corner to be the only safe spot in the car. That is where I was seated and I walked out of there later that night with only my father by my side.

That was the day I lost my mother and I thought it would be the biggest turning point in my life. However, that wasn't the only thing that happened.

It was also that day I realized I was different.

———————

This is the new edition of Supernatural Abilities! It is completely rewritten, giving it more depth, character development, plot, and other aspects that are needed for a good, exciting story. First chapter is still getting posted on Sunday, but I wanted to get this up to get you guys excited :)

Thanks for sticking around with me and I hope you like how this story goes. It is still the same characters but with a much better plot (though many main ideas are the same, just not presented the same way. Ja feel?)

Chapter One - The Dream

- -

My heart was pounding in my chest.

I struggled to stay quiet while someone creaked through the school. My eyes widened when I saw some mist swirling from underneath the door as if someone had opened a freezer. I wanted to make a break for the open window but I knew that they would hear as soon as I moved a single inch.

Slowly but surely, I began inching up to the corner and, while keeping my eyes on the door, made my way towards the window in the black room.

I saw a shadow pass from the crack, two feet moving so slowly and then paused for one moment, slightly turning--

Then suddenly, a hand covered my mouth and I found myself staring into black eyes.

I woke up with a start while I gasped for breath in my sweat covered state. I wasn't in that dark room. I wasn't being kidnapped. I was alone, in my bed, and completely safe. Taking another deep gulp of air, I collapsed back into my pillows and waited for myself to calm down.

Lately, nightmares have plagued my nights. Some worse than others, but this one seems to be a recurring one. It wasn't early enough to start getting up and because going back to sleep wasn't an option, I decided to wait out the time until the beeping of my alarm signaled the start of my day. I watched time go by until the numbers switched to 7:00 and I sighed in disapproval.

Beep, beep, beep.

With a groan, I flipped over and buried my face into the pillow while the alarm kept blaring on. With a sleepless night, I definitely did not want to have to endure eight hours of a useless school day.

"Taylor, get up already!" My dad called from his room that was adjacent to mine. I knew that he couldn't care less if I got up or not, but only really wanted me to turn off the alarm so he could enjoy sleeping in until noon like he usually does.

Regardless, I sat up and reached over to my nightstand to stop the unforgiving beeping. Light just barely peeked through my blinds but I was already squinting at it like I was looking staring straight up to the sky on a clear, sunny day. Slowly stretching my legs out, I got up and began my easygoing morning routine of getting ready for school.

After getting ready as easily and quickly as possible, I headed downstairs while dodging the mass amounts of leftover beer bottles that my father must have ingested the night before. His alcoholism started after my mother had died in a car accident. For the past five years he has turned to booze as his family and left me to fend for myself as much as I possibly could. Sometimes when I was younger, and lucky, I was left with babysitters who would take care of me more so than he ever did following my mom's passing.

My mother's death killed him too, in which some ways. He lost his job and hasn't gotten one since. More times than one has our house almost been taken away from us but he always somehow gets the money to pay off the bills and his alcoholic tendencies. We didn't have any other family and many times social services have threatened to take me as well, which is a scary thought. As much as my father and I don't get along, I would much rather be with him as opposed to living in some foster home.

"Dad, I'm leaving!" I called up to him but only got a muffled snore in response. Sighing, I headed outside and began the trek to school.

My only hope for getting out of this dull, small town was to be accepted to a college far from here. While my grades were subpar, I just hoped that I would be granted admittance to at least one of the many I apply to. However, I wouldn't only need acceptance. I would also need to scavenge up some kind of scholarships, loans, and financial aid to help me pay my way through. That way I'd be able leave my father to his own demise and away from the memories that swarm me here.

The walk isn't very long--maybe ten minutes or so--but around halfway there, a strange feeling went through my entire body. Taking a deep breath, I suddenly turned around, halfway expecting someone to be following me but received an empty sidewalk. After looking around for a few moments, I hesitantly turned back and continued moving forward but that uneasy feeling never left.

Once I arrived to school, that feeling just about vanished when I walked up to some peers all huddled up in a circle. "Hey, Taylor!" My best friend, Ryan, called out and pushed through the others to greet me with a large bear hug. Laughing, he finally set me down after a few crushing second and looked down at me with a wide grin. "How's my favorite girl?"

Ryan was my best friend. All the other people at my school were complete opposites of me: privileged and all about the high-school life. I stayed out of all the drama and rumors that I hear while walking down the hallways every day. It wasn't my forte nor did I want to be associated with people like that. It didn't necessarily mean that I hated everyone, but rather I chose to stay out of the social realm and closer to one person who truly stuck by me all these years: Ryan Campbell.

Despite being only one year older, Ryan definitely looked way more mature. I have the soft, baby face going for me and blond hair that made me look three years younger. The only thing 'striking' about me was my eyes; a sharp gray that stands out more than all of my gentle features. Ryan, on the other hand, had lost all the extra fat and went through the puberty rounds at an alarming speed. He looks more like a college student as opposed to a high school senior, especially once he lost his braces a few years ago. I've been noticing more girls giving him attention and I knew he would get around quite a bit. However, he always stood by me as a friend, and God knows how crazy I would go if I lost him as well.

"I'm good, Ry," I smiled back and we began walking into our school.

"You sleep well?" He asked and when I didn't respond, he gave me a sad look. "Taylor--"

"It was just another dream, no biggie."

"Yes, biggie," he countered with a concerned look on his face. "You've barely gotten any rest recently. You should go to a sleep therapist or something."

"It's just nightmares. I'll man up soon," I joked and continued walking to my locker just in time to grab my books before the warning bell signaled that class was to start soon.

Ryan clicked his tongue and shook his head. "I'm just worried about you. Please try to figure something out for my sake?"

I rolled my eyes at him and told him I would but had no intentions to. I've suffered from frequent nightmares and strange dreams since I was twelve. I wasn't a stranger to barely getting enough sleep.

After saying goodbye to Ryan, I left him to head to my homeroom. There weren't many students there considering how many seniors skipped nowadays, so I took a spot in back, near the window and relaxed in my seat. We don't do anything in the thirty minutes of homeroom every day, but near the end of the school year we will have to present our senior projects. That's in many months so I haven't even started, let alone picked a topic, so I chose to put my head down on my desk and try to soak up any ounce of sleep I could.

"Taylor?" My head shot up at my name and my teacher was holding the phone away from his ear and looking straight at me. "Principal Peters has a favor to ask of you. Could you head down to his office with your belongings?"

I nodded, gathered my things, and left with a ward of my peers' eyes following me out. I had asked my principal for a letter of reference earlier this week and he said if I stayed out of trouble, he would write me one. I'll do practically anything this guy says as long as he plans to give me one.

The hallways were strangely empty for being a Monday morning. I expected many late students shuffling down the halls or teachers gathering worksheets and equipment for the day but no one even passed me. Above me, the student announcements echoed through the emptiness around me and just like earlier when walking here, I got that unearthing feeling go through me.

I reached the main office and said hello to the receptionists that greeted me at the door before heading farther back and knocking on his door. Principal Peters answered it clad with his usual smile, striped shirt, and balding head before ushering me inside.

"Oh, Miss Buckley, I'm so glad you came down here!" He said with a big smile. "I have a huge favor to ask you."

I took a seat across from his desk and folded my hands in my lap. "What is it?" I asked, slightly disappointed that this wasn't the letter that I had originally hoped that I would get from this trip.

"We're expecting a new student any moment now and I would like if you could give him a tour of our school. His father requested that he gets one and I think you would be the perfect student to do it!"

"Of course," I said with a grin but was already internally dreading it. I'm not the most social person--That was Ryan--and I don't think I could handle the ample amounts of small talk this guy would put me through. "When?"

"Today," he answered. "You would have to miss your first period and maybe the second as well. Just make sure it's a good tour, answer any questions he could have, and be as nice as possible."

I gave him a fake laugh, "I'll try my best."

With that last sentence, another knock sounded at his door and Principal Peters got up and answered it with a smile. "Hello, welcome to our school!" He answered and reached his arm out to the people that I couldn't see yet. "You must be Cole."

"That I am, sir," I heard a deep voice answer.

Peters opened the door wider and in walked an older man, presumably this 'Cole's' father and a boy.

I first noticed his clothes. Dark jeans and a white V-neck. He looks like he has been out in the sun quite a lot, which makes me assume he's from a different place as our weather here only consists of clouds and rain. He didn't look like his dad at all, which was quite abnormal, unless he was adopted. He was attractive, to be honest. Tall, dirty blonde hair...

A cold feeling rushed through me as his eyes caught mine and I froze because I knew those eyes. I would never forget their dark, black color.

This was the guy from my dream.

———————————

Woohoo! Chapter one is now posted. Thank you SO much for all the love on the prologue! I plan on posting every few days so I can keep a rhythm but still be ahead by a few chapters. However, if there's enough comments/votes, I might post a bit earlier as a thank you :)

But in all honestly, you guys are the best. I hope you enjoyed this chapter and the beginning of the whole trilogy!

Chapter Two - The Beginning

I was too focused on this guy that I didn't even notice that Principal Peters was still talking until I heard him asking for me to introduce myself.

"Uhh..." I stuttered out and cleared my throat. "I'm Taylor."

"She'll be the one giving Cole, here, a tour this morning. She's quite a remarkable student so she can answer anything you could possibly want to know," Peters continued but I couldn't bear to let my eyes leave this boys'.

"Actually, I forgot I have a test in first period," I rambled. "Math, y'know, pretty important for graduating. There's no way I'll be able to do this tour with that--"

Peters interrupted me. "I'll talk to your teacher and get it rescheduled. This is pretty important and I can't imagine anyone else but you showing him around."

He continued on about our school while Cole and his father took a seat in the chairs next to mine. I held sweat beading on my palms while I tried to slow my breathing. I felt this Cole guy looking at me from the corner of his eye as I struggled to keep my cool. I knew I was failing even though I'm pretty good at keeping my emotions in check.

Maybe this was a coincidence. After all, it was just a dream. They don't come true.

But they do. Many times I have dreamt of something and later, days or weeks following that night, they end up happening. Minor things like acing a test or Ryan falling down. Some a little bit more important like my dad getting arrested or finding myself having to testify for him in court. Never has anything as scary as the dream I had last night has had even the slightest chance of actually happening. I know Deja vu is a real thing, but this is more than that.

"Taylor?" Principal Peters brought me out of my thoughts. I looked up at him and he had a slightly concerned look on his face while he looked at me. "Are you ready to go and give the tour now?"

I glanced over at Cole and he had an unreadable expression on his face. "Uh, yeah. Let's go then." Without even looking to see if he was following me or not, I practically ran out of the office.

It didn't take long for him to easily catch up with me. My great escape seems to have not been so fast or good. "So you're Taylor," he said as he strolled to my side. "My dad said that the principal kept going on about you and how you're such a good student when he requested a tour."

"Ha, yeah..." I trailed off. "He, uh, seems to like me."

"That's an understatement. You must be his number one student." I didn't reply to that so we continued on with that awkward silence that I was so worried about being prior to being introduced to Cole. Oh, how little my problems were ten minutes ago.

We walked around the school and I would point out different landmarks for him; the gym, music hall, auditorium. It's small around here, only a couple hundred students attending this high school. The town we lived in wasn't the biggest so everyone practically knew everyone.

"So what grade are you in?" He asked.

"Twelfth."

"Hey, me too!" I snuck a peek up at him and he was grinning back down at me. "It's a pretty nice school. Got any siblings that go here?"

"No, I'm an only child."

"Really? Must be lonely with just your parents around the house, huh?"

I clenched my teeth. I expected small talk, not a game of twenty questions. I liked the awkward silence more than this. "It's only my dad and I."

"Oh," he paused for a moment. "Divorce?"

"My mother died when I was twelve."

"Ouch, sorry to bring that up... Cancer, I'm guessing?"

Didn't this guy have any boundaries? This is a topic I have never liked nor wanted to talk about with anyone, let alone a complete stranger. Even Ryan hardly knew the entire story of my mom because I didn't like talking about her or what happened. He knew her before she passed away, we were best friends long before that as well, but he holds back from asking questions due to my feelings concerning the situation.

"No," I looked him straight in the eye with a standoff-ish glare. "Car accident."

He only hummed in response, obviously backing away from the forbidden topic, and continued walking in silence. The only sound that would break the reverie was myself occasionally making comments about the campus. He didn't seem too interested in the tour and acted more like his head and thoughts were in another place.

"Can we look at the field?" he finally asked. "I'm really into sports." Nodding, I started heading there.

The field was a bit separated from our actual school. It's on the same land, but a barrier of trees lined the outside. It was a regulation sized football arena, but didn't have the same pizazz as a larger, wealthier school would. It was still early morning so all of the gym teachers had their classes inside to save their students from getting cold in the dewy air.

"This is the field," I went on to say. "We're known as the Bobcats and--"

"Taylor Elise Buckley," he interrupted me. I turned around and he was leaning against a tree. "Seventeen years old. Daughter of Richard and Sarah Buckley. Born and raised in the same exact city, state, and house for your entire life."

I narrowed my eyes at him. "How do you know that?"

"I know quite a bit about you, Miss Buckley," he began looking at his hands. "From your entire background to the reasoning behind your eye color. Your parents have green and brown ones, so how exactly did you end up with gray? I'm not an expert in genetics or anything, but I'm pretty sure that's not how they work."

Putting my fear and wonder about how he knew all this information about me on hold, my mind stuck to what he was saying about my eyes. That question was always a mystery to me. No one in my family, let alone anyone I know, has eyes like mine. I'm not just talking about color, but overall appearance. When people think of gray, it's usually a bland color. However, my eyes are unusual, striking even, and bright. They stand out and while I liked them, it was always to go-to compliment for other people to give me.

Cole continued on without answering the question he proposed. "You were a bit of a mystery to us because you showed little to no signs of power besides that one day." His eyes met mine. "But just seeing you now, I know this lead was correct."

I gave him a confused look. "What are you talking--"

"You're different. Not just a little off meaning you like pulp in your orange juice or crunchy peanut butter or whatever other weird tendencies that people like or do, but I mean you have an ability."

I stared at him in utter confusion. "Okay, you're not making any sense and quite frankly, I need to get to class now. You saw every part of the school and I'm sure you can make it back on your own--"

I began walking back but he stuck his arm out to block me. I would have normally pushed past or went around, but when flames licked up his entire arm, I was taken by surprise. His arm was bare, no clothing in the way or anything as the fire flickered and I felt the heat radiate off of it. The air was damp so any kind of random forest fire would have been next to impossible, though it would make no sense because it was focused on him. However, above all, Cole looked fine--comfortable even.

"What the hell are you?" I jumped back. He had a slight smirk on his face as the flames disappeared and he crossed his arms over his chest.

"I'm just like you."

It's a short one, I know, but I promise the the upcoming chapters (after all this introduction business) are longer!

Well, thank you SO much for all the support on the last chapter! I hope this one spikes your interest as well. As always, thank you for everything and see you soon for chapter three :)

Chapter Three - The Explanation

Cole continued on like nothing was out of the ordinary.

"Well, not exactly like you. I'm a Fire. You must be a Mind. You communicate your ability through your brain while mine is mostly physical." He snapped his fingers and a single flame sprouted from the tip of his thumb. "Samuel said he felt the original burst of power five years ago, sound familiar?"

I wanted nothing more than to ignore what this guy was saying, figuring that he was playing some kind of joke on me, but his words rang in my mind. Five years ago was the car accident that ruined my entire family.

That day my mother died while I came out of it with only a few scratches. Everyone said it was a miracle because the car was hit at such an angle that made me be in the only safe spot in the car. I knew it wasn't some crazy coincidence but cast away the thought that I had made the car move because that's insane.

Or so I thought.

I must have had my emotions written all over my face because Cole smirked. "Remember now?" I didn't say anything so he chuckled under his breath at my stubbornness." Look, I have to be serious now. I'm not really here to go to some high school. I'm here to get you to training."

"What if I don't want any? What if I enjoy this high school?"

"Then you can stay here and die."

I froze and began breathing heavily. After all the joking today, Cole now has a serious look on his face.

"We're known as people with Supernatural Abilities and you're definitely not the only one. Once found by a Seeker, which is Samuel for this area, my fake father as you know him as, we send someone out to educate them, which is myself in this case. There are more of us and we're all training to survive. We're a dying species, Miss Buckley. We're being killed by Catchers, which are basically rogue supernaturals. They have these creepy pitch black eyes to tell them apart from us, not just the iris but the entire thing. They have powers but their brains only focus on killing rather than good. They're run by a single leader who changes them, makes them not know right from wrong but only to seek out and kill us. They're smart, cunning, and strong. Stay here and you'll die without any training."

The facts scared me, but I refused to believe it. While I hardly believe that I'm on some episode of Pranked, his words are nonsense. As much as I want to get away from this town, I need to finish high school. I need to graduate and move onto college so I can get a good job. If I've gone under the radar of this Seeker guy for so long, who's the say I can't stick it out with these catching things? That is, if they're even real.

Standing up a bit straighter to look bigger despite my short frame, I spoke in an even tone, "I kindly decline your offer."

He raised an eyebrow at me, "Oh?" I nodded, expecting him to fight me on it. "Okay then. Enjoy your life, Miss Buckley."

My eyes widened in surprise because I expected a much bigger fight from him considering how he was sent here to bring me back. "Really?" I asked in a disbelieving tone.

He shrugged and started walking away from me. "Can't force you, y'know. Goodbye, Miss Buckley. It was nice meeting you."

I watched as his tall figure disappeared through the trees and into the school. I stood there in utter confusion at all that went down in the last five minutes. Now, having time to process his words, the past four years now have made sense. All the weird things that I had cast off as unnatural puberty symptoms are now coming together. However, despite everything that has happened and I have seen I still almost didn't believe it.

Hesitantly, I raised my arm and pointed my hand at a fallen branch. Taking a deep breath and focusing all my energy into it just as I did the day of the crash, I slowly raised my arm and the branch followed along in the air. Never in my life have I tried to do something like this. I thought the car accident was some sort of freaky coincidence but then everything that Cole had said made sense. I am different. I'm not like Ryan or my father or anyone else in this school. I'm more like Cole.

Pulling my hand away, the branch dropped back onto the floor and I released the breath that I didn't realize I was holding in. Despite having abilities that I only realized today, I don't belong at that place Cole wanted me to go to. I've lived an almost normal life for seventeen years, there's no way I'm stopping that lifestyle now.

Straightening up, I pulled my backpack more onto my shoulders and headed off to class for the day. It went smoothly with no sign of Cole whatsoever. I guessed he just ditched the whole facade and went back to whatever life he was living before.

However, once lunch rolled around, I knew he wasn't leaving.

I should've figured that the 'goodbye' he gave me earlier was utter crap.

"Hey, Taylor!" Ryan called out as I approached our table. "This is Cole, he's new!"

I gave the fire boy a glare while I walked straight to the table in anger. Who was this guy thinking of when he decided to become buddy-buddy with my best friend?

"Already met," I deadpanned. "I gave him a tour this morning."

Ryan's eyebrows shot up. "Really? That's great! He's pretty cool, huh?"

I stared at Cole who leaned back and crossed his arms over his chest with a little smirk resting on his face.

"The coolest," I gritted my teeth together and threw my backpack onto my chair.

"God, what's up with you today?"

I continued eyeing Cole while I answered Ryan, "I must have woken up on the wrong side of the bed."

Ryan snorted and went back to eating his pizza. "I'll say..." he mumbled under his breath and I sat down in defeat.

Lunch was quiet with the occasional chatters by Ryan. He kept asking Cole questions about his life before moving here and while he never noticed, I heard the minimal replies that would keep Ryan happy but not give anything away.

"Hey, I actually need to use the restroom," Cole said near the end while getting up. "Taylor, can you show me where to go and possibly take me to my next class?"

"I'm sure you can find it yourself--oof!" Ryan kicked me from under the table and I huffed out. "Fine, I'll show you."

I grudgingly got up and left the cafeteria with Cole following suit. I saw a few people, girls in particular, staring at him while we walked by. Our school was rather small so getting a new student was rare, especially one that is attractive. The girls here have been around the same guys since kindergarten so any new face was a blessing.

Once we were a safe distance away, I abruptly turned around and he almost ran into me. I looked up at him and said, "Look. I know you don't really need to pee, so what do you want?"

"Can we meet up tonight?" He asked and all anger left my face and was replaced with confusion. "I can show you what it's like to have your abilities and how to control them. It's pretty fun stuff."

While I didn't want to, the curiosity as to all that Cole could do really interested me. "Where and when?"

"Here, about ten o'clock. I have a key so we can easily get into the school."

"You have a key?"

He laughed and showed me one from out of his pocket. "Samuel has a way with words," he said mysteriously.

"Samuel?"

"My"--air quotations--"dad, remember? He's a Mind just like you so he's pretty capable at being influential." He paused and continued a few seconds later. "So you'll come?"

"Why not?" I gave him a little smile. "I want to see all that you can do."

"Okay, see you tonight, Miss Buckley," He said and headed away.

"You can just call me, Taylor!"

He turned around as he continued walking, giving me that smirk that I have seen more times than not. "Nah, I don't think so."

————————

And chapter three is officially concluded!

Again, it's another small one but they're slowly start getting longer as there's more excitement going on. Thanks for everything you guys have done! I love each and every one of your comments and often find myself laughing at some of your guys' reactions :)

See you soon for chapter four!

Chapter Four - The Encounter

It's not hard to sneak out when your father is an alcoholic and doesn't care what you do or where you go anymore. Grabbing a jacket and my keys, I headed out in the cool night around thirty minutes before I was supposed to be there. The sky was already dark as summer was over now, so the air was crispier than usual. However, the walk was nice and comforting. Some might think that going out by yourself at night is dangerous but in a town where everyone knows each other, it's pretty safe.

Once I arrived at the school I headed up to the front steps to wait for Cole to show. I was here pretty early so I sat down on the steps and leaned against the front door. To my surprise, it slid out from under me and flew open. Cole must already be here.

Walking through the empty hallway was kind of surreal. Eerie, in a way. I called out his name several times but never got a response in return. I finally decided to head to the cafeteria, hoping that he would be there because it's such a central part of the school.

Once I reached the lunchroom and walked inside, I saw a single figure sitting with their back turned to me. In the moon-lit room, it was hard to see any kind of features but I saw dark hair and who else would be at the high school late at night?"

"Cole?" I called out and the person stood up rather quickly. In the brief moment it took for them to turn around, a cold wave rushed through my body.

The person wasn't Cole and despite the dark room, even I couldn't miss the pitch black eyes. This must be one of those Catchers I was told about.

I had initially expected some sort of monster-thing when he described them. After all, they're the enemy so they must look disgusting, right? But they looked human. The only part different was the eyes that were very unnerving to look into.

"So you're the new Supernatural," they spoke in a chilling voice that sounded almost robotic. "We finally felt you today. We have had suspicions about this area for a while now, but nothing was confirmed until this morning. You must have realized your potential, what you can really do, right?"

Gulping, I began stepping back without saying a word. I kept my eyes on them as a creepy smile spread across their cheeks.

"So what are you?" they asked. "Fire?" They started walking closer to me. "Water?" Another step. "Air?" They kept getting closer and closer. "Earth, perhaps?"

With every ounce of power and adrenaline I had, I flipped one of the lunch tables toward the Catcher and turned to run.

"Ahhh," I heard behind me, seeming unfazed by the fact a table hit them. "You're a Mind."

I sprinted through the halls and I knew they were following close behind. I took the chance to peek behind me and see they were really close. Without another thought, I turned around and threw my hands out in front of me focusing on time, just as I did with the day my mother died. When I opened my eyes, the Catcher was moving slower so I ran ahead to try to find a place to hide because slowing down time for a long period would only exhaust me.

I finally found an unlocked science room so I ran and hid in the corner behind some desks and breathed out as I felt the power slip from me and time turn normal again for everyone. Trying to control my breathing, I kept my eyes on the door hoping the Catcher couldn't figure out that I was in here.

My heart was pounding in my chest as I struggled to stay quiet while someone creaked through the school. My eyes widened when I saw some mist swirling from underneath the door as if someone had opened a freezer as I peeked from the corner. I wanted to make a break for the open window behind me but I knew that they would hear as soon as I moved a single inch.

It was in that moment when I realized this was a part of my dream. Instead of Deja vu like I always cast stuff like this off as, I knew it had to do with the fact that I have an ability.

Slowly but surely, I began inching up to the corner and, while keeping my eyes on the door, made my way towards the window in the black room.

I saw a shadow pass from the crack, two feet moving so slowly and then paused for one moment, slightly turning--

Then suddenly a hand covered my mouth and I found myself staring into black eyes.

I screamed out, expecting a Catcher but realized it was only Cole in the same moment that the thing following me burst into the room.

"God, you're such an idiot," Cole said through gritted teeth as he stared down the Catcher. "Why would you scream during a time like this?"

Without a second to spare, he threw me behind him and flames engulfed his arms. He threw a ball of fire at the Catcher but water escaped from its hands and disintegrated it.

I watched in both fascination and fear as the two began fighting with fire and water. Cole was obviously more skilled but the fact that he was facing his weakness gave him a harder time. Every time he would get the advantage, the Catcher would win it back by getting him off guard. Finally, Cole caught the Catcher at an angle where the fire hit its side and it screamed out in pain. In the brief moment of it being distracted, Cole jumped in and finish off the fight. The two grappled on the ground for a few seconds before Cole pressed both hands on its chest, scrunched up his face in concentration and the Catcher stopped moving. At that point, I knew it was dead.

"Let's go," Cole yelled at me but when he realized I wouldn't move, he grabbed my hand and pulled me along.

"What the hell did you do to it?" I gasped out while we ran down the empty hallways. I always thought entering a class right before finals was scary but this was way worse.

"Internally baked it," Cole said evenly while we exited through the main doors.

I was confused, "Wha--it's not a cookie! What about the body?"

"Samuel will get it, but we have to go," he pushed and pulled on my arm harder to get me to go faster.

We ran through the empty streets and what was previously a nice walk at night became one of the most frightening experiences I have ever gone through. We arrived at my house and it didn't even cross my mind to ask Cole how he knew how to get there. I saw that my dad's car was gone so he must be out at his nightly bar-hop adventures. I didn't know if that was a good or bad thing considering I was taking a boy I had just met today up to my room. We went upstairs and he grabbed my school bag from the bottom before tipping it upside down, letting all the contents fall to the ground.

"What are you doing?" I gasped out, trying to catch my breath as he began throwing clothes from my closet in the bag.

"They know you're here now. You can't stay here anymore or else you will die. Once one knows, they'll all find out. You're putting yourself, friends, and family all in danger by staying here. You need to come train so you can at least protect yourself."

I didn't say anything and watched as he packed my life away in a few simple bags. He grabbed a notebook and pen from my fallen school supplies and threw it at me.

"You need to write a note to your father. Say you're running away and not to go looking for you. It makes it more difficult that you're under eighteen, but Samuel will deal with the cops and any searches that go on. Right now he's dealing with the body so that'll have to happen tomorrow--"

"Can I say goodbye?" I finally spoke up and asked. "My dad and I don't have a good relationship but I know Ryan would be hurt by me leaving."

A look of pain, the most emotion I've seen out of him since this morning, crossed his face. "You can't give them anymore trails to people you care about, Taylor. We really have to go."

I didn't say anything but looked down and continued writing the note to my father.

Finally, most of my stuff was packed and we were running out the door and to a car that must have appeared there courtesy of Samuel at some point while we were gathering my belongings. Prior to us leaving, I grabbed a photo of my parents and I before the accident and threw it into my pocket. Cole tossed all my bags into the back of the car and we got in. As he backed out of the driveway, I looked up at the house that I spent my entire childhood living in while I left with a boy I met this morning.

We drove in silence for the first ten minutes or so before Cole spoke up.

"I'm sorry..." he said softly." I know today has been crazy but you have to do this."

"I know."

"You'll see them again, I promise to make that happen."

I looked at Cole and the smirking, cocky guy I met this morning was nowhere to be found. Instead I found a caring man who quite literally saved my life tonight. Granted, he also ruined it by taking me away from my whole life here but I knew this has to happen.

We drove for a while longer, passing city by city as we got farther from my home. "Cole?" I asked and he turned and looked at me for a second before turning back to the road.

"I thought you fell asleep," he commented. "What's up?"

"Can I ask where we're going?"

He was silent for a moment before he finally spoke.

"We're going to Supernatural Abilities."

__________I apologize if this one is a mess because I wanted to post a chapter this weekend but I'm working the entire time. So here I am, posting from work, without having proofread it before. I'll definitely come back and revise it soon, but I hope you enjoyed it regardless of the mistakes!

Chapter Five - The Drive

T hank you to @crookedaydreamer for the amazing cover above!!___________

We drove all night and the following day as well, only stopping for food, gas, and coffee. While I slept haphazardly through the trip, Cole kept driving without even mentioning getting a hotel or stopping to sleep in the car. In the times that I was awake, I would ask him questions about Supernatural Abilities.

"The leader is a woman named Patricia Galen, but you should only call her by her last name. There's five types of abilities: Mind, Fire, Water, Air, and Earth, but you can be roomed with anyone regardless of their ability. We have five different levels based on advancement, power, and ability to handle themselves in the real world. Five being the strongest and about to 'graduate' per se, while one is the start and where most of the newbies begin. To determine your level, you'll be tested--"

"Tested?"

"A fight with people of all abilities. They base how hard they go and difficult they are based on how you continue to perform. Don't worry, there's no right or wrong way to do it. Just try your best and you'll be fine."

Later that night, I was awake with Cole while he drove on the highway. We were the only car there considering how it was so late. I looked at Cole who looked absolutely exhausted. Dark bags hung under his eyes and his eyelids were half closed. His coffee was gone but apparently we're close so he won't get another.

"Do you want to stop for the night?" I asked, a bit worried about his state.

"No, we have to get there."

"You're about to fall asleep--"

"I'm fine."

I shut my mouth and relaxed in my seat again. After a few minutes of looking outside at the dark night, I felt myself dozing off. I was almost asleep when a horn went off and I jolted up.

In the split second, I noticed oncoming headlights straight in front of us and Cole dozing off. Their horn was blazing so in a brief moment of strength and adrenaline, I forced the car to the side causing our car to skid into our correct lane as a semi-truck flew past us.

During this, our bodies slammed into the sides of the car and Cole woke up, immediately realizing his mistake and righted the car, coming to an abrupt stop on the side of the highway. The only sounds in the eerie night was my heartbeat pounding in my ears and our mangled gasps of air as we had narrowly avoided death.

"Well..." Cole started. "I think we should get a hotel for the night."

Unable to talk, I just nodded in agreement and he slowly began driving towards the nearest exit. We drove in silence through a tiny town until we parked in front of a quaint motel with a gas station across the street.

"You stay here," Cole said while getting out of the car. "I'll book us a room."

I watched as he headed off to the inside of the lobby, leaving me in silence and darkness.

I was exhausted--Completely ready to pass out right then and there. I'm sure it had to do with the mass amounts of power I had to expel in order to save both of our lives, especially since I've been sleeping all day. In comparison, I felt as if I had ran a marathon.

Cole finally came back a few minutes later with a sheepish look on his face. "Bad news," he said. "I didn't expect a night stay before leaving, so I only had enough money for a single."

"Oh, that's fine."

"You sure? I can get the floor or couch or something--"

"Cole," I gave him a look. "I know you're not going to start anything and we're both ready to crash for the night. I couldn't care less, this isn't elementary school."

He gave a little chuckle and grabbed a bag of his and one of mine as we headed up to room 104. When he opened the door we were greeted by a dingy room and, as promised, only one double bed. Being a motel in the middle of nowhere, this was about as much as expected.

He put our bags in the closet and fell onto the bed with a moan.

"It isn't much, but this might be the most glorious moment of my life."

I laughed and sat down on the side, eyeing the bathroom in the corner. I've been in a car for over a day and the only thing I want to do is clean off all the muck and grime from the adventures.

"Mind if I shower?" I asked and his groan that he answered me with was taken as a yes.

The bathroom and its component were all small but I couldn't care less. After shutting the door, turning on the water, and shedding my clothes, the warm shower became a heaven. Granted, their complimentary soaps and hair products weren't ideal, but it was enough to get the job done.

However, showers were always places to think. I'm sure Einstein came up with all of his discoveries in one of them, if they were available during his time. I mean, how would I know? I just ran away from public school and any chance at graduating.

48 hours ago I was having the nightmare about an event that would occur 12 hours later. It's crazy to think that none of this--Cole, Supernatural Abilities, Catchers--happened years ago because it does not feel like it's only been two days.

I wonder how my dad is doing or if he even noticed me gone and the note I had left. I'm sure Ryan is freaking out, wondering where I am. I haven't had much time to think about all that I had left behind because I've been numb to it all. Being in Cole's presence made me feel like I had to be tough and powerful like him, but now, in the comfort of this water and my own being, I was able to reflect on all the crap that has happened to me in the past few hours.

I felt the tears fall before the sob escaped my throat. The mixed with the shower water but I could already feel my face puffing up. I was like that for a while--crying while standing in water until my skin pruned up.

When I finally got it all out, I turned off the shower and stepped out, wrapping one of the towels around my body. Wiping off some of the steam on the mirror, I looked at myself for the first time in two days. In all honesty, I looked like a mess but at least I was now a clean mess.

I dried myself off and pulled on some new, comfier clothes to sleep in before stepping out. Cole was lying with his back on the bed and his arms shielding his eyes from the light. When he heard the door open, he peeked out from the cracks of his elbows.

"You okay?" he asked and I gave him a nod. "Sure you are." He sat up and gave me a knowing look. "Need a hug?"

"I'm fine--"

"Your red eyes tell me something differently. Give me a hug."

"Cole--"

"You need it."

Giving in, I sat down and gave into his embrace. I felt his face go into my hair and I was surprised that, despite the hours spent sitting in a stuffy car, he still smelled good. After a few seconds, we both pulled back and I mumbled out a thank you to him.

"No problem," He smiled and reached out to turn off the light. I hadn't even noticed that he changed into a t-shirt and shorts to sleep in. Once it was dark, I snuggled into the uncomfortable bed, stretching my legs out.

In was silent for a while until Cole broke it. "Hey, Taylor?"

"Yeah?"

"I want to say thank you for the whole car fiasco earlier."

I flipped over to my other side. "No problem. You saved me with the Catcher so we're even now."

"I guess so," he mumbled and was quiet for a moment until he spoke again. "But you have to admit, the moving the car thing was pretty cool."

I cracked a smile and shook my head without realizing that he couldn't see it in the darkness. "Just making sure we don't die too quickly."

And with a little chuckle on his end, both of us relaxed and finally went to sleep.

———

I woke up from a blissful sleep to the sound of glass breaking.

I expected the worst--Catchers breaking in, a fight about to ensue, the jist. However, once my eyes focused after being woken up, I found myself staring at Cole fresh out of the shower with a towel wrapped around his waist and brushing his teeth in front of a mirror. Looking down, I saw broken glass and water everywhere.

Cole swore under his breath and he gave me a sheepish look. "Sorry for waking you up. I didn't realize that I still had soap on my hands when I tried to pick up the cup."

"It's fine," I said as I gave him a little smile and he turned to continue getting ready to leave.

I found myself looking at him and I never expected him to be as fit as he was. Under his clothes, he seemed healthy, yeah, but not nearly as muscular as his body actually is. I guess from training for a long time to fight, you're bound to end up looking good.

I finally looked up and he was smirking at me in the mirror while he continued brushing. Blushing, I turned away and stretched my arms out to relieve some of the kinks that sleep had given me.

"How much longer until we get there?" I asked while getting up and going through my bag for clean clothes.

"A few hours," he noted while stepping back into the bathroom and spitting out the toothpaste into the sink. "We should be there mid-afternoon."

I hummed in approval and opted for some jeans and t-shirt so when we do get there, people don't think I'm some sort of slob.

"Hey, Taylor?" I looked up and saw Cole throwing a bottle of shampoo right in front of me. "Catch!" I watched as it fell in front of me, a few feet away.

"That was an awful throw," I commented as he gave me a look.

"That's because I wanted you to use your powers."

"Oh," I dragged out the word. "I get the game now."

He shook his head with a little grin on his face. "Okay, ready now?" I nodded and he threw it again.

Focusing all my energy into that single bottle, I stopped it mid-air. I saw as Cole nodded and held out his hands as I threw it back to him.

"Good," he said and placed it back in its proper place. "So you have telekinesis, what else you got?"

"Well..." I messed with my fingers because this was always a forbidden topic for me to think about, let alone talk about. "I can slow down time."

He nodded. "Time manipulation. Can you speed it up or make it stop all together?"

"I don't think so."

"This is what Supernatural Abilities will teach you. Odds are you can't or won't learn every ability that Minds can have, but you'll be learning a lot more. There's healing, shields, teleportation--"

"What?" I asked, my eyes practically popping out of my head. Teleportation? I mean, I always wondered how celebrities would be in a new country on the other side of the world every day. However, I think it is more likely due to the vast amounts of money they have available to waste as opposed to crazy, unnatural superpowers.

He laughed. "Yes, it's a real thing. I've heard it's really taxing and energy consuming, but some Minds can do it."

Nothing much was said after that because we began getting ready to leave. Cole finally got dressed and I was able to also brush my teeth and change as well. After an hour or so, the two of us checked out and were on the road again. This time, we were both well rested and more comfortable with each other having spent the night in a cheap, dingy motel together.

After a few hours of driving, we pulled over and got some food for a late lunch and ate it while continuing on. I knew we were pretty close by now and nerves were already taking over.

"How does this place work? Are there schedules or is it a free-for-all, or what?"

"You train with your levels or abilities every day. It's a mixture of learning information and then hands-on training and fighting. Usually mornings are sit-down lessons and after lunch we train."

"So it's like a school," I concluded and he shook his head.

"Only if you count people getting burns, frozen, hit with rocks, blown away, and mentally controlled a school all while learning how to properly kill someone."

"Fine, you're right." I paused before speaking again. "So what level are you?"

"Five."

"The highest?" He nodded. "Wow."

"After years of training. I can see you being a Three or Four. You're pretty good, but definitely not able to protect and save yourself by any means."

"But that's why I have you," I teased and he chuckled.

"Only for now. Once you finish your training, you'll be sent out on your own."

"Alone?" I asked in fear.

He nodded. "There's not enough of us to go around for pairs. You're usually on your own unless you marry another Supernatural or something. They don't separate partnerships like that."

I was about to ask another question but we turned off the paved road and went into the forest. I grabbed the handle in fear as he continued off-roading like nothing was out of the ordinary.

"Is this where I find out that you're actually a kidnapper and you're taking me in the woods to murder me, hundreds of miles from my home?"

"Relax," he said nonchalantly as he swerved to avoid a fallen tree. "This is just the way to find the place. You can't very well have a training area full of kids with supernatural powers right in the middle of a city, can you?"

I mumbled out a few swear words as he continued driving. After a few minutes the trees finally cleared to show a gravel road and a barred fenced area with a single gate leading in. The land was huge with not as many trees as the forest but enough to provide cover. Far into the distance I could see people running around with several huge buildings in the middle. I had only expected some tents and some ponds, but that's it. This place was much bigger and better than I had anticipated.

Cole must have been waiting for my reaction because I heard a chuckle come out of him while he stopped the car so I could have my few seconds to stare.

He held his arms out as wide as he could in the car.

"Welcome to Supernatural Abilities."

____

As promised, this chapter was way longer! The story is actually beginning now, and next chapter you'll be seeing a few familiar faces :)

I hope you all enjoyed! Thank you all for all the support. All views, comments, and likes are always appreciated and I genuinely read each and every one (And tend to laugh at some of your reactions). I noticed we got into the 200s for fantasy books! Let's try to get it even closer to that #1 spot by spreading the word about it and like/comments, yeah? :)

See you all in a few days for the next chapter!

Chapter Six - The Meeting

Thank you to @skyler1135 for the amazing banner! _________We pulled up to the gate with a single kiosk in the corner that held a bored looking teenager who was playing on some handheld device. Cole cleared his throat and the boy immediately perked up.

"Oh! Hi, Cole," he said while fumbled inside with unseen buttons. The gate finally opened and the boy gave him a sheepish smile. "Go right on in."

"Thanks, Johnny," Cole called to him as we drove through the gate and on a gravel road lined with tall, old trees. As we neared the school, more and more people began showing up in the grassy, forested areas around us. Most were just sitting around and talking, but some were messing with their powers. Rocks were in the air, water spun around... it was so crazy to me.

We finally pulled along the back of the building where most of the people were gathered around eating. It was around dinner time and a nice day, so many of them were sitting at picnic tables or on a blanket on the ground. There were only a few parking spots and cars as Cole pulled into one and put it in park.

"Listen," he started. "People are going to stare at you and whisper and such, it's all very high school. You're new and we don't get many new people around here. They all mean the best but they're not very inconspicuous about it."

I shrugged and he got out the car as I following suit. All the chatters of the common area dwindled down as it seemed that all eyes were on Cole and I. He ignored everyone and went to the trunk to grab our things. Once he did, he nodded his head towards a door for me to follow him.

While the outside of the building was pretty, the inside was the same. There were few doorways but Cole and I went down the hallway until the very end that held double doors leading into a room. Cole knocked and the doors opened to reveal a middle-aged woman sitting at a desk.

"Hello, glad to see you're back," she said while getting up and holding out her hand to me. "I'm Patricia Galen. It's so nice to finally meet you, Taylor."

"Likewise," I smiled as we all took a seat.

"So I see that you all ran into a Catcher along the way," she raised an eyebrow up from underneath her glasses. I must have had a confused look on my face because both her and Cole laughed. "I'm a Mind," she answered the questions that hung out in my head. "I can read your thoughts."

I got uncomfortable at that point because I have always liked my head and thoughts being my own but that isn't the case here. She cracked a slight smile at my discomfort but continued on without saying anything about it.

"This is Supernatural Abilities, the place where people like us train to protect ourselves and kill those who threaten us--The Catchers. I know Cole has told you other specifics so I won't bore you with all that again. We will let you get all settled in tonight and tomorrow we'll test you on where you place in our ranks."

"Where is she going to live?" Cole asked and Galen turned towards the computer to search for something.

"Why don't we put her with Claire? After all, Bethany left a month ago and she's your friend as well. Might as well introduce her to your friends while we're at it, right Cole?" I was confused at her words but Cole gave her a face while Galen laughed. She turned towards me and said, "You're going to like it here, I can tell. You'll learn so much but at the price of leaving the people you love behind. As Cole said, it's for their protection as well as yours that you do this."

"I know," I mumbled and she gave me a small smile.

"Well, if that's everything, I'll let Cole show you to your new home for a while. Claire is a nice girl. Loud, but very nice. See you tomorrow, Taylor, and if you have any questions, feel free to ask anyone here."

The two of us bid Galen a goodbye and I following him through the building once again. We went up a few flights of stairs while Cole went on about my new roommate.

"Claire is really nice. We've been friends since she got here. She's dating my roommate, Alex so you'll be seeing him around a lot as well. And me too, I guess, since you're living with part of my group of friends."

"Oh, darn. I bet you wanted to ditch me as soon as we got here," I joked, bumping my hip with his.

A smile spread onto his face. "How'd you know?"

We continued walking until we found ourselves in front of a door labeled '201.' Cole fished out a key from his pocket and unlocked the door, going in first. When he opened it, a squeal was heard from the inside of the room.

"Cole! You made it back--" She stopped when Cole stepped out of the way to reveal me.

There was a girl sitting on one of the two beds in the room and next to her was a boy. They looked around the same age as me, but much more joyous and excited. Well, the girl was.

"Claire, this is your new roommate, Taylor," Cole introduced. "Taylor, this is Claire and Alex. Mind and Water respectively."

Claire jumped away from Alex and off the bed to come give me a big. "It's so nice to meet you! We all heard about what went down with your pick-up. Bad luck, huh?"

I gave her a sheepish, shy smile. "Yeah, little bit."

"Well, it's a good thing that you made it back here in one piece. Cole must have been your knight in shining armor--"

"Okay, enough, Claire," Cole interrupted her before turning to me. "I'm going to head out now if you're all good to go. I have a lot to do before tomorrow and you need to get some rest before your test." Now he looked at Alex. "Hey, man. Wanna come with me? Leave the girls to their bonding rituals."

Alex stared at Cole for a second before giving Claire a peck on the lips and following him out. Before the two boys left, he turned around and said, "Nice to meet you, Taylor. Hopefully Claire doesn't drive you crazy too."

I gave him a smile while Claire shouted out an objective, 'hey!' and then they left. Once the door fully shut, Claire snorted.

"A lot to do, my ass," she mumbled. "He just wants to go see Vanessa before lights are off."

"Vanessa?"

"His girlfriend," Claire answered and I felt a little frown rest upon my lips because Cole never once mentioned any romance here. "She's the worst but I guess he likes that kind of girl."

"What?"

Claire gave me a look. "Let's just say she's not the most decent person out there."

I nodded once and put my bags down on the extra bed. The room was small, but as expected for a 'dorm' room. There was two of everything: beds, dressers, and shelves. There wasn't an attached bathroom so now on top of getting used to being at a place filled with people with magical powers, I have to shower in front of them too. It wasn't decorated or anything because I assume Claire was also practically abducted from her home prior to coming here and didn't have time to go decor shopping. It's a room, not a home.

"Did Cole show you around?" Claire asked and I shook my head. "Here, I'll give you a tour. Drop your bags and let's go!"

I found myself walking about Supernatural Abilities while Claire talked a mile per minute. She showed me the mess hall, the training rooms while were lined with state of the art exercise equipment, and even the ladies showers, something that I was very disappointed to see.

"So how did you find your powers?" I asked while we walked around outside. There were only a couple students out right now since it the evening air had a slight chill in the air.

"I was fourteen and trying to cheat on a test," she admitted with a slight red tinge on her cheeks. "The person in front of me was a child-genius--smartest one in the school! I was focusing so much on them that I heard their thoughts in my head and I knew all the answers they were putting down."

"So you can read minds?" I asked.

She shrugged. "Only if I want to and focus. It's not like I hear a million voices in my head all the time. It's only when I put in the effort to, which I usually don't because I feel that it's pretty invasive."

That relaxed me more. I was already put off from Galen being able to read into what I'm internally thinking, but having my roommate able to do that too? That would be awful.

We started heading back to our room after seeing everything that I needed to. I still didn't know how to get around but I have Claire and maybe even Cole to help me out while I get used to being here. My roommate was easy to get along with and talk to so at least I didn't have to pretend to like her. She was a bit too eccentric at times, but it was all in good fun and easy to get used to.

"Tomorrow you have your placement test," Claire stated as we walked up to our room. "Don't stress about, it's not a big deal to anyone anymore."

"Why not?" I asked in confused at how she stated her words. Why would anyone else care?"

"We've all seen so many placements that it's kind of a normal thing by now."

I didn't say anything while the words soaked in. "Wait," I stopped once the realization reached me. People watch?"

"The whole place does," she crinkled her eyebrows together as she used her key to open up our room's door. "Didn't Cole tell you?"

Peeved off, I huffed and slumped down on my bed. "No, he must have forgotten to mention that."

She laughed at my angry posture and patted my shoulder with one of her hands. A little smile played on her lips. "Don't worry, no one will judge you by how you do... You know, except the judges."

"Thanks, Claire," I deadpanned as she laughed. "Means a lot."

Another, very introductory chapter! But don't worry, the next one is all exciting and stuff :)

I just want to say thank you SO much yet again! Please (if you celebrate) have a good Thanksgiving and weekend! I'll be posting the next chapter in a couple days like usual.

Chapter Seven - The Placement Exam

The amazing banner above is made by @micahthewriter!

The next morning I found myself being woken up by a knock on the door. I had crashed pretty early from both stress about the test and exhaustion from the trip over. I groggily wiped the sleep from my eyes and slumped over to the door where I found Cole behind it.

"Cute," Cole commented on my sleepy appearance. "It's time to go get ready now."

I yawned and rubbed at my eyes some more. "Now?"

Cole nodded once. "Yes, now so come on."

"Let me get dressed first--"

He grabbed my arm and began dragging me through the hall. "No one's up yet and you need to get ready."

I took my arm back and I began waking up more to actually support and walk myself. I followed Cole through and out the dorms to the outside where I was greeted with a blaring sunrise and surprisingly warm weather.

"We're going to the arena," he said. "But first you need to get dressed in your proper attire in the locker room."

I barely remember Cole pointing out the arena but it was pretty far through the trees so we didn't actually get up close. This time, we actually headed there and I found myself face to face with a dome, net covered arena in the ground with bleachers lining around it. I felt like I was in some gladiatorial era.

He didn't bring me in the ring, but rather down some stairs to a nicely lit hallway. He opened up a closet and looked me up and down. "Extra-small?" He asked.

I raised an eyebrow. "For what?"

"Shirt and shorts."

"Medium and small," I mumbled as he tossed me some purple workout gear and white shoes that he had correctly guess the size. I looked up at him in surprise and he shrugged.

"Shoe size was in your information they gave me before I picked you up. Shirt and shorts? Never got. Kind of weird because I got a lot of other sizes."

I nodded, kinda feeling self-conscious that he knew all this information about me. What else could he know? My feelings should have shown on my face because a smirk rested on his lips.

"What other sizes?" I asked, suddenly turning nervous.

"A little of this, a little of that," he snickered.

"Even..."

"First thing I looked up," he winked and I felt myself turning bright red as I self-consciously crossed my arms over my chest.

I didn't say anything else and took the clothes to change in the locker room while Cole stayed in the front. They were both a light purple and comfortable enough to go on a ten mile hike in. Judging by the warmth of early this morning, we were due for a hot day so the clothes were lightweight enough to not cause any unneeded heat.

I stepped back out to the lobby area and Cole nodded in approval. "You'll start your placement test in around twenty minutes. I recommend warming up, stretching your brain, or whatever else you Minds like to do."

"I know about as much as you do about this," I muttered but decided to sit down and start brainstorming what I should be expecting. I wasn't given much information about this and was left in the dark about it all. The only thing I really got was not to worry too much about it.

"Listen," Cole said while sitting down next to me. "I get that this could be stressful to you, but like I said before, you can't do anything wrong out there. Just showcase what you can do and you'll be placed into your appropriate level. Most people get levels one or two but I think you're better than that so you'll be sure to surprise some people. I mean, a person has gone out there and all they could do was lift a pebble off the ground. You can do that, so there's nothing to worry about."

"Thanks..." I trailed off and I could start to hear footsteps and chattering above us.

"You're starting soon," He said and got up, motioning for me to follow him.

We went farther down the hallway until we found another staircase that led up to a rock wall.

"Once that drops, you have to go out there to the arena. That is your queue that the test will start. Remember, you can't really mess up or do wrong. You just need to give it your all and you'll be good. By the end of this, you'll be placed into your level which goes from one through five."

I heard someone start talking above us, presumably on a microphone but their words couldn't be deciphered. Suddenly, the rock wall dropped along with my stomach as people cheered from the outside.

Gaining confidence, I went up the dark stairs to where a door of light was at the end. Before heading out I stopped to take a deep breath to gain my composure before taking the last step to my ultimate doom.

"Hey, Buckley?" I turned around and saw Cole leaning against the wall, just like he was doing when I was giving him the tour of the school and he told me about Supernatural Abilities. "Don't be afraid of hurting anyone. Be offensive, not defensive."

I gave him a little smile and stepped out into the arena. It took a moment for my eyes to be adjusted to the sudden brightness but found myself looking at an unpaved area with rocks, a stream, and a full 360 of people in the bleachers. Directly across from me was a room lined with windows and adults sitting and focusing on me, one I recognized as Galen. Behind me, the rock wall sprung back up, locking me in the arena.

"Taylor Buckley," my name echoed through a now quiet setting. "Your placement test will now begin."

It wasn't even second after the announcement stopped that a rock came flying towards my face. Gasping, I jumped out of the before realizing that I should have used my powers. A flood of energy was coursing through me as a man rose out from out of the ground with his eyes trained on me.

He raised his arms up, making all the rocks in the arena start floating. One by one, they came soaring towards me but the adrenaline in my body gave me an advantage. Using my mind, I began throwing them off course so I wasn't in their line of target.

In the middle of this, Cole's words replaying in my mind.

Be offensive, not defensive.

A big boulder came at me but I braced myself. With my hands out in front of me, I stopped the boulder mid-flight but instead of letting it fall, I lifted it up with an unseen force until it was above my head. Dirt and pebbles fell on top of me as I gritted my teeth in concentration. With a grunt, I let the rock fly forward, straight towards my assailant.

The man held out a fist and the rock split into two, going on either side of him. However, he gave an approving nod and went back down into the ground. I caught my breath as the crowd remained silent all around me. Something inside let me know that this test was just beginning.

Then another person literally flew down from the sky, right in front of me. Her eyes were a very light gray, almost scary looking. Mine were darker, but still weren't anything close to black. Her eyes were almost white, but were eerily still pretty. She gave me a little smirk and blew on me, having the force of a car that blasted me in the wall of the arena.

Grimacing, I slowly got up as she flew up into the sky. The air around me starting picking up, forming a tornado. I found myself stumbling but shot my head up to the sky where the girl was floating and twisting her arms in a circle. I fell down to my knees and gasped onto the grass as the wind picked up. Using one hand, I reached my arm up and focused all my energy on constraining her with my mind. Finally, the air around me slowed and returned to normal as the girl was struggling against my mental grip on her.

When I finally had to drop the telekinesis, she looked down at me from the air, winked, and flew away.

At this point, I was beat. My body and mind ached as I struggled to take breaths. If they were going with the same pattern, I still had three types of abilities to go through until I was done.

Then, everything around me was on fire.

This didn't surprise very much considering that I was with Cole for a few days. A man popped down from the stands as fire swirled around him. The air filled up quickly with smoke and I felt it in my lungs as it kept rising and growing closer to me. The man across from me drew his arms together, forming a large ball of fire. A few seconds later, it started flying straight towards me.

It was that moment that I didn't realize what I was doing. Focusing all my thoughts into safety and healing, I watched as the fireball came right for me but as it was supposed to hit me, it acted as if my body was some fireproof barrier, flames bouncing off of me, and I couldn't feel anything.

It wasn't telekinesis. It wasn't time manipulation. It was something new that somehow came out of me in a time of danger and adrenaline. I had learned a new skill.

I know on my records that it only showed those two because that's what I told Cole. I looked up at the windowed room and saw them looking through papers and down at me with confused faces. Even the Fire man across from me looked surprised. He shrugged, jumped up, and climbed out of the arena while I felt this new type of Mind power fade out.

Three down, two to go.

This time, a girl came out of the pond seemingly dry and with the prettiest blue eyes. She wasted no time in drenching me in gallons of water, making me fall to the ground in a wet heap. She began pulling up strings of water that she froze along the way and shot them at me. I dodged each by scrambling out of the way but not doing anything to retaliate in my exhausted state.

She finally rose both arms up, creating dozens of icicles before firing them all at me.

I might have been ready to pass out and wanting nothing more than a nice bath or maybe even a massage, but I somehow was able to pull out enough energy to slow time down. The once menacing and quick frozen water was now traveling at the speed of a slug. In fact, everything around me was, except myself.

I got up and began hitting each and every one, making them slowly shatter with time being half the speed. To those watching, everything seems like real time so I must have been looking like I was some kind of speed runner. Once the last one was broken, I made time go back to normal and the girl looked taken aback. In a brief moment, she, too, disappeared.

The last Supernatural Ability was Mind, the one I obviously am. However, judging from what Cole had said before, the Mind ability has so many dimensions to it so each of us has different powers from one another. The next person is a Mind, guaranteed, but also a complete mystery.

That's when I blinked and found myself back in my old house.

I had no pain and when I looked down, I found a pair of jeans and a t-shirt that I would normally wear. The house wasn't destroyed like it was when I left, but rather cute and clean. It smelled not like booze, but rather chocolate chip cookies.

I followed the smell into the kitchen where a blonde woman was leaning over into the oven. When she got back up, my heart stopped.

"Oh, Taylor!" my mother said with a cheery smile on her face. "I didn't even hear you come home!"

"I-uhh--" I stuttered out while my father came into the kitchen, clean shaven and dressed well to give my mother a kiss on the cheek.

"I'm going to work now, see you two ladies when I get home," he said without the smoker's crack in his voice that I have grown used to.

"What is this?" I asked out loud while my parents looked at me in confusion.

"These are cookies," my mom said while she showed me the sheet I hadn't realized she was holding. "I'll say, they have to start teaching you more in school--"

"You're supposed to be dead," my eyebrows furrowed together.

My mother's mouth dropped to a frown, something I rarely saw during my childhood. "Did you have a nightmare last night, Taylor?"

I shook my head as she advanced towards me. The concerned look in her eyes made me almost forget what I was talking about, but I turned away, formulating my jumbled thoughts into words. "No, I watched you die. You're dead. This isn't real."

"Taylor," my father held out his hand. "Are you okay?"

That's when I noticed that his left arm had a watch on it, usually signifying that he was right handed. However, that wasn't true. My dad's dominant hand was his left, so he would wear it on the opposite side. A common mistake someone could make.

"This isn't real," I repeated and shut my eyes tightly together. "Go away, this isn't real!" I screamed and when I opened my eyes, I was back in the arena.

I didn't even realize I was crying until I blurrily looked out to see a woman with a very surprised look on her face. The arena was completely silent, not one peep out of anyone. The people up in the room all looked down at me in shock, except Galen who looked pleased.

"Taylor Buckley, your test is now over. Please stand by while we configure your results."

The girl in the arena stared at me for a few moments before heading towards the wall where the rocks when up and down once she walked through. I rubbed at my eyes, trying to erase all that remained of my tears while I felt hundreds of eyes on me. My heartbeat threatened to escape my chest as all the adrenaline, power, and energy slowly started escaping my body, leaving me ready to knock out.

"Taylor Buckley," the voice came back again. "You are placed in level five. Congratulations, we will see you in training tomorrow."

I looked out at the crowds and people looked stunned. There were some whispers and opened mouths but once the initial surprise left, the crowd exploded in cheers. It was so loud that I didn't even notice that a rock wall behind me dropped and Cole was helping me up.

"You did amazing," he whispered in my ear so I could hear. He supported some of my weight as we walked back down where I had entered. Behind us, the wall went up once more and we were greeted by a muted applause.

"Nothing to worry about," I took a breath, "my ass."

"Usually they don't go that hard on newbies, they must have known what you could do."

And that, my friends, is when I blacked out.

———————

It's this chapter that really made me realize how much I missed writing this story. I hope you enjoyed reading it as much as I did writing it :)

Sorry this update took longer than usual to get up. I still have many chapters already done but I'm in the middle of pre-finals week and too busy to even sleep. I hope the next one will be up sooner than this one was, but no promises!

As usual, thank you for reading and see you next chapter!

Chapter Eight - The Introduction

Shoutout to @sarcasm4jessi for the amazing cover!! _______________When I came to, I was greeted by bright lights shining directly into my eyes. Squinting, I turned away with a little groan.

"Oops!" I heard. "Sorry, I'll close the shutters." I heard a bit of shuffling and sure enough, the room became dark enough for me to open my eyes with ease.

When I was able to focus on things, I found myself in a room with Cole, Claire, and even Alex all sitting across from me. The couple was close together on a small love seat while the guy I've spent ample amounts of time with was on a single armchair.

"Where am I?" I asked while rubbing at my eyes. I felt a sharp pain in my shoulder and I had to stifle back a moan in pain.

"Medical ward," Claire answered while pressing a button on the wall. "Cole had to bring you here after you passed out."

I felt myself turning red and I fell back against the pillows. "Oh, man. That's embarrassing. How long was I out for?" Looking at Cole's clothes, it couldn't have been too long because he was wearing the same thing from this morning.

"Only for an hour or so," he answered when he saw me looking at him.

"And embarrassing? After what you did? I find it hard for anyone to think of you as embarrassing," Alex commented while leaning back in his seat. It wasn't until this moment that I could notice just how blue his eyes really were and how well they stood out against his black hair.

"What do you mean?"

Alex snorted. "You placed as a level five, the highest you could've gotten. Don't you know how rare and phenomenal that is?"

"You did everything right," Cole said with a smile. "But there is some bad news..."

I raised an eyebrow, "What?"

"You're a little beat up, which isn't anything serious. You'll feel it for a while but you can still train and what not. The healers will try to get rid of them as much as possible," Claire answered in her usual, upbeat voice.

"Oh, that isn't bad at all--"

"And a few inches of your hair was burned off."

My eyes widened as I reached behind my head to my ponytail. Sure enough, part of the ends were singed off, leaving a few strands on my fingers. Luckily my hair was long before, probably needing a cut anyways, so it wasn't the end of the world.

"Don't worry," Claire started. "You're still pretty. I'll chop off the ruined parts tonight."

I gave her a thankful smile and relaxed in the bed as a woman walked in, clad in scrubs and tightly pulled back hair.

"Hello, sweetie! How are you feeling?" She asked while coming to take my vitals.

I shrugged. "Fine, I guess. I have a headache and I'm ready to nap for a century but other than that and a few sore muscles, I'm good."

She hummed in approval, "That's good and expected considering all that you did this morning. I'll try my best to ease the pain as much as I can."

She pulled the blanket off of me and I was surprised to find a few scarce burns and scratches lining my legs and torso. I watched as she would press her hands against the wounds, burning from the pain at first, but then having it slowly recede to a dull ache. When she pulled her hand away from the worst of the burns on my side, I was surprised to find that it was mostly gone. I felt my eyes widen and the people in the room chuckled.

"I'm a healer, dear," the woman said as she moved on to my legs, utilizing the same technique. "Well, I'm a Mind but healing is my main ability. I might not have gotten all those crazy moves like you did, but I like being able to help people," she smiled and focused back on my ailments.

After around twenty minutes of being healed, I was finally released from my room with little to no marks from the placement exam this morning. Even my headache had resided and the only thing I truly felt was exhaustion and hunger.

"Hey, do you mind if I go and get something to eat? I don't want to inconvenience anyone so you guys don't have to join me but if I could get some directions--"

"Nonsense!" Claire butted in. "I'll come! We don't have training today anyways so all of our afternoons are free!"

I smiled at her and began the follow the three Supernaturals to a large building lined with many windows. There was a good number of people in there, ranging from around twelve years old to some around their forties or even fifties. There were many tables all around and at the front was a buffet-style arrangement of foods. I grabbed myself a slice of pizza while the others took their favorites among the rest of the choices. We opted for a seat in the corner and as we walked there, I felt the eyes on me from everyone in that cafeteria. In some ways, this place was more like high school than the one I actually attended. However, I tended to blend in there but at Supernatural Abilities, everyone stares wherever I go.

We were eating in a comfortable silence before a shriek interrupted it.

"Cole!" A girl near the door yelled, looking straight at the guy across from me. As she approached, I could see that she was really pretty with dirty blond hair and black eyes that signaled that she was a Fire like him. She ran over and wrapped her arms around his torso, pulling him out of his chair. In a second of brief confusion, I watched as she grabbed his face with both hands and kissed him.

So this must be his girlfriend that Claire was talking about.

Cole broke the kiss first with a disheveled look on his face. The girl giggled and then noticed me looking at them.

"Oh my goodness!" She exclaimed and held out her hand to me to shake. "Where are my manners?" At that, I heard a little snort come from Claire and peeked over to see Alex nudging her. "I'm Vanessa, Cole's girlfriend."

I gave her a fake smile and reached to grasp her hand. It was hot, unnaturally so. The look in her eyes told me that she knew that it was uncomfortable and obviously her doing. If that's the way she's going to be, so be it.

"Nice to meet you," I replied and dropped her hand. "I'm Taylor."

"Oh, I know who you are. I mean, I was there when you had your placement test today! Good job by the way. Hopefully we'll be training together soon," She dropped her fake smile and turned to Cole with dark puppy eyes. "Want to come to my room to watch some movies? We just got some new ones in while you were gone."

Cole looked over at us and said, "You guys need anything from me?"

Alex gave him a look. "Why would we?"

His friend sighed and turned to me. "I meant it more towards you. Need anything before I go?"

I shook my head and watched as the two walked away, Vanessa grabbing his hand on the way out. It was weird. I never imagined him to be into a girl like that--loud, shrilly... and kind of rude, to be honest.

"Well, she seems nice," I said sarcastically when they finally disappeared.

"Yeah, she hates you too," Claire said while leaning into Alex and stealing one of his fries. "The stuff she was thinking... I don't even think I can repeat it without needing to clean my mouth out with soap."

I was surprised by this. Never in my life have I had someone truly dislike me. Well, besides my father not wanting anything to do with my life, but I don't think he hated me. But judging by the way she tried to burn my hand off, I guess it isn't too much of a shock.

"Can I ask why?"

Claire shrugged. "She's overly jealous. She thinks something happened between Cole and you before you guys got here. Obviously nothing did, but in her mind just him spending the time to get you is a big no-no."

"Well, that wasn't his choice to get me so why would she freak out about that?"

"He wanted to go get you. He was the first to volunteer when it came to your case for some reason. He didn't have any information on you but jumped up at the first mention of this. And this is Cole we're talking about. He hates pick-up missions so him wanting to go for once surprised everyone."

"Can't you read his mind or something?"

Claire pursed her lips. "Girl, that meeting was at four in the morning. I could barely get dressed, let alone try to use my head."

I laughed before getting up and throwing my trash away. When I came back, Claire was standing and motioning for someone to come over.

"Allyson!" She yelled and I watched as a girl with dark, black hair approached us with a smile.

"Hi, guys!" She said while sitting down across from me. Her eyes gray eyes focused on me and she waved. "I'm Allyson, nice to meet you!"

"She came here not too long ago," Claire exclaimed before sitting back down and leaning into Alex.

"But I didn't place nearly as well as you did on your placement test," Allyson laughed. "So I'm probably going to be here twice as long as you are!"

"Hey, level three isn't bad!" Claire countered.

"Compared to level five?" Allyson said an eyebrow. "It's kind of shabby. You did great, Taylor. Everyone I was around couldn't believe it."

"Thank you," I replied while being interrupted by a yawn escaping my throat. I smiled sheepishly and rubbed the back of my neck. "I'm pretty tired... I think I might head up and take a nap."

"Okay!" Claire nodded. "You need help getting back?"

I shook my head. "I should be fine. If not, I can just ask someone."

The all said goodbye to me and I headed out on my own. Unlike this morning, my hair was now basically singed off at the end and I was in a level five, something apparently unheard of here. People eyes followed me while I walked to the dormitory. Luckily Cole had brought along a bag full of the clothes I had changed out of this morning and it held my key in the pocket of my shorts. As I searched around to find it, I heard someone clear their throat behind me. Straightening up, I turned around and saw Vanessa standing there with a few movies in her hands and Cole was nowhere to be found.

"Oh, hi, Vanessa--"

"Listen," she interrupted while her eyes narrowed in on me. "I don't know what happened between you and Cole on that trip you had together, but he's with me. You can get whatever fantasies out of your mind about him because as soon as we both leave here, the two of us are going to be partners and you'll be stuck at this place. Got that?"

Her words made me angry and her psycho-jealous persona was exactly how Claire described it. "I totally understand," I deadpanned and turned her back on me to continue searching for the shorts that held my key. I can't stand girls who feel the need to 'own' whomever they're dating. Keeping my answer short and simple would hopefully make her leave and get off my back about it all.

She made a little noise before stalking away with her movies and into a room not too far down. Great, I was neighbors with someone that wanted to burn my insides to a crisp. When I finally fetched my key, I practically groaned in relief. I threw the bag on the ground once I was inside and fell onto my bed for a much needed nap.

____

Thank you so much for everything you do for me! I still have a good amount of pre-written chapters ahead of this but that stack is getting smaller and smaller since I haven't been able to write so often due to fall quarter ending and a million assignments being due all at the same time. When the time comes that I am writing upload-to-upload, it could range from two days between updates or more than a week. Unlike my other stories in the past, I'm not going to force myself to write and produce something mediocre. I want this story/trilogy to be great, regardless of how long it takes me to write :)

Chapter Nine - The Training

I gently pulled at the ends of my newly cut ponytail in lieu of being nervous.

"Oh, just relax, Taylor!" Claire said while reaching down to tie her shoes. "Right now is just our sit-down training course. There's not going to be a pop quiz or anything!"

"But you guys know so much more than I do. I'm basically like a third grader who is entering high school," I grumbled the truth. I know everyone starts out this way, but I hated not knowing what to expect or going into something with little to no information on a topic. I might have the power to be at this level, but definitely not the brains.

Claire laughed and reached over to pat my shoulder. "Don't worry, you'll catch on quickly."

I groaned and followed her out of our room. Several others were also heading out for the day and would peek glances as the two of us walked down and out of our building.

"When are they going to stop with the staring?" I mumbled to Claire who shrugged in response.

"They'll stop when something more exciting happens here, which is rare."

I sighed in defeat and continued walking to the buildings around the arena area of Supernatural Abilities. There were several doors all marked with numbers one through five on them.

"I'm only level four so I'm in a different room than you. However, Cole, Vanessa, and Alex are all in five so you're not alone. If you don't want to sit with the couple, Alex would be more than happy to be with you."

I thanked her and said goodbye before heading in. Sure enough, the three mentioned were all sitting together in the third row. In some ways the room reminded me of a college lecture hall. There was a variety of stadium-like seating and a whiteboard, computer, projector, and screen all at the front. With my head ducked low, I made my way over to them and sat down next to Alex.

"Hey!" Alex said while straightening up from where he was practically falling asleep. "Glad you made it here okay."

"That's only because Claire drags me along and shows me everywhere."

Alex laughed. "That won't change even after you get used to this place. You're stuck with her for the long run."

I smiled and soon the whole room hushed down once a woman stepped out to the front and began talking about the importance of and how to be one step ahead of your opponent. While the information was interesting, I couldn't help but not understand some of the diction she used. Unlike most of the people in this room, I was bumped to the top. They had the previous training and knowledge while I was being thrown to the fishes.

We sat there for two hours while the woman demonstrated various techniques and talked how and why each would be important to utilize when fighting to kill someone. When it was finally noon, we were able to stretch our limbs and leave to go get some lunch.

"So how was your first lesson?" Alex asked while we waiting for the swarms of people to leave ahead of us."

"Confusing," I muttered under my breath.

"You'll learn quickly like we all did. It's going to suck the first few days but I know you'll catch on."

When we got to the lunch room and got food, I followed Alex to the same table we sat at yesterday where Vanessa and Cole were already there. Vanessa was clinging onto him as if her life depended on it while he was trying to take a bite of his sandwich.

"Hey, guys!" Cole said when we showed up before he turned to speak directly to me. "How'd you like your first class?"

"It was alright." I sat down across from the couple while Alex went by Cole. Claire must be either still in her class or in line to get food because she wasn't anywhere to be found.

Cole snorted. "Come on, it was boring."

"It's not as boring as it was confusing. I don't understand anything they're saying!"

Cole laughed and sat up straighter, scooting closer to the table which ultimately made Vanessa be pushed away a little. Her eyes practically had flames in them as she stared between us.

"I can always help you. I have no problem going over the stuff you should know. It's great and all that you got placed at such a high level but I understand the lack of information that you have."

I almost laughed at Vanessa's face. Now I wasn't one to try to backlash, but I gave him a smile and nodded my head. "I'd appreciate that."

While Cole was all smiles, Vanessa looked like she was going to explode in fury. Claire, only making things more hilarious, walked up as bright and cheery as she has been every other day. With a grand hello to everyone, she pecked Alex's cheek and sat down next to him, taking a spoonful of her soup into her mouth.

"I have to go," Vanessa said abruptly and pushed away from the table.

"Oh, okay," Cole focused his attention on her now. "See you in training?"

"I don't think so," she muttered and stomped away. Cole looked after her confused but shrugged it off and continued eating.

"Well, isn't she a pile of joy," Claire said under her breath and Cole shook his head.

"She's been so pissy lately. I don't know what's going on with her."

Alex gave him a look. "So you're not going to do anything about it?"

"Not my fault that she has a bad attitude all the time."

Lunch went more smoothly than when Vanessa was still here mostly because that awkward tension was gone. Without her, Cole is more jubilant. He still wasn't like that guy I saw the night in the hotel room when I broke down, but he was livelier when Vanessa wasn't around.

Finally, our thirty minute lunch came to an end and I found our group making our way to the arena. Claire explained that we needed to change into our various work out gear, the purple clothes I wore yesterday, and meet outside in the open field of grass outside.

While we were changing, I noticed all the colors. Mind was represented by purple. Fire was red, Earth was obviously green, Water was blue, and Air was coded as white. When Claire and I were done, we met the boys back up where a group of people were gathering.

"Okay," a woman dressed in black called using a megaphone. We're doing partner trainings today. Nothing too rough is allowed. Grab someone of a different Ability and begin offensive and defensive maneuvers."

Oh, great. Everyone's picking partners and I'm the lone wolf in the corner who just joined the pack.

"You're with me, Buckley," Cole grabbed my arm and pulled me to an empty spot next to Claire and Alex.

"So what are we doing?" I asked.

"I'm going to try to hit you with something that you'll deflect, then we'll switch roles. Nothing too crazy, right?"

I shook my head as we backed a few feet away from each other. I gave him an 'OK' sign in which he returned with a little ball of fire being thrown my way. I gave him a look and easily took one step out of the way of the blaze.

"Come on, I know you're better than that," I called out to him.

He gave me a wide smile. "Just trying to get you warmed up to this, that's all."

I looked around and saw a fallen tree branch behind me. Using all my focus, it rose and I threw it over my head and directly towards Cole who ultimately burned the thing to nothing.

This time, he didn't waste any time and I found several lines of fire coming straight for me. Not wasting a second of thought on in, I slowed down time and rolled on the ground to avoid getting hit just as they flew over my head. Bringing time back to normal, Cole nodded in approval as I narrowed in on him and sent an unseen force right at him. At the initial touch to him, he realized I was using telekinesis to push him back and he sent another blaze towards me.

After a few more minutes going back and forth, the instructor wanted us closer for a more hands-on approach to it all.

"You actually fight?" I asked, bewildered that they taught this. 'Like with your hands? Punching?"

Cole laughed and cracked his knuckles. "Yeah, you just expel your power into it so it's stronger."

I shook my head. "I've never fought anyone before."

"Well, this is a week of firsts for you then. Punch me."

My eyes widened. "What? No!"

Cole gave me a look. "Punch me, wimp. I'll give you pointers."

I sighed in defeat and looked down at my hand. In no way was I strong enough to hurt someone with my fist, let alone by kicking too. "Where?" I asked and he pointed to his cheek. "No!"

"We have healers everywhere around here if you do some damage! Come on, I've been hit dozens of times. One more won't kill me."

I shook my head, "I'm not going to hit you in your face."

Cole shrugged. "Fine, I'll get Alex to come punch me. God knows how much he probably wants to after all the stuff I've put him through these years...."

He was taunting me just like he did the day I left home. Groaning, I formed a fist and he shook his head. "No," He stepped forward and grabbed my wrist to bring my thumb to a new position. "There. Hold it like that and punch."

Biting my lip as he held out his cheek to me, I did the same fist arrangement he showed me and brought my arm back before bringing it forward to connect it with his jaw. In the moment my eyes opened, I noticed his rubbing at his face with an impressed look.

"Not bad, Buckley," he complimented. "Needs work, but not too shabby."

He showed me a variety of other fighting techniques and I never realized just how handsy fighting was. His hand would sometimes find my waist or I'd accidentally be touching his chest. It was like dancing, in a way, if that was dangerous and painful.

As the last technique, Cole faked me out and brought me down onto the ground with a grunt escaping my throat. He gave me a sorry smile but as many times as he was able to bring me down today, apologizes were out the door a long time ago. He offered a hand which I gladly took and got back to my feet.

"That was fun," He said while still rubbing at his face from earlier. That might have been the only good, strong mark I put on him today while others were mostly accidents. "We can do some more of this in a few days."

My eyes furrowed. "Why not tomorrow?"

"We have arena exercises tomorrow. We'll be fighting one another."

I groaned because, sure enough, I was being thrown into something just like I have been the entire time I've been here. My body was still slightly sore from my placement test and I knew my beat-down from Cole today would only make myself worse.

"Do I have to go?"

Cole laughed, "I didn't drive miles to get you and then fight a Catcher in order for you to drop out on your first day."

"This is technically my third day," I sarcastically pointed out and he rolled his eyes.

"First day of actual training," he clarified as we walked towards the locker rooms. "You'll get used to it and become better. You already picked something up just by having your placement test. You'll be one of us in no time."

I said goodbye to him and disappeared to go change. Once I was done, I noticed Alex, Claire, and Cole all talking outside of the arena. When Cole, who looked very disinterested in what the couple was flirting about, saw me, he perked up and motioned me over.

"We're going to go swimming down by the lake, wanna come?" He asked.

"Lake?"

Claire nodded excitedly. "It's kind of hidden among the trees and in the outskirts of SA. Not many people know about it so it's fun to go and get away from everyone once in a while."

"Plus, it's hotter than Cole right now," Alex interjected. "And I don't mean that in a 'you're attractive' kind of way."

Cole gave him a look. "Gee, way to boost my confidence, man."

His friend smiled, "That's my job."

On the way to the lake, we stopped by the dormitory to change into our various swimming clothes before heading out again. The walk there didn't take too long and 'lake' is quite the exaggeration. A deep, large pond is more accurate and it was nestled right in the middle of a large amount of trees. Despite my observations, Alex jumped right in with a yell. When he came up, he was full of smiles.

Claire shook her head at his fun and stripped out of her cover up before turning to us. "I'm not even going to get in myself because I know he's just going to do it," she said right as a line of water wrapped around her waist and pulled her in with a splash. Inside the water, Alex was laughing hysterically as he came back up, gasping for air.

"I hate you!" She squealed and threw water at him playfully.

Alex raised an eyebrow at her and suddenly, a huge bubble of water came out of the pond and above Claire's head. "You really want to play that game with me?"

His girlfriend gave him a nervous smile and went over to the Water-user with her best puppy eyes. He laughed at her and pulled her under where I could see a patch of air underneath the water.

"They can't stay under too long," Cole said as he looked down at them as well. "While he's able to move the water out of the way, he's no Air user and can't keep it circulated. Alex is able to breath underwater but Claire can't so they'll eventually have to come up."

"It's weird how connected all the abilities are," I commented. "You need Water and Air together. Then Fire and Earth to make lava. You need the Mind with a lot too. There are tons of examples of them all working with one another, you never realize it until you're actually putting them to use."

"Good job, Blondie," He complimented. "A lot of people don't realize that right away."

"You know, you could try calling me Taylor because it's my name and all," I joked.

He waved his hand like it was a preposterous suggestion. "That's no fun, Brain."

I raised an eyebrow, "Brain?"

"Well, you're a Mind so it makes sense."

I laughed and watched as Claire and Alex came up for a breath of air just as Cole predicted. "That one wasn't any good."

"Trust me, I have awhile to come up with some really good ones," Cole warned as the couple went back down for their own privacy.

"I expect all of them written down and in alphabetical order by the time I leave here."

A grin rose onto his face. "Consider it done."

————————

Enjoy as always! This time we got up to around #220. SO close to the 100s! We'll get there eventually, but I still appreciate every single one of your comments, votes, and reads on each of my stories :)

Chapter Ten - The Match

As I had predicted the day before, the next morning I was incredibly sore and Claire basically had to drag me out of bed.

"Here, you crybaby," she said while pressing her palms onto my shoulders and closing her eyes. Within a few seconds, my pain started to subside to a dull ache.

"You can heal?"

She shrugged. "Not as much as the actual Healers can do, but enough to help."

Yesterday was fun at the so-called 'lake.' We stayed there for a few hours just swimming and playing around until our basic needs came to our attention and we headed out to get food and sleep.

After we got ready for the day, the two of us headed a different route today than before but the building we walked into was nearly identical to the one yesterday. Instead of numbers lining the door, there were symbols. One was a flame, another was a water droplet. Next was a leaf then some swirls. The last was an eye.

"Today is ability based lessons where new skills are taught or refined depending on who you are and what you know," Claire told me as we headed towards the door with an eye on it. "Our symbol is kind of lame, but what else is a tell for a Mind? Don't even say brain because that's just tacky."

This classroom was more open and larger than the one yesterday. It looked more like a small gym than a place for learning. However, there were some tables and chairs so Claire and I took two open ones next to each other. Other people were pouring in and we were a huge cloud of purple from our clothes. It was weird being around so many people with the same eye color and abilities as my own and even weirder knowing that most of them were watching my every move.

Luckily, it didn't take long for some people to walk in. One I recognized as Galen and the other... I froze in my place.

I whispered to Claire, "That's the girl from the... uh--"

She gave me a sympathetic look, "That's Sophia. She's the Mind from the placement test."

I watched as she scanned the crowd until her eyes fell on me. Immediately, a frown rested on her face as she turned away. Next to me, Claire snickered under her breath.

"She must not feel too great about you getting out of her power. No one has been able to do that since she began doing those tests. She's the hardest one because she takes you to a different place and most of the time, people don't realize it and would live there forever."

"I noticed a flaw," I muttered and sunk down in my seat.

"Really? What?"

"A watch."

Claire looked like she was going to ask another question but Sophia interrupted her. "Head Leader Galen here is going to sit in and watch today," She announced to everyone here. "It's a normal day, so we'll get right back into telekinesis."

I watched as everyone began to spread out and focus their minds on items. Some people narrowed in on pencils that would only move a few inches or so. Others went towards balls or chairs to move. Claire brought me to the side where some weights were and gave me a sheepish look.

"I'm not the best at this, so bear with me," she said as she tried to lift some of them. One ten-pounding rose a few feet before crashing to the ground and she huffed out in frustration. "Judging from your test, you can do this pretty well. Why don't you try?"

Doing as told, it didn't take much for me to lift up the rack of weights quite a few feet up before bringing them back down gently with a deep release of air. Claire looked at me dumbfounded and stomped her foot.

"How are you so good at that!" She groaned. "You obviously got the offensive part of the Mind ability!."

I laughed and was about to reply until a hand rested on my shoulder. Turning around, I froze when I saw that it belonged to Sophia.

"Taylor," She spoke in an even tone but almost as if she was forcing herself to be civil. It was then that I noticed Galen was behind her. "Do you mind coming with us for a moment?"

I only nodded and snuck a peek at Claire as we walked away. She looked confused like I was as the three of us exited the gym to go outside.

"We understand that telekinesis is one of your abilities that you came in with," Sophia commented once we were a little ways away. "However, it's quite an advanced technique, especially with how much you can lift. Galen and I were curious as to how much is too much for you?"

"Well, what do you want me to pick up?" I asked, feeling self-conscious under their gazes.

Galen looked around and pointed to a bike leaning against the building. "Let's try that first and we'll work our way up until it becomes too much."

Vanquishing any other thoughts from my mind that didn't concern the bicycle, I gently made it rise up and then down before turning to them in confirmation. I found myself lifting a multitude of other things such as boulders, bushes, small trees, and even the two of them.

At the fifth or so item, Sophia nodded to a large truck filled with wood. "Try that."

This time I met some resistance. Grinding my teeth together, I struggled to lift the vehicle up and only managed a foot or so before I had to bring it back down. Turning back to the two, I found them exchanging a look.

"That's quite impressive for someone who hasn't undergone any training," Galen complimented. "What else can you do?"

"Well, that... I can control time too--"

"What do you mean?" She asked. "During your test we saw you moving at alarming speeds for some of it but running that fast isn't associated with the usual Mind ability."

"I can slow down time for everyone but me. In your eyes, everything is the same but I look as if I'm going twice the speed. To me, everything is going at half the rate as normal. It takes a lot of energy so I can't do it for too long."

"Interesting..." She trailed off before asking another questions. "What else?"

"I'm able to see future events..." I muttered and rubbed the back of my neck. "I can't control it and they come as dreams."

"What was the last thing you saw that happened?"

"When Cole came in the middle of the Catcher attack."

Sophia snorted. "Most of the girls here dream about Cole... I wouldn't put it down as a skill--"

"Oh, Sophia, please keep your thoughts to yourself," Galen warned here.

She raised an eyebrow. "Thoughts to myself? Really? Around here?"

Her superior smiled. "You have a point there." Galen turned back to me. "Anything else?"

"Well, the whole blocking thing that happened during the placement test. Cole said it was some kind of shield but it just sort of happened back there."

She nodded. "Fascinating. You're a strong girl, Taylor. More so than we had expected from Cole's notes he wrote on you."

"Oh really?" I asked while crossing my arms over my chest. "What did he say?"

Sophia laughed. "Basically that you didn't do anything when the Catcher arrived--"

"Sophia!" Galen interrupted her. "That is private information."

She shrugged. "What? Obviously they're a good laugh now that she's Wonder Woman around here. I'm going back to everyone in there to see if I'm needed. Goodbye now," she waved and disappeared back into the building.

Galen shook her head after her. "She used to be so positive before she left...Trust me, she used to be the sweetest girl but going out into the real world really changes people." She sighed and turned back to me. "Despite her animosity, she's impressed with you, as am I. You still have a lot to learn but that'll come with your training. Keep practicing and you'll be stronger than ever."

"Thank you," I muttered, slightly embarrassed from her compliments towards my ability.

"I'll let you go back but I'll be around to keep track of how you're doing," she smiled. "I have high hopes for you, Taylor."

I nodded once before heading back inside where people were still practicing their telekinesis. I found Claire in the same spot as before and while she was doing better, a sheen of sweat lined her forehead.

"What was that about?" She asked while raising a light chair up a few inches before it crashed back down.

I shrugged. "They wanted to know all that I can do. I guess the placement test didn't show too much."

The rest of the morning went by easily. We went over some skills that I knew and others that I didn't and wasn't able to do before lunch came around. By the time we left and grabbed what we were going to eat, we were the first ones at the table. It didn't take long for Alex and even Allyson to show up and start eating with us. Around halfway through, we were still missing someone.

"Where's Cole?" Allyson asked the question I was wondering.

Alex scoffed. "He's talking with Vanessa somewhere. Apparently she's done being a cold-hearted nightmare for the time being."

So everyone didn't like Cole's girlfriend. Wouldn't that tick him off that maybe, just maybe, she's an awful person? Or, in the both literal and comical sense of the word due to her ability, she's a bit of a hot head?

After lunch, my nerves began to grow. As Cole said yesterday, today was time for our actual sparring and fighting with other students. I know I did well during my test, but going to against people my level really bothered and scared me.

I expected us to head in the way of the arena but we went straight instead. After a few minutes of walking and following other people dressed in their appropriate Abilities' gear, I found myself standing in front of several smaller versions of the place I had my placement exam.

"These are essentially the same things as the main arena," Claire told me while walking around them to the back. "They're just smaller and have more resources to you. The main stadium is to mimic the real world. People will also have their exit exams there too."

She and Alex brought me to two large boards with various names on them. Apparently the only ones that have this training exercise are those in levels four and five. I found my name near the middle.

TAYLOR BUCKLEY... MIND. REBECCA NEILSEN... WATER.

"You got Becca?" Alex asked and a smile spread grew onto his face. He leaned in to whisper into my ear and said, "She's not the best so you'll easily beat her."

For one of the first times since I got to this place, I breathed out a sigh of relief. Alex was only a few fights before me while Claire, on her separately scheduled matches, was one of the first groups to go. Cole and Vanessa were going at the same time, but not fighting each other, near the end.

While we took our spots in the stands to await the first fight and Claire went down to get ready, Alex laid down the guidelines for me. We had five minutes to unhinge our opponents and get them into a position that would kill them if you delivered the final blow. Obviously we wouldn't be doing that but this allows conclusions to be drawn about the end.

There were a total of four places for people to fight. In the middle of the round arenas was a tower that help people watching and monitoring all the fights from above as well as at least one other person refereeing each match from the inside. Each were identical on the inside, having a water tub, rocks, dirt, lit torches, and apparently, as said by Alex, advanced air circulation in there. I watched as four couples stepped into their various fields and prepared themselves. Suddenly, a beep blared from the middle, a large timer flashed above, counting down from 5:00, and everything went wild.

It was a mess of water, fire, air, and earth flying around. Unseen forces were hitting and knocking people around which could only be done by Minds. It was crazy, as well as sort of beautiful to watch. All the elements were clashing and moving around with each other that it made for a mesmerizing sight. From one of the fights, I heard someone cry out while their opponent took the opportunity of their distracted state to roll forward, pin them onto the ground, and hold a boulder above their head.

"Done!" The referee in that stadium called and the winner jumped off of the loser. In a good show of sportsmanship, he held his hand down to help the other up.

The first round of fights came to a close. Some ended early with a winner while others went to the end of the five minutes, concluding a draw. The next group of fights held Claire and her opponent was some guy I've never seen before. From next to me, Alex groaned.

"What?" I asked.

"She's against someone pretty good," he admitted. "Claire is strong, don't get me wrong, but more of a defensive, helper type instead of a fighter. This guy is going to cream her."

The buzzer went off and I saw Claire intensely looking at him. If I could guess, she was using telepathy to read his mind and see what his first move was. Sure enough, he ran forward, throwing waves of fire at her which she easily dodged. They continued like that for a little bit, cat and mouse sort of action. Slowly, the two inched closer to one another and it became harder for Claire to dodge.

Finally, her opponent was close and as he fired a gust of flames at her, I jumped out of my seat when she just stood there. Besides me, Alex chuckled.

"Just watch," he said while leaning back in ease.

And I did. The fire flew right through 'Claire' as if she was nothing but air and suddenly, she appeared behind him, knocked him off his feet with a swift kick to the legs. I laughed to myself and sat back down, enjoying the fact that my friend wasn't charred to bits.

The match ended soon after that with the boy pinning Claire in a corner until the referee announced his victory. The two shook hands and disappeared down to lockers below to change and get checked for wounds, as I was told by Alex.

I watched another fight with him until Claire came back up, clean and bandaged, to join us. She seemed proud at her fight and Alex gave her a loving, congratulatory kiss. Not too long after, Alex had to head down to get ready for his own fight.

Watching his fight was way different than the others' I have seen so far. He was very skilled and calculated every move of his. I always thought of water as free-flowing but he made it precise and exact. It didn't take long for him to dismantle his opponent and claimed the victor of the round without any marks hit on him.

"He's really good," I commented to Claire who nodded exuberantly.

"He should be ready to head out to the real world soon," she said with a slight twinge of sadness in her voice. "He's one of the best Supernatural Abilities has ever seen."

Alex came up quickly after his fight was over, probably skipping the check-up with the healers all together. From a fight against two Water Supernaturals, I expected him to be soaked but he didn't even have a single drop on him.

"Good job," I complimented and he smiled at me.

"Now it's your turn, Miss Level Five," Alex joked and slumped down next to Claire. "Go get your first win."

I waited until another fight concluded before heading downstairs. I was scheduled to be in arena four and I followed the signs until I reached my desired place of entry. There was still another fight going on at the moment so I took the time to stretch out. I found it rather weird, considering I was a Mind and it's not like I use all of my limbs like the others to fight.

I heard the beep of the current fight, signaling that it was concluded. Overhead, an automated voice echoed, "Next session, please enter your arena."

Taking a deep breath, I opened the large metal door in front of me to enter into the sunlit stadium. Across from me, a girl with red hair also came in. The two of us sized each other up until the horn blared, announcing that our fight was to begin.

I was taken aback because she whipped some water at me a split second before the fight even started. Luckily, I was able to duck fast enough that it never hit me. My eye caught a large piece of metal and, using telekinesis, I threw it in front of me to create a shield as a mass amount of water came gushing by.

While this girl was definitely a fighter, she was sloppy in every move she did. I allowed her to take a couple of shots while I analyzed her movements just as Alex did in his. After a few seconds, I noticed that she favored her right side, leaving her left vulnerable.

My opponent threw another stream of water at me, almost like a power shower nozzle. Slowing down time, I ran forward while breaking every line. While this would have definitely hurt due to its speed in normal time, being slowed down made it soft and easy to interrupt.

I allowed time to go back to normal and I watched as her expression changed to surprise, now attempting to make another move towards me. The lining was perfect and, as expected, she left her left side open. With some power, an unseen force driven by me came at her open side, making her crash to the ground. In a split second, I was on top of her, holding her down with one knee on her chest and telekinesis as an extra precaution.

"Done!" Our referee called and I jumped off of my opponent who I vaguely remembered behind named Rebecca. I reached out to help her up which she gratefully took before huffing off in disappointment.

Leaving the arena victorious, I found myself slightly wet but unhurt. I walked by the attached medical clinic and shook my head when they asked if I needed to get cleaned up. A couple of the Supernaturals in there looked at me in awe as I continued on.

Not going to lie, I was kind of proud of myself. After only a few classes I was slowly becoming an actual fighter--one who judges before going forward. Thinks before doing.

I hid my prideful smile and went back to be with my friends.

I was going to post this today, but plans totally got in my way of doing so. However, I hope you enjoyed this long chapter!

And GUYS. We made it to #165. That's crazy! Thank you SO much for all the support :) I'll try to get the next update out before Christmas because I have some time off and also write a ton of new chapters too to get even further ahead.

See you next update!

Chapter Eleven - The Backstory

Alex and Claire started slow clapping as I walked up to them.

"Brilliant," Alex said in a fake posh voice. "Just brilliant."

I rolled my eyes at them and sat down. Claire was all smiles as she began talking really fast. "You did great! I saw what you were doing out there, looking at the best point of action. That was smart! You're completely running through the ranks and training of this place without even learning it!"

I laughed and shook my head. "I still need a lot more training, but thank you."

Despite being able to leave after your fight is over, the three of us stayed to watch Cole's fight. I haven't seen him all day, but when he stepped into his arena for one of the last fights, he already looked pissed.

In the arena next to him was Vanessa, who was facing off against some girl I didn't recognize. When the buzzer sounded, I watched as she went straight in with a tornado of fire.

"She really doesn't waste any time, does she?" I muttered under my breath and Claire laughed.

"She's the definition of a hot-head... Literally"

Alex nodded, "The two of them probably got into a fight before they got out. Look at Cole, he's fuming."

I turned and watched the guy's fight to see him burning everything that the Earth he was fighting threw at him as he walked closer and closer. I have only ever seen Cole fight that Catcher and that was pretty quick. Here, Cole took his time and, as I did, calculated the movements of the person he was fighting. The Earth threw a large clump of rock, dirt, and debris at him which Cole immediately returned as magma. His opponent jumped out of the way as it sizzled into the side of the arena. Cole then created a wall of fire on either side of the Earth, making it impossible for him to run away. Sure enough, he had his opponent down on the ground and the referee called the fight over.

Looking over at Vanessa's fight, hers was already announced over and I saw her brushing off some ash from her clothes with her own opponent clenching their knee of the floor.

Alex was the first one of us to get up. "Well, I'm going to make sure Cole doesn't murder anyone." He turned back to us, "We can all meet up at the lake afterwards because it's pretty hot out. If I'm not there in twenty minutes, call for help and the fire department."

"You're a Water," Claire pointed out. "Extinguish yourself."

Her boyfriend put a hand on his heart as streams of tears immediately began falling from his blue eyes like an over animated cartoon. "Claire, you hurt me so."

She pushed him with a groan. "You know I hate when you do that!" He began laughing and the tears stopped. "He learned how to make water fall right by his eyes so it looks like he's crying," she explained to me. "Sometimes he makes it realistic just to make me feel bad and he knows I hate it!"

Alex continued chuckling and kissed her on the forehead before heading down to where Cole presumably was. The two of us headed down to where the lake--totally a pond--was and she immediately jumped in, still clad in her workout clothes. She floated up to the top and relaxed on her back.

Taking off my shoes, I decided just to put my feet in the water while she swam around until the guys got there a little bit later. Alex looked as cheerful and jolly as usual while Cole looked about ready to burn down the forest that surrounded us.

As predicted, the couple jumped in and joined each other in the water while Cole took a spot on a rock a few feet from me, rested his chin on his hand while he slumped down.

"What's up with you?" I asked, watching as Alex and Claire had a race to see who could hold their breath underwater the longest. Obviously Alex won.

"I'm just fine, shorty," Cole grumbled and I smiled at his new nickname.

"You don't look like it."

He plastered a fake smile on his face and looked at me. "See?"

I shook my head with a little laugh. "Now, I might not be a genius but I know that you're lying."

He sighed and ran a hand through his messy, dirty blonde hair. "Vanessa and I got into a fight today."

I raised an eyebrow. "Oh? What about?"

He gave me a look. "You know, you're a bit nosy."

"Says the guy who knows basically everything about me from reading some papers," I eyed him. "Even some things that weren't necessary information or important to know."

For the first time today I saw him laugh and put a cheeky smirk on his face. "You got me there." He turned more serious as he answered my question, "She's mad over the fact that I didn't tell her where I was during class this morning. She thinks I was seeing another girl, yada-yada-yada, that I'm an awful guy, yada-yada-yada, and we fought about it."

I fought the urge to roll my eyes over her over-clingy nature. "It doesn't sound like you're too happy to be dating her."

"We're not dating," Cole said abruptly. My eyebrows crinkled together in confusion. The two definitely looked and acted like they together. Even Claire and Alex told me they were. Cole sighed and moved down to sit by me while the couple swam around us, not paying attention to Cole and I whatsoever.

"We're not official," he mumbled under his breath. "At least, I never made it so."

"Then why does she act like you are?"

He shrugs, "She got it in her mind that we are a thing and I haven't really done anything to make sure she didn't think that. It's kind of my fault, I guess."

"How long have you been 'together?'" I asked, using air quotations on the last word.

"Two years or so." My eyes widened and he turned defensive. "Don't give me that look!"

I raised my hands up in surrender, "Hey, I'm just surprised, that's all. Do you want to be with her?" He shook his head. "Then why don't you end it?"

He gritted his teeth. "I owe her for something."

"It can't be enough for you to make you unhappy for two years."

"I'm not entirely miserable," Cole said while leaning back on his forearms. "I mean, she's a nice girl, one of my best friends, but she is an awful 'girlfriend.' I mean, let's face it. The girl is nuts."

I laughed and caught a flicker of a smile on his lips. "I still think you should just end things."

"Why?" He raised an eyebrow, turning on his sarcastic facade. "You want a turn at the ole' Cole, here?"

I shook my head, "Please. I'd rather fight a whole swarm of Catchers."

"Sure you would, girl," Cole laughed. "I saw you looking in that hotel room."

I immediately felt myself turning red, remembering the time when he was fresh out of the shower. "What did you expect me to do? It's not every day I wake up to a naked boy!"

Cole snickered again and it didn't sound forced. "I'm just messing with you."

I huffed out in embarrassment. "So what favor do you owe her?" I asked and he froze. "Come on, you know my whole backstory and I know next to nothing about you."

Cole eyed the couple in the water who was laughing as Alex dragged Claire down with a bubble surrounding their bodies.

"A year and a half ago, I was hanging out with Vanessa off-grounds," he muttered under his breath. "I was a level two because I had just gotten there a month earlier and knew little to nothing about my powers. She was a three and the two of us were just messing around and having some fun."

"How'd you even get out?" I asked.

Cole shrugged. "It's pretty easy, actually. We dodged some security Supernaturals and jumped over. I don't remember why we thought it was a good idea, but it happened. We were out there for around an hour, just exploring... maybe drinking a little from a bottle we stole from the kitchen... then a Catcher found us." He sighed. "Long story short: I froze, just as you did when you saw your first. I stood there, completely still, while Vanessa jumped into action and was able to kill the Catcher after a long fight. I sat back and watched because I was in shock. Vanessa ended up saving us, but not without getting hurt herself. We got lucky that it was a new, untrained Catcher because we would surely be dead if it knew what it was doing. The Catcher ended up dropping a boulder on her leg while she was down and it broke it. She was still able to char the thing to bits to kill it while she was in pain. I ended up carrying her back to the infirmary and sticking by her the entire road of her recovery. Since then, everyone has just assumed we were together."

"So you owe her because...?" I questioned, not really understanding how this is linked to them being together for this long without him wanting to.

"She saved my life. I knew she liked me before that whole thing, so I thought I owed it to her to make her happy."

"And I take it that Alex and Claire don't know this?"

He shook his head. "No one does. We said that a tree fell on her while we were sparring and our fire went out of control. I don't want anyone thinking I'm weak."

I resisted the urge to roll my eyes at his masculinity being threatened. "So why are you telling me?"

He shrugged. "You seem trustworthy, Buckley. Besides, I do know a lot about you while you know hardly anything about me. I think we'll be even now even though I still know your br--"

"Stop!" I interjected, not wanting him to finish his sentence about the stuff that was put in my papers. "Getting back on topic, that was two years ago. I'm not trying to boost your ego, but you're kind of amazing out there now. No one will think you're weak for something that happened when you were a level two."

Cole shrugged. "I've gone along with it too long that telling people would only get me and her in more trouble."

"Well, like I said, it was a long time ago. You have got to stop being with Vanessa when you obviously don't want to be. You're leading her on, which is probably worse than you 'owing' her anything."

He took in my words for a few moments and sat up. "I guess you're right and, honestly, if I'm with her for another five minutes I might lose my mind." He gave me a genuine smile. "Thanks, pinky."

"Pinky?" I asked in confusion.

"Because your cheeks get all pink when you're embarrassed."

"Hey, I have pale skin!"

"Oh, I know you do. I saw it in your papers," he winked while getting up.

"Stop talking about that!"

Cole laughed and began walking away, hopefully to go talk to Vanessa. "Nope, it will never get old."

———————

Enhancing on character backgrounds from the first version is just so nice.

Anyways, I hope you liked it! We got up to #107 on the last one!! Thank you so much for all the support as usual. Please have a good break, happy holidays, and a Merry Christmas (if you celebrate!) tomorrow!

Chapter Twelve - The Girlfriend

The next day was sit-down classes with everyone in my level. Like yesterday, Cole and Vanessa were not to be found so I took a spot next to Alex.

Today's class was talking about various techniques to maneuver out of a Catcher's grip if they get you. It was interesting, but still basically a foreign language to me as they went over all the steps that I would need to practice later today.

After this was lunch so the two of us joined up with Claire and headed to the cafeteria to get some food before training starts today.

I was growing used to the routine here. People still gave me interested looks, but not nearly as much as I got when I first showed up. Sure enough, my five seconds of fame was slowly diminishing and I couldn't be happier.

I still thought back to home quite a lot. What was my dad doing? Did he even care that I was gone? What about Ryan?

I wanted to eventually, when I had 'graduated' from here, go back. I know making contact with them would only allow them to be a target for Catchers, but I do want to see and know how they are doing. While I think my father probably doesn't care, I can completely see Ryan freaking out about this whole thing.

"Taylor?" I shook myself out of my inner thoughts and looked at Claire. "What do you want to get for lunch?"

I looked at our options and shrugged. "A burger is fine with me."

We got our food and headed over to the table that Allyson was already seated at. Her young features were excited as we sat down around her.

"You guys are never going to believe it," She started. "I just saw Vanessa down by the dorms and she was fuming. Even the ends of her hair were on fire."

Claire snorted. "That is something I do believe. The girl is crazy--"

That's when we heard a scream of anger. Hesitantly, I turned around and noticed that everyone is staring at Vanessa who was standing in the doorway of the building. Her dark eyes were searching the crowds until they rested on me and she began stomping over here, flames licking the air was she continued forward.

"Oh shit," Alex muttered under his breath. "Who is she looking at over here?"

"You're a real gem, Taylor," Vanessa said to me as she got closer and closer. "A real gem."

I briefly looked over at Claire who was staring at me in surprise. "What the hell did you do? Did you murder her cat or something?"

She came to our table and I stood up with my best 'please calm down, I'm only a civilian in this case' face.

"Vanessa--"

"Since when did you think that running your little mouth and meddling into another person's relationship was a good thing?" She seethed. I could see waves of heat coming off of her skin because she was so angry. Now is the time to place nice guy and not get burned to a crisp.

"Look, I was only trying to help a friend--"

"A friend who is my boyfriend and helping my relationship! You've only been here for a week, you know nothing about us!"

"I was just trying to help--"

"You got it through Cole's mind that he needed to break up with me. Me! Why'd you do that? Because you want him? You think that because you spent a few days alone together, you actually have a chance with him?"

I grit my teeth together to stop myself from going off on her. I might have been placed into level five, but this girl has it out for me right now and she could probably easily hurt me.

"That is between you and Cole. I just offered some advice on the situation he told me yesterday--"

Her eyebrows furrowed together. "You were hanging out with him!?"

And that's when everything went down. She pointed her hand out to me and some fire came storming right to my spot. There was a brief moment of pain that I felt on my left arm before what felt like a gallon of water fell on top of me. Then, another arm pulled me out of the stream from my right.

Once the water was gone, I gasped for air and spluttered water out of my mouth as I coughed. Claire was grabbing my arm while Alex was out of his seat, eyes on Vanessa who was now thrashing around on the ground with two guys I didn't know holding her down. They both had dark eyes like her and judging by their lack of pain from the fire radiating off her body, they were both Fire Supernaturals.

I didn't even notice Cole running in until he was angrily looking down at his now ex-girlfriend on the ground. He kneeled down to her level and spoke in an even tone. "This is why I broke up with you. Not because of her. It's because you're an awful person. Next time you go on a rampage, take it out on me rather than an innocent bystander."

Vanessa glared at him but stopped her thrashing enough for the guys to bring her to her feet. They still didn't let go as she stared between Cole and myself.

"Bring her to Galen," Cole told them. "She'll obviously know what happened and can take it from there."

I watched as they took her out of the cafeteria and everyone slowly watched her leave. Once she was gone, Cole turned towards us, almost looking surprised that we were even there.

"Well..." he started. "That could have gone better."

Claire dropped her hand from my arm and I turned to her and Alex with a grateful smile. "Thanks, guys."

Alex shrugged, "Sorry you had to get drenched in the process."

We laughed but Cole was silent, his eyes resting on my upper arm. "She got you." I looked down to where he was looking to see a newly made burn blistering my arm. It was pretty gross, but not too big. "Here, I'll take you to the infirmary." He turned towards the others, "We'll meet you down at training. You guys can stay here and finish up lunch."

Without another word, Cole put a hand on my back and pushed me out of the cafeteria with a ward of following eyes from the rest of the Supernaturals that were watching this event proceed.

Well, looks like my fifteen minutes of fame are back.

"I can walk myself, Cole. You should just go--"

"No, I want to. This is my fault."

I rolled my eyes. "Please. That girl has been out to get me the minute I stepped foot in this place." I was silent for a moment as I carefully chose my words. "So how did it go? Before her rampage, I mean."

He shrugged. "She seemed fine, really. Like she understood but then she excused herself and came here. I told her that I wasn't feeling the relationship anymore and that we'd be better as friends like before. I said that I had a conversation with a friend who helped me realize some things so this wasn't a decision I had made on the spot."

"Then she came to kill me," I joked and he gave me a sheepish smile.

"Sorry about that. I didn't think she'd turn to violence."

I laughed as we continued on. As my initial short burst of adrenaline wore off, I found the burn on my arm growing more painful. We walked into the clinic and one of the healers looked at me in surprise.

"What happened?" she asked while bringing me over to one of the beds they have in the back. "Training isn't for another ten minutes!"

I was about to answer until Cole beat me to it. "Trust me," he said while she gently touched my wound, making me wince. "You'll find out soon enough."

She didn't say anything in response, but only focused on my wound. Her fingers were light across the burn and the pain disappeared as it began slowly healing itself. It was interesting to watch something that looked pretty bad turn into a light pink scar. The whole process didn't even take long, maybe a minute or so. I hope that with more training I could do something like this too.

"There you go, honey," she said with a grin while helping me up. The pain from my burn was now gone and my arm felt as good as new again. I thanked her and then followed Cole back outside and in the direction of the training areas.

"Today's partner practices," Cole said while we approached the area where people were already doing their things. "Wanna team up?"

I spread my arms out and sarcastically said, "I know I have swarms of people dying to work with me, but I'll make the exception for you."

He rolled his eyes and grabbed my arm to drag me along to an empty spot in the grass. "Come on, Blondie. You're such a hoot."

We began doing basic exercises of meager attempts to hit each other that were easy enough to dodge without losing any energy. When our instructor announced that we would be switching to close combat, the two of us moved from fifteen feet away from each other to five.

"Have you learned how to use your power when close together?" He asked while stretching out his arms. When I shook my head, he hummed in response. "Okay, let's try it. You're used to fighting from far away, not so much when you're close together."

"How do you--" I couldn't finish my sentence because he tackled me to the ground, pinning me easily in place. I'm a small girl, short and petite, but Cole was tall and had muscle packed on him.

He leaned over me, letting his dirty blonde hair flop in front of his face while he held all my limbs down so I could barely even struggle.

"Try it. Use your telekinesis to move me," he said in an easy, untired voice.

I continued struggling out of his hold; unable to control my mind long enough to even focus on attempting to get him off of me with my powers. I found myself losing energy in this endless, unforgiving, and impossible fight between me and Cole the superhuman.

Superhuman... because Cole's strength is the only thing unnatural about him. Bad word choice, Taylor.

"I can't," I said through gritted teeth and continued thrashing around while he watched in amusement.

"You're working physically, not mentally like your ability suggests. Think, don't move."

I thought about his words and was able to move my fingers just enough to expel some power from where he held my wrists. Using telekinesis as suggested, I threw him with the unseen force onto his back and found myself now on top, holding him down with the power. He struggled to get up for a moment before falling back down and bringing his hands behind his head to relax with a smile on his face.

I dropped the power and he nodded. "Good job. Now do that next time before flopping around on the ground like a fish."

I rolled my eyes and got off of him, helping him up as we practiced the same sort of thing some more. I found out new ways to get someone away from me when they were holding me down or too close. Cole was a good teacher, but still strong enough to completely annihilate me if he so wanted.

"Class is over!" Our instructor announced and Cole dropped the ball of fire that he held inches from my face. He patted me on the back and threw me one of the bottles of water that we had grabbed halfway through.

It was always so hot here and I kind of wished I was a Water to drench myself or an Air to blow some cold wind on me. I felt sorry for the Fires, they were hotter than they needed to be and probably even more so in this heat.

"Good job, Shorty," He complimented while grinning at his new nickname for me. "And congrats on your first week here."

I gulped down a few swigs of water and realized that I made it an entire week here without dying once. A few bumps along the way and one enemy, but still alive. "Thanks!"

"We'll have to celebrate on our day off tomorrow," he commented while Alex and Claire walked up.

"Celebrate what?" My roommate asked and Cole explained. "Yes! We can have a kickback at the lake with a group!"

She began talking excitedly about who would be invited and what would be needed. It's kind of weird. In high school at home I would rarely ever go to parties or be invited and would only go if Ryan wanted me to. Coming here I had a good group of friends, not that Ryan was not ever enough for me, but it was just a change in scenery. I liked it. I liked having a roommate who had enough energy and happiness for everyone else and another friend, her boyfriend, who was both a comedic relief and a mediator of the group. Then Cole, the literal hot head of the group, who now would hopefully act more like the guy I see when we're alone now that he's done with Vanessa.

Thinking of the guy, he caught my eye and rolled his eyes at how excited Claire was at a single idea that now had to happen or she would surely go crazy. I just smiled back and continued listening to her planning for my one-week Supernatural Abilities anniversary.

————————

And hello once again! I hope you all had a good holiday and also a happy new year that is coming up VERY soon! I placed a little poll on my message Cole about romance vs. only adventure/fighting stuff, so please place your input there!

Thanks again for all the support and I'm so happy to say that we're getting closer and closer to #1 on the fantasy section! See you soon with a very exciting chapter coming up :)

Chapter Thirteen - The Darkness

T o say I am a people person is a total lie.

So how exactly did I find myself down at the lake with my room-mate, her boyfriend, Cole, Allyson, and a few other people that I've only seen but never really was introduced to until tonight?

Claire, that's the answer.

I remember back to this morning when she practically had to beg me to look nice and wear something other than sweats and a t-shirt that I would normally wear on days off back home. The girl was persuasive, I'll give her that. When she almost dropped some tears I knew were fake, I had to give in.

So here I was... sitting on a rock with a drink in hand with some of the others would swim underneath the moonlit sky and the rest were sitting around talking and laughing.

Even at my own celebration I was basically alone.

"Hey!" Allyson came and sat down next to me. Her eyes were unnaturally gray tonight, even compared to other Minds. "You enjoying yourself?" she asked.

I shrugged and took another sip. "I'm just not so much of a party person, I guess."

She nodded and leaned back to watch the people screwing around in the water. "So how was your first week? Learn anything new?"

"I guess. Nothing too crazy. I still get people staring at me all the time for no reason which is pretty annoying."

"You're strong, Taylor," She commented. "Of course people are going to wonder about you. You're probably one of the toughest people here to have made it all the way up to level five so quickly."

"Not like I asked them to do that," I grumbled under my breath and she looked at me with a questioning gaze.

"So how'd you get up there?" She asked suddenly and I regarded the question with confusion.

"What?"

"To level five. How'd you do it?"

Her tone changed from just small talk to now gathering information. "I don't know, I just fought with what I have."

"But no one has ever looked like that before. You knew what you were doing. Did you train with another person before coming here or did you just practice on your own?"

"I didn't do anything," I mumbled. "It was just second-nature, I guess. I never even truly experimented with my powers like that until that day."

"But you had to have some sort of training," she insisted. I noticed her eyes changing, not becoming as gray as before and almost turning a different color. I blinked once and they were back to normal. "It's nearly impossible for anyone to have done that!"

"Why are you asking so many questions--"

"Hey!" Cole interrupted and I've never been so thankful for someone to do so. Allyson looked a little put off before excusing herself and leaving.

"Thanks for that," I muttered to him. "She was playing a game of twenty questions with me."

He laughed. "She does that sometimes. She's young and wants to be better so I just give her pointers. You're new, someone she hasn't annoyed yet, so you're an easy person for her nosiness."

"Well I hope she got enough out of me."

His cheeky grin told me otherwise. "She'll probably ask more tomorrow. So how do you like this party?" I gave him a look and he laughed. "I figured as much. Like I've said, I know your profile pretty well. You were always home or at your friend's house."

I shrugged, "I was never much of a people person. Ryan was always enough company for me."

He hummed in response before asking a question. "You must miss him, huh?"

I nodded. "We've always been close, even before and after my mom died when I shut everyone else out but him. I haven't had much time to really miss anyone or think back to everything I left behind, but it is still pretty hard."

"I get it. We all do. I left behind my parents, friends, and a little sister who probably looks nothing like how I left her."

"So we don't get any contact with them whatsoever?"

He shook his head. "Not until we leave here and even then it's rare."

I didn't do anything but sit there in silence. Had my mom still been around, I'm sure this separation would have been much harder. The only person I truly believe misses me is Ryan and even then he was probably brainwashed by a Mind just like the police and my father were after I left. Who's the say that anyone would even remember me if I went back? I know the Mind, Cole's fake father on the day he picked me up, did damage control after I left, but just how much did he change in people's minds?

"Hey," Cole bumped my shoulder when he realized my silence meant sadness. "I promised I would make sure you saw them again, didn't I?"

I smiled and rolled my eyes. "Yeah, and you better make it happen."

"I don't break my promises, Blondie."

We were silent again, but this time it was much more easygoing as we watched the others swim around in the so-called lake. Alex and Claire were both there, of course, along with three other people whom I forget the names of. Standing off to the side talking, I recognized the two Fires that held down Vanessa when she tried to kill me and a few others. Allyson was now nowhere to be seen but that thought disappeared when a question popped into my mind.

"Cole?" The boy in question raised his eyebrow to me as a signal that he was listening. "Is the past couple of days a good estimate of what the upcoming weeks should be like?"

He thought about it for a moment before shrugging. "More or less. It's just classes and training with the occasional excitement of a new Supernatural coming in. Departures and new levels are given out every new season and they're always followed by big parties for each level."

I practically groaned. "More parties?"

He laughed, "Supernaturals are really into fun. I guess being locked into an area in the middle of nowhere really gets to people."

"Well, I'm not a big partier. Guess I'm different from everyone."

He grinned and said, "Then I must be too."

I was about to smile back when a familiar feeling spread over me and I wasn't sitting next to Cole while overlooking the party anymore. I was in the dark, frightened and confused. While I recognized this as a vision, I couldn't help but be more immersed in it than ever before. It was like I was already there and a shiver shook down my spine.

I felt someone behind me before their words escaped, their mouth only centimeters from my ear.

"You're one of them," the voice hissed and I was jolted out of the state to find Cole shaking me with many worried eyes looking down.

"Are you okay?" Claire, now dripping wet and huddled next to Alex, asked as I struggled to regain my breath.

"I had a..." I gasped out. "A vision. I saw the future. I saw... Something."

Cole snapped from concerned to Supernatural-slash-Catcher-killer mode. "What happened? What did you see?"

I was about to describe the darkness and the voice when I felt something on the right side of my back and shoulder that immediately took my attention away from the question. The feeling went from merely uncomfortable to pain and Cole released me from where he held me up, clutching at his own back. A struggled breath escaped from Alex next to me as my eyes closed in pain and a scream erupted from my throat.

It felt like fire spreading across my skin, burning deep and was seemingly unstoppable. When I opened my eyes, black splotches lined my vision as I saw the people from the party confused and helping Cole, Alex, and myself.

"What the hell is going on?" I heard someone yell, but it was heard as if I was underwater as my eyes squeezed tightly once more.

"What is happening with them?"

"I can't heal them!"

"Get them to the infirmary now!"

I heard another scream, initially deeming it as Cole or Alex, before realizing it came from me. The pain somehow continued getting worse, something that I would cast off as impossible before it grew more and more unbearable. I forgot where I was. I forgot who I am. The only thing was the fire burning through the veins and skin on my back and shoulder before it finally overtook everything and I was greeted by darkness.

———————————

Dun dun, DUN! I hope everyone had a good New Years! Let's make 2016 the best year yet, yeah?

As always, thanks again for all that you do for me! I read each and every comment you all leave me, and also frequently reply to some as well so be sure to check there in case I say something interesting :)

Chapter Fourteen - The Marking

I was back in darkness; the same place I had my last vision.

This time my breath was shaky. I knew I wasn't in a definite place or room, but rather a limbo state. I wasn't dying. I wasn't dreaming. I was just being.

The same voice sounded behind me. With just one word, I shivered.

"Soon."

That's when I opened my eyes to the same hospital room I was in just days earlier after my placement exam. The only difference was that it was dark outside and the only light came from the radiance of the moon and a light peeking out from the bottom of the door. I could see shadows fading in as soft words are being spoken in the room behind it.

"This is the beginning," A voice I recognized as Galen said.

"The prophecy says six, but only five of them are here with no other reports coming from the outside. The other is still out there in a place with no Seekers," Another, Sophia, said.

"They'll turn up soon enough. Right now we must deal with the others."

"Have any of them woken up yet?"

"No. I expect it shouldn't be too long. She might have all the power but not enough to kill them all just from the Marking." Galen was quiet for quite some time before speaking again. "Cole Trainor. Alexander Carpenter. William Phillips. Leona Carter. Taylor Buckley... Who is the sixth?"

That's when the room faded out once more.

———

The next time I came to, it was bright. My eyes blinked, slowly adjusting to the sudden light as a pair of arms wrapped strongly around my body.

"I was so worried!" Claire said while holding me. "Are you okay? How are you feeling?"

She pulled back and I could see that her eyes were red and bags lined the bottom. For a girl who spends ample amounts of time on her appearance most of the time, I knew she must have been here all night.

"I'm fine," I mumbled. "What happened? Where are Alex and Cole?"

"Alex woke up a little bit ago and is being looked at by one of the nurses. Cole is still out." She bit her lip. "There's two others that came in just like you guys. I don't know what's going on, they won't tell me anything. But..."

I raised an eyebrow. "But what?"

"I'm not allowed to say. Galen warned me and said she needed to be the one to show you all--"

She was interrupted by a nurse and Sophia walking in. She looked well put together, despite knowing she was up and about last night too. Apparently the witch can't look tired because it's a sign of weakness or something.

"Good," she said while crossing her arms over her chest. "You're finally up. Sit tight and we'll be having a meeting when everyone's awake."

"What's going on?" I asked but she shook her head.

"Have some patience. You'll find out soon enough," she said and turned to leave the room. Before completely exiting, she stopped and looked over her shoulder at me. "Welcome to the beginning of the end, sweetheart. It'll be a long road coming."

She finally left but I sat there in complete confusion and fear. What's going on? What even happened last night? What the hell am I?

Claire sat there quietly, something I would have otherwise thought was impossible, while the nurse gently took my vitals. She asked me to lean forward, which I did, and when she lifted up my shirt, my friend gasped. I peeked up at her and her gray eyes shined in disbelief at what she was looking at on my back.

"What?" I asked her while the nurse gently prodded at my upper right shoulder making it sting in the same place that was burning yesterday. My friend only shook her head quickly and averted her eyes downwards.

I was about to say something else but I heard some yelling in the room next door. Claire's head bopped up and she gave off a small sign. "That must be Cole up. Mind if I go check on him?"

"No, you go on," I said and she practically ran out of the room.

The nurse continued checking up on me before gently wrapping my shoulder and back in dressings. It was tender to the touch and while I recognized the familiar feel of Healers doing their thing, the pain was never lessened. Was what happened to us truly that serious?

After the nurse tried and failed to heal me, she sat there to ask me some questions about how I feel and other random things such as how my time at Supernatural Abilities has been. After quite some time of awkward small talk, Galen walked in and the nurse scurried off.

"Can you please come with me, Taylor?" She asked and I nodded, getting out of bed while feeling the dull ache from my back and shoulder.

She walked pretty fast and I struggled to keep up. We went through the hospital in SA to a room that I had no idea was there. It was obviously for conferences or something similar, with a large table in the middle and chairs lining its outside. There I saw Sophia, Cole, and Alex all sitting there in silence with two others, a girl and boy whom I have only seen but never talked to also joining us. I took the empty spot next to Cole, both of us sneaking confused looks towards each other, while Galen took the head of the table, Sophia on her right.

"Last night, all of you faced the same problem," She started out, carefully measuring her words. "You all were hit with a burning pain that was so incredible that it forced you to pass out. This was to be expected for some of you, but not all, and definitely not so soon.

"You five all are of different elements. Taylor Buckley with the Mind. Cole Trainor with Fire. Alexander Carpenter with Water. Leona Carter and Earth. Then William Phillips with Air. All of you show immense strength in your abilities and have probably discovered that you are much stronger than your peers."

Galen then took a deep breath and bowed her head, as if to think about what she was the say next. While I know that Cole and Alex are very strong, I still had a lot to learn. I couldn't even think of a time that I saw this Leona or William fight so I can't vouch for their strength.

"This is not a coincidence," She continued on, her head still down. "You all are the strongest of your particular elements and all found yourselves in pain last night. That was the beginning of a great war, much larger than the one we have already been fighting. But you all are the heads of it, the only ones able to put an end to decades of death and fighting with the Catchers."

Her head then rose up, catching my eye in particular before scanning the others. Her next words went deep; beginning the chaos that I knew would ensue.

"You are part of the Big Six," She began. "The only ones who can kill the leader of the Catchers."

Of all the things that went through my head, the one thing that made an appearance the most was: What the hell does that even mean?

I looked over at Cole and he seemed perplexed in his thoughts. Galen gave us a moment to think about what she had said before continuing on with nonsense that seemed more like a two AM sitcom than my real life.

"There have been old Supernatural relics and prophecies from centuries in the past and they have all had a way of coming true. This was the last one, pertaining to a group of six individuals of different abilities who must overcome the leader of the Catchers. She is overwhelmingly strong and not only has the ability to make an entire army of reprogrammed Supernaturals in the form of Catchers, but also has possessed all five of the elements that you know. Last night, she gave you the Marking that signifies who you are. The pain was a signal to you, naming you as one of the Big Six to everyone.

She has the ability to get in your thoughts, but after the Marking, there is no way she is able to hurt you from afar."

I thought back to the so-called 'visions' of the darkness and the voice. They must have come from the Catcher's leader.

"Once our meeting is over, you can go back and view your Markings in private," she told us. "However, one of you seems to be missing. After all, you're all deemed the Big Six, but there are only five of you and five known abilities."

"So you're hinting that there's something we don't know?" William asked, a surprising accent lining his words.

"Surprise, surprise," Cole muttered from next to me, leaning back further in his chair. "Another thing we had to idea about? Wow."

"We didn't want to enact fear without knowing when this was going to happen. It could've happened ten years ago or centuries in the future. We had no idea," Galen told Cole who didn't say another word. She then continued on with what she was saying before the interruptions. "The last element is Electric, meaning the user is the only one able of conducting electricity for his or her power. They have not been found or brought in but there is a good chance that they will soon because the Marking has been placed on them. It's easy to hide a power, but not so easy to do that with your Marking."

"So how is everything going to change?" Alex asked. "We all have the Marking now, are we just placed in an all-out brawl?"

Sophia is the one who chimed in now. "Katherine likes to play cat-and-mouse. She'll tease you, but will want you to go to her to fight. You will train here, learning more abilities and growing stronger, while she waits for you to come."

"Katherine?" I found myself asking and Galen shot a look towards Sophia.

"That's the leader's name," Galen sighed. "What we haven't said yet, is that years ago, Sophia and a few others were sent out to find Katherine and her home. She is the only one who came back."

For the first time since I got here, Sophia's tough girl act faltered and I saw sincere sadness on her face. She masked it quickly and crossed her arms over her chest, holding her head high.

"When the Electric turns up, we'll send two of you out to get them depending on their location. We want it to be a quick, easy trip but we expect a lot of hiccups along the way. But, as said, Katherine is waiting you out, growing stronger herself, so we can't wait too long until you're all sent out. This is a mission that could not only cost all of your lives, but possibly thousands of others as well if you fail."

Well, that definitely doesn't calm my nerves.

"We will tell the public tonight. Please keep it under wraps until then and we'll see you in the conference hall at four. Until then you can have all the privacy that you want. I'm sorry you all have been dragged into this, but you must understand that you are our only hopes for survival. Without you, we will all be killed."

The meeting was adjourned and the five of us all walked out in silence while Sophia and Galen stood there. When we got outside, Claire was standing by a tree and immediately threw her arms over Alex, asking a million questions that none of us could answer. Leona and William left the group first, going to their separate ways without a goodbye. The rest of us went to the dorms, Alex and Claire stepped into his room immediately, making Cole turn to me.

"Mind if I come over for a bit? I don't want to hang out with the couple and don't want to be alone."

I only nodded and brought him into my room. It was left just as before the party happened yesterday with millions of outfits thrown across the floor. Cole didn't look bothered and took a spot on my bed, myself sitting down next to him.

"And I thought last night was going to be fun," he joked around.

"That is exactly why I don't like parties," I muttered and saw a line peeking out from the collar of his shirt. "Did you want to look at the Marking?"

He froze on the spot before relaxing. "Can I see yours first?"

I nodded and turned around, gently lifting to back of my shirt to reveal my back to him. I heard him gasp, just as Claire did in the hospital room and I almost jumped as a finger gently went across my skin.

"Wow," he breathed out. "At least this Katherine chick did a good job."

I situated myself so I could see my back from a mirror on my wall and found myself staring at the right side of my back that was filled with intricate lines that mimicked what a tattoo would look like. However, tattoos looked like they were placed there while the Marking had the appearance of being natural, as if it belonged there, in dark coloring.

I let my shirt fall back down in place and turned towards Cole. "Your turn," I mumbled and turned away in embarrassment as he shed his shirt.

"What?" He asked and I could almost hear the smirk in his voice. "Not like you haven't seen it before."

"And you gave me a hard time then too," I shot back and raised my head when he turned around, exposing his back and newly made Marking to me. His was more masculine, but just as detailed. Just as he did, I found myself reaching out and trailing my fingers down the lines. I expected them to be rougher or bumpy due to welting as tattoos would be, they were just as soft as his skin would be. His back tensed as the initial contact before relaxing as my fingers traveled around.

"This is so weird," I mumbled. "I never wanted a tattoo in my life but now that I have something like it, it feels like it's supposed to be there."

"So you're groping my back because...?" Cole joked and I pushed him away.

"Oh, shut up. You were doing the same thing to me."

He got up and looked at it in the mirror, humming in approval. "I like it, but yours is way cooler. Katherine must have a thing for Brains like you so she made yours better."

I rolled my eyes at him and watched as he leaned back in my bed, making himself comfortable without putting his shirt back on. I felt myself turning red and turned away to turn on the small television in our room to watch some mindless sitcoms.

"It's kind of weird," I said to him while making myself comfortable as well. "I've known you for over a week but yet it feels like longer than that."

"That's because I'm the man you've been dreaming about--" He stopped when I hit his arm. "I'm kidding, but that's how things go around here. Life seems to move twenty-times faster at Supernatural Abilities because who knows how long we all have together, especially now that we're at the frontline for this war."

"Do you think we're going to fail, Cole?" I asked, my voice turning small.

He didn't respond for a bit but when he finally did, he said, "Hey. We're going to train our asses off and you're going to be the best Mind this whole place has ever seen. Hell, you probably already are."

I snorted. "Yeah, right."

"Yeah, I am right. You'll learn plenty of new abilities in no time. Though, I do hope you don't learn how to read minds."

I raised an eyebrow at him. "Oh? Why not?"

He shrugged, a smile lining his lips. "I like to keep some things under wraps, Munchkin. I already have Claire going through my mind and getting into my business so I definitely don't need you doing the same thing."

"If Claire could go through my mind, how couldn't she see that you didn't like Vanessa?" I asked.

"Some things I don't like to think about and block them out as much as possible," He muttered. "She only really butts in when she knows I'm lying about something and I was always pretty good at not letting my emotions show."

"But yet you tell me."

"You're just easy to open up to, I guess."

I smiled at him and found myself laying down next to him on the small bed, but not in a sexual way. More in an 'I'm-so-exhausted-from-all-the-events-that-happened-recently' type. We were quiet for a bit, only watching the stupid shows that we got on the television before I found myself falling asleep to the noises of a romantic comedy and Cole's steady breathing.

———————

Had to keep you guys waiting on that last one :) Hope you enjoyed and thank you so much for everything you do for me.

AND NOTE. PLEASE do not post any spoilers. It's getting to the point that I have to delete so many comments that have spoilers from the original. I have many first-time readers on this story and I would hate for the plot to be ruined for them. Just monitor what you're commenting and posting if you're original fans of the series :)

Chapter Fifteen - The Announcement

"Well, well, well," Alex's voice boomed in my room, making me wake up with a start. A groan sounded in my ear and a hand on my waist tightened as I found myself looking at Cole's face who was still trying to sleep.

"Just five more minutes," Cole mumbled and subconsciously pulled me closer.

Somehow in the few hours we got to sleep, Cole and I ended up cuddling on my small bed in my room and I found myself looking at Claire and Alex who stood in the doorway with knowing gazes.

"Quite a position we've found you two in, huh?" Alex asked, humor lining his words.

It must have looked bad: Cole's arms around me. His shirt still off from when we examined our Markings. Both of our hair completely messed up from the nap.

"Cole," I hissed quietly while shaking him awake. "Get the hell up!"

My friend opened his eyes, realized he was holding me, and jumped up, successfully falling off the bed. Claire nearly died laughing at him and Cole got up with a grumpy expression on his face.

"If you saw us in cahoots, why did you bother us? He muttered and my eyes widened.

"We were just sleeping, I swear!" I exclaimed and the couple in front of us gave me a disbelieving look.

"Our love is not something to be ashamed of, Blondie!" Cole cried out with sarcasm lining his words and his hand falling over his heart. "You're so cruel!"

"You're such a liar--

"Anyways," Alex interrupted. "We came to get you guys for the assembly. You know, the one we have to be at." He gave us a stern look and peeked over at Claire, giving us the impression that he didn't tell her what had happened yet just as we were supposed to do.

"Okay, just let me get dressed real quickly," I said, getting up with a stretch and grabbing an outfit off the floor that had been left there from the night before.

I watched as Cole also got up, exposing his back to us and Claire gasped just as she did with seeing my Marking. She looked away with a hurt look, knowing that we were all hiding something from her. There was no doubt in my mind that she's probably read all of our thoughts to know what was going on but didn't say anything to preserve some privacy. When her eyes caught mine, I knew I was right and I gave her a small frown in return as a silent apology.

I quietly went into the bathroom and changed quickly to come outside and find that Cole had finally put on a shirt. Once we were all ready, the three of us headed to the auditorium while everyone around us buzzed about what this mysterious conference could be about.

"I bet it's a special guest," one girl told another who shook her head.

"I think there's going to be a tournament or something fun like that announced!"

Oh, how wrong they were.

I tucked my head low, pulling my collar up to further cover my shoulders from any wandering eyes that might accidentally see my Marking. I've already been the center of attention, but now I'll be looked upon for everything. All these people's lives are at stake and the six of us are the only ones who can keep them alive. I began to breathe quickly, shaking from the fear and unwanted pressure put on me. Cole noticed and looked down at me from his superior height before placing his hand on my upper back, steering me out of the main crowd and off to the side.

"You okay?" He asked, leaning me against a tree.

I shook my head. "All of these people are going to be looking towards us, Cole. Their lives are all in our hands. What we do from now on will not only affect ourselves, but every Supernatural as well."

"You're not doing it alone, though. It'll be you and me, Alex, and the three others. Galen, Sophia, and so many others will help make sure we're more than ready. You'll never be alone in this. Even if you have no one else, I'll be there."

In this extremely sappy moment, I couldn't help but smile at him, taking more deep breaths to calm myself until my heartbeat was back to normal.

"You good?" He asked and I nodded. "Great. Now shall we go get exposed to our peers?"

I chuckled and stood up straighter as the two of us followed the last of the Supernaturals heading into the auditorium. Alex and Claire saved us spots in the middle and we sat down, still hearing the chatter and guesses as to what this would be about.

After a few minutes, the curtain opened up to show an array of seats filled with instructors that I have both seen and worked with during my short, but seemingly long, time here. Galen stepped out to the microphone and the entire stands grew quiet.

I phased out for most of what she was saying, not wanting to hear the bitter truth for yet another time. I have never heard such a place filled with so many people be so quiet besides the one voice announcing the beginning of an even greater war than the one everyone thought we were in. Galen never mentioned any names until the end.

"Now only five of the people in the Big Six are at Supernatural Abilities today. Will Leona Carter, Alexander Carpenter, Cole Trainor, Taylor Buckley, and William Phillips all stand?"

With my head down, I did as I was told and I heard the shifting of people as they looked around at all of us. I felt like an animal at a circus. Instead of dance, monkey, dance, I get fight, Mind, fight.

My eyes caught Vanessa's from several rows ahead and she looked both angry and scared. For once I got something other than complete hatred from her as we stared at each other. After a few moments, we all sat down and Galen marked the assembly as over.

"If you have any questions, please address your instructors," She said as people began erupting in shouts of confusion and fear. "Classes will go on as scheduled tomorrow."

Alex, Claire, Cole, and I fought through the crowds to get outside while so many people tried to stop us. They asked us what our plans were, how we were going to go about this, and how we would save them. All questions that none of us could answer.

"Everyone knows where our dorms are so they won't be safe until curfew. Claire and I will get some food and meet you two up at the lake," Alex said to Cole and I.

I didn't have time to respond until Cole nodded once at his best friend, grabbed my hand, and ran in the direction that I vaguely remember the lake to be in. Thankfully, we were one of the first people out and no one was able to stop us as we made our breakaway. It only took a few minutes of running until the clearing came in sight and we slowed.

We didn't say anything but both sat down on the rock we were on the previous night. The initial wave of fear from before was now replaced with anger. I kicked at some dirt before noticing another boulder across the way and used telekinesis to lift it up before pounding it back down, causing chunks to break off.

"I can't do this," I gritted my teeth and threw one of the smaller chunks against the tree. "I didn't sign up for any of this when I came here. I never wanted a death sentence."

"None of us did, hot shot," Cole muttered. "But it's time to grow up and live with it."

I glared at him. "You're saying this to a seventeen year old girl. I should be in high school, worrying about whether or not I'm going to the prom with my crush, not having an entire species relying on me and the rest of us!"

I threw telekinesis at a tree, successfully making it fall down with a large crack. For once in my life, I actually felt the power that ran through me, the strength that granted me a spot in the Big Six, and I hated it. I wanted nothing more than to go back to my easy-going lifestyle of wanting to get into college to escape my broken home.

"You can have this time to have a meltdown, but after this, it's game time," Cole spoke in an even, yet stern voice. "There's no time for playing the Damsel-in-distress act. It's time to grow up and accept the burden that has been placed on you."

"Accept it? I yelled, turning towards him in anger. "I can't just accept the fact that I could potentially die in this situation."

"News flash, Princess," He said, his dark eyes trained on me. "Everyone dies. Might as well do it for a good cause."

I held up a branch, ready to throw it at him but once it was mid-air, he quickly burned it to ash and pushed me against a tree, holding my hands in such a way that prevented me from firing at him again. My chest huffed out in exasperation from all the energy I had expelled while he sternly looked straight into my eyes.

"No more of this," He warned. "You're better than some temper tantrum."

I glared back at him until I no longer felt the fight inside of me. My whole body relaxed and he let go of me as I let myself fall down in a heap.

"I just don't know what to do, Cole," I mumbled as he took a spot next to me. "This is all too much."

"It'll seem impossible, but you'll learn. You have to grow up quickly now more than ever."

I only nodded before groaning. "And I thought you were supposed to be the hot headed one."

Cole shrugged. "Well, I am hot, but most of the time I can handle my emotions. Now you? I understand how this could be a lot to take in, but you can't do that all the time."

"I think I'm good now... Thanks."

"Of course, Shorty," he said while messing up my hair. "Anything for my little Blondie."

I rolled my eyes at him and stripped off my shirt to a sports bra before jumping into the water. It felt good in the heat of the day, especially from being around Cole so much. The boy felt like the sun and this water made me relax.

It didn't take long for Cole to do the same thing and follow me in. The water's temperature rose a few degrees, but still felt great. I watched as he swam around, the Marking on his back showing easily under the clear water. In some ways, it was easy to forget the past 24 hours and the events that unfolded, but they were always in the back of my mind.

Claire and Alex joined us a little bit later, carrying armfuls of snacks and dinner items for us to munch on until it was safe for us to go back with little confrontations with the other Supernaturals. After some time spent on swimming, we all sat down on some rocks and had a dinner in quiet until Claire broke it.

"So what are you going to do?" She asked in a low voice. I could hear the fear laced in her words, but she tried to mask it.

Alex shrugged and put his arm around her. "Live with it. Train. Fight. As long as we're prepared we'll be able to do what we need to do."

"But you could die," She almost whispered.

"It needs to be done, regardless of what happens to us," Cole interjected. "If it wasn't us, it would have been someone else. The six of us will have to succeed if we ever want our future generations to live in safety."

Nothing much was said after that.

It seemed like Cole and Alex have accepted this fact, while I still felt the various emotions about it all. It was unfair that this has been put on us. It was scary to know that all Supernaturals rest in our hands. There were so many other things to feel rather than just letting it happen.

After eating, the four of us swam around for a bit longer until the sun went down making us have to pack up and head back to the dorms. Alex and Claire headed out rather quickly while Cole hung back and waited for me to dry off and put all my clothes back on. The woods were dark, so he made a ball of fire in his hands in order for us to see where we were going.

"We're probably out a little later than curfew," Cole stated. "But, honestly, who is going to get mad at us about it? We have a lot of power now."

"We shouldn't abuse that though," I muttered while pulling my jacket closer to my body. He saw my attempts at warming myself and placed a hand on my shoulder, letting heat radiate out from his palm. "Thanks," I told him after my teeth stopped chattering.

"I'm not saying we will," He continued on with our previous conversation. "But they can't expect us to be all gun-ho about this thing. We're still young and deserve to have fun."

I was quiet until a question popped into my mind. "How old is young exactly for you?"

He laughed. "I just turned nineteen a few months ago."

"Wow. I turn eighteen in a few weeks."

A smirk rose onto his lips. "Oh, I know. The papers told me."

I turned a little red at his comment. "Stop talking about those papers! We all know you know every single unneeded detail about me!"

He laughed and we continued to the dorms while only making little small talk. As predicted, curfew just passed so the entire campus and hallways were bare, allowing us to walk easily into the building without an issue. Cole escorted me to my room, bid me farewell, and made his way to his own place. Once inside, I saw Claire lying on her back while staring up at the ceiling.

"I never expected this out of your one-week Supernatural Abilities party," she admitted. "And I'm not too happy about it either."

"But it did happen and now we just have to go on. Alex and Cole did, so now it's our turn."

I changed into some comfier clothes for sleep and laid down on my bed just as my roommate was doing. She snuck a peek at me with a little smile lining her lips.

"Speaking of Cole..." She started and I groaned, knowing where she was going to go with this.

"Goodnight, Claire," I stopped her and turned off the light while her laughter rang in the dark room.

———————————————

So I'm at the point in my updates that it has caught up to all the extra chapters that I have written in advanced, so I'm going to start making Fridays my official update days! However, please keep in mind that I am a working, full time college student so updates might not happen right on time every week. But, unlike many of the others stories I have written, I LOVE writing this and work on it every time I am free.

But, as always, thank you so much for all the support! See you in a few days :)

Chapter Sixteen - The New Instructor

I was woken up by my bed flipping over, making me fall to the ground with a groan. When I sat up I found Sophia casually standing in our doorway.

"What the hell was that for?" I asked angrily while rubbing at my side that had hit my nightstand.

"Galen wants a meeting and called upon me to rally the troops. Get dressed in your work out attire and come on," She said while turning around and walking out, closing the door with telekinesis on her way out.

Claire was now awake, sitting up and rubbing at her eyes before spotting me with a mattress on top of my body.

"Was that Cole?" she asked, her voice groggy and still filled with the sound of sleep.

"Sophia," I grumbled and threw the mattress against the wall. Instead of going back to sleep like I so wanted to, I did as was asked of me and quickly changed and got ready before heading out to where Galen's office was.

The sun was just barely rising now so the entire campus was most likely still asleep. Once I got to the building, the doors opened before I could grab the handles myself and I took a spot next to Alex. There was only four of us here: Galen, Alex, myself, and Leona who looked like she woke up with a smile. I mean, really. Who wakes up at this time and already looks like they've been awake for hours?

It didn't take long for all the others to show up as well and Galen address us all. "You will no longer be training with your levels. You five will all get one-on-one sessions with the best of your ability at SA. You will still join your peers in the arena, but please do not go too hard on everyone. They will all feel it is unfair that you'll still be participating, but you need that experience in order to grow."

She paused and opened the double doors leading into her office to allow for several people whom I have seen during various classes or trainings. They all stood along the wall and Galen nodded at them in approval. She began naming off all of us and the instructor that we would now be working with. All was well until she got to me.

"Taylor, you'll be working with Sophia."

"What?!" I almost yelled before thinking. Galen's second in command, and now my personal trainer as well, didn't look quite as happy to be put with me either.

"Yes, Taylor," Galen eyed me. "Sophia is now whom you'll be reporting to."

I slumped in my chair and I saw Cole smirk at me from across the table. I glared at him and the boy had the audacity to hold back a chuckle.

Galen continued on as if nothing was wrong. "There is a classroom set aside for you five. There, you'll be learning much more advanced techniques and testing them out. After class, you'll still have lunch then have either training with your instructors or arena fights. You'll be both separated from the rest of the Supernaturals here and joined up. Expect a lot of angry and worried people coming up to you all in the upcoming days. This is news to all of us, so just stick it out until the shock of it all goes away."

I scoffed, "Like that'll happen..." I muttered under my breath, knowing that I've heard those words plenty of times before only for them to all become lies and my name be on everyone's lips in story after story.

The meeting was adjourned and we were all immediately taken into the empty classroom specifically for the Big Six. The day for everyone else wouldn't be starting for another hour, so the entire campus was empty.

The room was just as big and stocked as the other ones I've been in and our individual instructors immediately took us all away from one another. Sophia looked as grumpy as ever and squared me up as soon as we got our own spot.

"Do you remember the placement exam?" She asked me while leaning against the wall with her arms crossed over her chest.

"How could I forget where we first met?" I asked sarcastically and she narrowed her eyes at me.

"Let me be more specific," she clarified through gritted teeth. "Remember the time I made you cry in front of dozens of Supernaturals?" When I glared at her, a smirk rose onto her face in victory. "Good, because so do I. We do background research on everyone before they step foot into the arena for the first time. You family life and house were all things that I both know and have seen. I used that information and formulated a scene in your head that you couldn't help but think it was real. Well, not so much. You were able to catch a flaw, but most people can't. This is called mental manipulation and I'm going to try to teach you how to do it. It could prove useful when fighting Catchers that are protecting Katherine, but I don't think it would have any effect on her."

She began sending pictures into my mind, showing me how she is able to control her brain and propel power onto another person's. She would mess with mine, sending me to random places, such as the jungle or New York City, or doing something terrifying like making me believe I was drowning.

"You see how it could be a weapon now?" She asked while I coughed and struggled to catch a breath a horrible dreamlike state.

I gasped. "Got it."

It was different than the other abilities that I have, as those have never been involving another person. To reach into someone's mind was a difficult thing, and I was having problems completely investing myself within. While I could get a touch of it, I couldn't reach in and plant myself entirely inside.

"How do you expect to kill the person in charge of the Catchers if you can't even learn this one thing?" Sophia groaned, exasperated over my many failed attempts.

"I've been here for hardly a week, bear with me a little," I said with a glare aimed towards her.

"You're useless," she muttered and looked up at the time. "And it's time for lunch. We'll meet up later for more training."

She stalked away leaving me breathing heavily and taking sips of my water. After a tough couple hours of training, sweat was already dripping down my face and I probably looked like a mess. I bet I looked better during the placement exam compared to today, and I was awful then.

Cole came over to my in the middle of my recovery and stood over my exhausted form. He looked like nothing had happened today, just a normal day of training and light exercise.

"You don't look too good," He commented and I glared up at him.

"You know, you shouldn't say that to a lady."

He gave me a look. "Pretty sure you can take the truth, Sweaty. I haven't lied to you yet, and I don't plan to."

He offered me a hand which I gratefully took before he helped me up. The others were all still finishing up their own trainings so Cole and I took the initiative to just leave to get lunch. As soon as we exited the room, the Supernaturals hanging out outside, having just got out of their own sit-down lessons, stopped talking and stared.

With my head tucked down, Cole led the way while the eyes followed us out. It was unnerving and uncomfortable, but luckily no one engaged us to ask questions or voice their concerns. I remember Galen mentioning our Markings during the assembly yesterday to entire place, so I saw some eyes trailing down to see if they could catch a peek of it on my back. All of us were wearing our short sleeved workout gears today, so there would be a very slim chance of anyone seeing any of ours.

When we made it to the cafeteria without any controversy, I was relieved to see that Claire was already seated at a table that was a bit more secluded than the others. She gave us a smile when we sat down, both fit with plates before turning back to her own food.

"How was training?" she asked while taking a bite of potatoes.

"Awful," I said at the same time Cole replied with, "Pretty good." My roommate only smiled and proceeded to continue eating.

While I consumed my food, I noticed that the dining hall was much quieter today than usual. Looking around, I saw people with their heads tucked low and other sneaking glances over at our table, namely Cole and I. It didn't take too long for Alex to make his way over, only looking a little flustering from the earlier training.

Apparently I was the only one who went through hell and back today.

Allyson came and joined us around halfway through lunch. She didn't ask us any questions, which was weird because she bugged me for answers the last time I had seen her. When lunch was over, all of us, except for Allyson who was still too low in levels, headed to the training fields. Claire went to her own group while Cole, Alex, and I went to our specific instructors that were on the other side of the grass. I could see the other Supernaturals glancing over at us and hardly working on their own training.

I walked up to Sophia who looked as demeaning and expectant as ever. Instead of the nice clothes she wore this morning, she had switched into some work out gear that matched my own.

"We'll do some team fights today between you and I," she said. "Basically try to hit me while expelling your power correctly. Try to reach deep into your brain for something, anything, new, just like the placement exam."

She began by pushing a force against my torso that made me fly a few feet back. I got up quickly and watched as brick came coming straight for my face. Using my own power to slow down time, I was able to grab control of it and fire it back. I was surprised to see that Sophia had somehow managed to turn it into dust halfway to her.

This back and forth motion continued for a while until Sophia must have gotten bored of it all. She then fired ten weights straight for me, coming at all sides, and I initially panicked. With a split second to think. I grasped onto the shield that I had barely practiced with and watched as the weights hit an unseen force a few feet away from me before falling to the ground. As I dropped my protection, Sophia looked at me in surprise.

"You can propel your shield," she commented. "That could actually be useful against Katherine. How far could you go?"

I shrugged. "I don't know. Maybe a bit more?"

"We'll have to practice that tomorrow."

I almost groaned at the thought of having to endure this human training me for however long it takes to be great. Peeking over at the other Big Six members, I saw them all doing similar things with their own mentors. Sophia noticed my lack of attention and ordered me to start again.

We didn't train for too much longer and once she let me leave, I made a beeline for the communal girls' showers. There were a few people already there, eyeing me as I walked in. Luckily, I was able to sneak past without any word from them and pull the curtain closed so no one could disturb me.

I ended up being in the shower for quite awhile, long surpassing the time it took for my fingers to resemble prunes. When I got out, I wrapped a towel around my torso and peeked out of the curtain. When I saw that no one was here with me, I released the breath I didn't realize I had been holding and walked out to grab some fresh clothes from my locker.

I didn't want anyone to question or see the Marking until they had already become accustomed to seeing someone else's. Just judging by Claire's reactions to both Cole's and my own made me not want anyone else to be surprised or curious about me.

I was about to start changing when a throat was cleared behind me. Turning around, I saw Vanessa leaning against the wall and all my defenses immediately went up.

"Relax, I'm not here to murder you," she said while getting up and sitting down on one of the benches. "Nice Marking by the way. I didn't expect it to look like that."

"It's different for all of us," I muttered. "So maybe your expectations will be met with someone else's."

"Of course you would know," She eyed me. "Considering how much time you spend with Cole, I'm sure you've seen his Marking quite a few times already."

I was about to refute her remarks but she held up a hand.

"That's not why I'm here. We broke up, I get it. I just want you to know that this whole shit fest, the Catcher leader, you guys, everything, is big. If you ever need help or training, let me know and I'll give you a fight that'll challenge you."

Her words caught me off guard. Her helping me? Vanessa actually being nice?

"Don't think this is a whole identity switch, the whole mean girl going nice because it's not. I still hate you. I just want to make sure that Cole is going to be alright and you need to be in top shape to make sure that happens."

"Oh," I mumbled. "Thanks. I'll, uh, take you up on that offer one day."

She nodded once and turned around, her hair whipping across her shoulders. "By the way, you might want to get dressed. I'm sure people will be back in here any moment."

When she left, I did just that. Sure enough, some girls walked in as soon as I pulled on my shoes. They regarded me with caution before proceeding to do their own thing.

I grabbed the last of my belongings and headed back to my dorm room, taking comfort in the silence and time to myself for once. I didn't head down to dinner, but instead relaxed on my bed, watching some mindless, cable TV sitcoms and worried about little to nothing.

____

As promised, it is Friday (Well, for me, anyways) and I have updated! This will now be the day you should get an update, with possible Saturday/Sunday updates as well if I'm especially busy the week I could be writing.

Thanks, as always, for the support and see you in a week!

Chapter Seventeen – The Proof

There was screaming all around me, but I couldn't see any faces through the dense smoke and dust. It was a mess of all the elements, fighting while I stood in the middle doing absolutely nothing. Completely frozen, in shock.

"Taylor!" I heard a familiar voice yell at me. "Get the hell out of there!"

And that's when I woke up.

I was gasping for air while my skin shone with sweat. Beside me, Claire was still sleeping away as if nothing was happening. I envied her, but these visions came along with my Mind ability.

Looking at the clock, it was almost time for me to get up anyways and because I knew I wouldn't get back to sleep after having a vision like that, I decided to start getting ready for training with Sophia.

I had undergone several sessions with her in the days that have passed but never truly achieved much. I felt myself understanding more and gaining a better grasp of the power that was inside me, but I was never able to hold on to any of it to bring out new skills and because of that, I faced the wrath of Sophia.

But today was different, as we would now be put into the rink to fight against other Supernaturals who were not in the Big Six. Some have already thrown fits about this, claiming that they're being set up for failure. The only response to that is something along the line that if we, meaning the Big Six, don't have practice then everyone is doomed.

You know, happy thoughts.

Pulling on my usual Mind attire and after doing my daily bathroom activities, I headed out into the already warm and humid outside despite it being the morning. I decided to just go to our training room and start warming up. Hopefully Sophia would appreciate the fact that I was taking the initiative and starting my day off early and right.

As expected, I was the first one to the specified Big Six training room. I eyed some weights in the corner and picked one up, bringing it over to myself. I wasn't the strongest physical person, but would lifting this count as doing arm curls?

The door suddenly opened and in walked Leona, making me drop the weight with a bang. Her prominent green eyes showed surprise when she saw me in there, most likely not expecting anyone, let alone the person who usually oversleeps to be here already.

"Oh, hello there," She said, her voice gentle. I hadn't really had the chance to connect with Leona or William yet, the other two people in the Big Six. I'm not too good at making new friends but if I had to work with these two, I guess I had to become an expert at socialization as well as my ability.

"Hey," I said and gave her a smile. "Couldn't sleep so I got up early and came here. Are you usually awake before the sun rises?"

She shrugged and put down her bag. "Once the earth's up, so am I. It's a characteristic of most people with my ability."

"Huh, I didn't know that."

She grinned, showing off some white teeth that shone brightly against her dark complexion. "You're still new here and getting the hang of things, so I wouldn't expect you to. However, I am surprised that you're learning so quickly. You seem to have really gotten used to this sort of life in the couple week you've been at SA."

"Kinda had to," I muttered, rubbing at the back of my neck. "Especially with this whole Big Six stuff, I never had the choice to just give up or say no."

Leona gave me another little smile. "And you're doing a good job here, from what I can tell."

"Thanks," I said in both surprise and happiness at her compliment. "That really means a lot."

She nodded once before silently beginning her own warm up method: yoga, stretching, the relaxing business. For someone who has to use their body to fight, I imagine they would have to be pretty fit to do that. I mean, look at Cole. The boy has muscle.

But with me, the one who primarily fights through their mind, all that isn't very needed, but could prove useful. In a physical fight against a Catcher, I would die immediately. I need to train both my mind and my body.

"Care if I join you?" I asked, taking a spot next to her where Leona was doing some crazy twists with her body. She shook her head and tried to mimic her position.

And that's how Cole and Alex found me later and almost died laughing when they saw stance I was in thirty minutes later.

"Pretty sure that's not right, Taylor," Alex said in the middle of his cackles.

Leona was at a perfect angle and arc, while I probably assembled the Leaning Tower of Pisa more than anything else. I dropped my body to the floor in a lump and huffed out in frustration. When they looked down at my crumbled form, I glared.

"Huh," Cole commented. "Your papers didn't say that you're the most inflexible person ever. Looks like I won't be calling you Twisty anytime soon."

"Well, sorry for trying," I groaned while adjusting myself to a sitting position. "I just want to be strong and physically fit like the rest of you guys."

"And you're not?" Cole asked with his eyebrow raised. "Taylor, you look great--"

"It's not all about looks, you know," I eyed him. "In the event that my powers magically disappear and I'm left with pure strength, I'm toast!"

"And how would that even happen?" Alex challenged. From next to me, Leona watched our conversation in joy.

"Gee, I don't know. How'd the hell did we end up with superpowers? Or this thing on our backs? Or how did we all magically pass out from pain at the same time? I know I haven't been here too long, but I'm starting to see a pattern of things that seemed impossible happening."

Alex didn't say anything as Cole gave me an impressed look. He offered a hand that I gratefully took.

"Then let's go," Cole said and I gave him a confused look. "You're being trained a different way. Let's go on a run."

Alex laughed as Cole grabbed my hand, despite my objection to running, and led me outside. When I finally was able to pull away, I faced him in defiance.

"I'm not interested in running--"

"It's needed, Princess," Cole grinned while stretching his quads for a few moments. "Stamina is really important."

"I'm not--Ow!" When Cole shot tiny balls of flame at my head, I jumped back. However, he didn't stop and I get going and moving out of the way until I eventually had to start running. After some time of him shooting fire at me from behind and myself further ahead, he finally stopped and caught up to me, the two of us running through the wood side-by-side.

"See, it's not so bad!" He said exuberantly while I was already gasping for air.

"I... hate you so much," I wheezed by continued on.

Cole grinned at me. "That's not what I'd say to you, but I'll take it."

He thankfully didn't take me on a long run and once we circled back to the training room, everyone was there and I collapsed onto the ground in a mess of heavy breathing.

"That... was awful," I gasped while Cole chuckled.

"You're fine... Unless you need some CPR? A little mouth-to-mouth resuscitation?"

Alex laughed from next to him while I felt myself turning redder than I was before from the heat. "Oh, shut up," I got out.

The others in the Big Six were whisked away for their own trainings not too long after that while Sophia actually gave me an easy day after seeing the mess I was in after the run.

"Cardio isn't a bad idea," she commented. "I want you to start running before we start training everyday. You usually work on strength and stamina during level three, but because you skipped that, you're like a twig with the lungs of a smoker. Go work out your body for once."

"Gee, thanks for the vote of confidence."

She smirked before getting back to business. "Now for arena training today. Like Galen said before, don't go too hard. Focus on trying to get those new things we have practiced to work. These fights are for you to learn and practice all you new skills, not primarily to win."

I nodded and she let me head off to lunch with Alex in tow. Cole was still training and doing his own thing so we left him in favor of getting ourselves fed. In the middle of getting food, Alex cleared his throat.

"So... " He trailed the word off. "You and Cole?"

"What about us?" I asked, not catching onto what he was saying.

"You two are pretty close now, huh?" I thought about it for a moment and nodded.

"Yeah, I guess so."

He hummed in response, a little smile on his lips. "Claire and I can tell. Pretty close." He had grabbed the last of his food and the two of us went to the table where my roommate was waiting for us. "Right, Claire?"

"What?" She asked through a mouthful of salad.

"Cole and Taylor are getting real close, right?"

Claire's face immediately brightened, a smirk lining her lips. "Definitely. Really close."

The couple in front of me were looking at each other, as if communicating telepathically and honestly, that's probably normal in this place. I finally sighed and stared at the two of them expectantly.

"Okay, why are you two acting weird?" I asked and the two just blinked at me.

"You're right, Claire. She's in denial and blind," Alex whispered to her and I groaned.

"I can hear you, you know!"

"She can hear me?" Alex whispered much too loudly to his girlfriend while she giggled. "Must be some crazy Mind trick!"

I was about to say something else but instead I heard a, "Hey, Shorty!" and turned around to see Cole taking the spot next to me. The couple exchanged a look.

"Still not done with the nicknames?" I asked and went back to my food when Cole shook his head.

"When are these names going to turn into 'babe' or 'cutie?'" Alex asked, raising an eyebrow in humor. "'Cause you two are getting pretty close."

I could feel myself turning red but Cole remained calm. "The answer is easy," Cole started. "Whenever she finally accepts her love for me."

The table started laughing and I rolled my eyes at my friend. "You're hilarious, Cole. Absolutely gut-wrenchingly funny."

He reached over and ruffled my hair. "Nah, don't worry about it, Brain. You're just fun to tease, that's all. We're just friends, of course!"

I hummed in approval and continued eating until it was time for us to go to arena training. It kind of unnerved me to have to fight someone who wasn't Sophia or in the Big Six. I wasn't necessarily worried about overpowering them or anything, but more scared that they could beat me and make me out to be a fool in front of everyone. I'm supposed to be one of six people who are the strongest of our kind and if I can't win a fight against one of my peers, who would trust me to beat the leader of the Catchers?

When we reached the board, it said I would be going against someone named Sam Jeon. I didn't recognize the name, but he was a Fire so we would see how this went. Considering I got burned in a second with Vanessa, this might not end well.

My fight was one of the last ones to go, so I took a spot near the corner with my friends. People would peek over at us, specifically Alex, Cole, and I, with angry expressions, probably mad that we are put into this exercise with them. I watched as everyone went, including those in the Big Six and Claire, who happily won her battle. As predicted, Leona, Cole, Alex, and William were all successful in their fights, making the people around me mutter in disdain every time they were pronounced the winner.

Then it was my turn. Like last time, I headed downstairs and did some light stretching before finding myself in the arena, looking across to see a boy in red clothing similar to my own. Once the buzzer went off, I took the initiative and made the first attack.

Unlike my last fight, this Sam guy was good. He dodged everything I threw at him while returning it with blasts of his fire. I started growing frustrated at this and slowed down time, running forward, and blasting a wave of unseen power straight towards his chest, making him fly back.

Apparently that made him mad because the next thing I knew, a giant tornado of fire came straight for me. I only had a split second to put up a shield and run through the flames. Sam's initially happy expression was gone when he saw me emerge because he probably thought that move was going to be the finisher. Using his moment of shock, I forced him against the wall with one hand while grabbing whatever I could using telekinesis in the other, holding it over him as a threat to drop it, successfully ending the fight.

When I dropped everything to the side of him and let the force that held him still fade out, Sam just stared at something to my right in shock. Looking down, I saw that the side of my shirt was scorched to a crisp, revealing the side of my sports bra and body. I must not have projected the shield far enough out to include the loose shirt while going through the flames, allowing the flame to catch hold of the thin cotton.

Normally, this wouldn't be an issue. However, with the right side of my shirt scorched off, everyone could see most of my Marking. All around me people stared in confusion, awe, and a million other emotions that I couldn't make out. The others and I have carefully hid our Markings in the days following the meeting, not wanting the extra attention to be brought upon us. While we all knew they would see it eventually, none of us wanted to be the first to show in and, of course, this wardrobe mishap is also the first time all of these people are seeing what mark the Big Six as one of our kind.

In some ways all of this could have been a lie to them: The Big Six, Marking, Katherine, but now there is physical proof that all of them could see. It shouldn't have been a big deal, but it was. With such intricate lines, it looks so natural and beautiful, but is also a sign of what is to come and the symbol of a possible death sentence.

That's when I found myself pushing past Sam and the referee in my arena and out the back door. I didn't stop to get healed, knowing that I must have had at least a couple burns on me. Instead, I tried running of the place only to be stopped by Cole.

"Hey, slow down there. It's fine. It's just your Marking--"

"It makes it real, Cole. All of this," I spread my arms out in exasperation. "They were mad before, but now they have proof that all of this is seriously happen. It makes me and you and the other four all freaks. It makes us responsible now that they all believe in this crazy story."

"They'll calm down like usual. They'll talk about it for a while, yeah, but why wouldn't they? You have the Marking and yeah, it means something more than you being in the Big Six, but it's still you. It's still your skin. You're still a short, little Brain. Have them gawk and get angry at us all they want, but the power is out of their hands now. It's on us and worrying about how you're perceived will only hurt you in the long run."

I finally released a big breath, realizing that he was right. While these people have been waiting and searching for any sign of our Markings, it doesn't change anything for us. I can't keep worrying about what everyone else wants when I'm still training to be the best Mind I can be.

"Thanks," I muttered, giving him a little smile. "You're pretty good at calming me down."

He laughed and threw his arm over my shoulders, leading me out of the building. "Ever since day one, Shorty, I knew you would be a panicky one."

We began walking back to the dorms, ignoring the last of the fights that were still going on in the arenas.

"Hey, one more thing," Cole piped in around five minutes into our walk.

I raised an eyebrow at him. "Yeah?"

"Next fight, you might want to keep your clothes on."

I felt myself turning red from both embarrassment and anger and pushed away from him while he laughed at my reaction. "It wasn't my fault he was a Fire!"

In the midst of his cackling, Cole was able to deliver another sentence, "I'm a Fire too and while I have a different method of getting clothes off, that does not include it happening in front of dozens of Supernaturals. Just refrain from stripping next time, okay?"

I rolled my eyes at him, knowing that he was just teasing me like usual, and continued on with our walk back to our homes.

This would've been up WAY sooner if it weren't for Wattpad being some maintenance!

This is kind of a lame, filler chapter, but they're needed once in awhile to continue the story on. As always, thanks for everything and see you next week!

Chapter Eighteen - The Memory

"You made quite the scene yesterday," Sophia commented the next day while she watched me do my pre-training workouts. "Nose to the floor, Buckley."

I stifled back a groan while I pushed my body even further down before going back up. "Yeah, I tend to do that a lot," I got out in several breaths. Having just gone on a couple mile run, these pushups were even harder than they would be on normal circumstances.

"Ever thought about not making any shows? That seems to be all you're good at."

I gritted my teeth from her jabs at my incapability of learning anything new. I pressed my body down for another push up but my arms gave out, making me fall to the ground. From above me, I heard Sophia scoff.

"Five minute break and we're starting up training," she said and twists on her heel to go grab some equipment to use for the next several hours of torture.

Following the arena training fights, Cole, Alex, Claire, and I just stuck it out in my dorm, not wanting to hear any nonsense or complaints from any of the other Supernaturals. Coming in today, I heard Sophia and William's trainer talking about how people have been demanding more answers and say in the matter. Looks like they are now taking what happened more seriously.

After the blissful five minute break was up, Sophia immediately ordered me to lift some of the items she had pulled out. She would stand behind me, judging my stance, shifting my position around when she determined I was doing it wrong. We would continuously go up in weight, even having to move outside, until I reached the most I could carry: a small bus.

"You're going to have to lift more than that," She said when I dropped it.

I put my hands on my knees and hunched over, trying to regain my breath. Sophia stood over me, arms crossed, and the usual angry expression on her face.

"I'm trying, okay? I'm not going to become the hulk in only a couple weeks."

Sophia rolled her eyes. "Don't know how you even got into the Big Six," she mumbled just loud enough so I could hear. "Obviously Katherine made a mistake."

I felt my anger growing, which in turn impacted my persistence and stubbornness. "Let's do something else."

She raised an eyebrow at me and motioned to get up, then to follow her. We went back into the building where the rest of them were all doing their own training, happily and merry. Unlike me, they all had good, nice, supportive trainers while I was stuck with the spawn of Satan.

"We'll do one-on-one fights," she said while leaning down to tie her shoe laces tighter. "Give it your all--"

I immediately shot out a wave of power at her chest, making her slide back. Surprise was written all over her face while she righted herself. I was going to get something else with my telekinesis, but an unseen force twisted my arm back, making me cry out from the brief moment of pain. It made me fall to the ground and once she dropped her own telekinetic power on me, I rubbed at my shoulder to ease the tension she built up.

Sophia stalked over to me, confidence in her walk, and looked down.

"Next time, try to have a stronger opening." I was about to respond, but she waved me off, walking out of the gym without another look towards me. "Go to lunch and come back ready for a real fight."

I groaned, but got up and practically stomped my way to the cafeteria. Because Sophia let me out early, I was one of the first people there and got my lunch pretty quickly before picking the table we usually sat at. With my head propped up by my hand and the other scooping cooked vegetables into my mouth, I watched as more and more people made their way into the building and went to get their own food.

Cole was the first out of my friends to show up and caught my eye as soon as he walked in. Instead of getting food, he headed over to me with his eyebrow raised as he looked at my unhappy form.

"Rough training day?" He asked while sitting down next to me, popping one of my chicken nuggets into his mouth. When I failed to comment on him stealing my food, he moved his hand up to his mouth in mock surprise. "When the hungry, hungry hippo doesn't say anything about her precious meal being eaten by another person, that's when you know she's not very happy. What happened?"

"Sophia was a bitch," I muttered, my eyes cast low.

His lips formed an amused smile. "Like usual?" I shook my head. "More?" When I nodded, he faked a gasp. "Wow. I'm so sorry."

I had to grin at his support for me and this ridiculous, ongoing situation with my instructor who did more degrading than helping. He reached over and patted my back before standing up to go get his own food.

"Thanks," I told him sincerely and he gave me an over-the-top bow as Alex and Claire walked up.

"Anything for my lady," he winked. "Now, may I go get some food, Princess Buckley?"

Rolling my eyes, I said, "Anything, Mr. Court Jester."

My friends started laughing and with one more parting look at Cole, I said hello to the couple. They gave me the usual 'you're such a liar about you and Cole' face but didn't say or do anything else about it.

It didn't take long for him to return, both himself and the ever-so funny jokes that he seems to pull out of his sleeve every chance he gets, and we all continued eating until it was time to get back to training.

"Please don't make me go," I practically begged Alex and Cole. Claire already headed off to her own outdoor practice, while the rest of us were held up by me complaining.

"Do you really want Sophia to have yet another thing to get mad at you about?" Alex asked while Cole pushed me from behind.

"As long as I can deal with her tomorrow, I'm fine with it."

When Cole realized that getting me there was going to take hours, he reached down, wrapped his arms around my waist, hoisting me up and over his shoulder. When I began yelling, Alex threw some water in my face to make me shut up.

So when we walked up to where the Big Six was practicing, we were quite the sight to see. While the others laughed as Cole put me down, Sophia looked less than amused. I walked over to her she looked at me expectantly.

"Are you ready now?" She asked. She was around my same height, maybe slightly taller, but the girl seemed to tower over me.

Grinding my teeth, I got out, "Let's do this."

We spaced ourselves out and despite the others having their own different training sessions at the same time, I could see Cole peeking at us from the corner of his eye while he practiced firing with precision.

Sophia made the first move by trying to hit me with a leftover branch from a windstorm earlier in the week. With a low duck and a little time manipulation, I avoided it easily and swung it around to bring it back to her at a faster speed. This back and forth motion continued for a while and I knew she wasn't giving it her all.

"For someone who so easily navigated her way through the placement exam, you'd think you'd be doing a lot better," Sophia said while easily stepping around a thrown tire.

"Maybe I would be if I had a better trainer," I shot back and her eyes narrowed.

That's when I found myself looking at my worst fear: Two Sophia's. They flanked either side of me and it was impossible to know which one was real. I slightly panicked when they both used telekinesis to fire a force at me from both sides. My head immediately felt like it was going to explode but I was able to pull up my shield before it did too much damage.

"You're just a bad student," The two said. "You proved you're strong enough to get to a level five, but not enough to stay there. You're the weakest one of everyone in the Big Six. You're the reason why they'd fail, ending everyone. It'd be your entire fault."

That's when I found myself in another alternate universe. I recognized the scene to be from back home. My house was in the same shape it was prior to me coming here--degraded, beaten down, a mess. Everything seemed bigger than before, as if I were looking at it all through the eyes of a child. When I heard a door slam shut, I turned around and saw my father as drunk and disgusting as he was the day I left.

"You're a disgrace," he spat at me. "You're the reason why your mom is gone. It's your entire fault."

"But I tried to help--" My voice, higher than it is now concluding that I was, indeed, myself as a child, said but was cut off when he threw the bottle he had been holding down on the ground. The glass shattered everywhere and I had to shield myself to stop the shards from hitting my face.

"Yet she's dead but you're still here," he seethed, taking a few steps towards me. "You're alive while she's in the ground."

"Daddy, please calm down--"

My dad was never physically abusive so while I knew this was all a manifestation made by Sophia, this fake scene felt so real. I remember the guilt I felt when my mother died and the pain from all the harsh words my father would say to me when he was intoxicated. She was trying to hurt me in ways that would really sting and it was working.

I wasn't the one to break away from the image so when I found myself in a heap on the grass back at SA, I knew Sophia has dropped it. She stepped forward, leaning over me, her eyes flashing in anger.

"You'll fail everyone here just like you did your family," she fumed. "You're useless. Prove me wrong by doing something. Show me that all this training isn't being wasted."

From behind me, I heard Cole yell, "Sophia, that's enough. You're going too far. Leave her alone."

While the gesture was nice, I couldn't focus too much on it while my instructor and I were in a glaring battle. My heart pounded but not from the painful scene she made, but from anger. I reached my hand up at a tree, ripping it out of the ground, roots and all, making it fly straight for her. Leona, who had been working on her Earth ability around there, jumped back and watched the fight unfold.

Sophia kept trying to unleash more and more scenes into my head, to hurt me from within, but I kept shaking myself out of them as soon as they entered. I grew increasingly frustrated as the fight went on until I eventually fired the most power I have ever manifested only to have her jump out of it easily.

With my teeth gritted and my focus on Sophia, I yelled out, "Enough!" and that's when everything changed.

For weeks I hadn't been able to reach inside anyone's mind except my own to harvest and release power. She is able to do that easily, to see what I'm thinking or to propel different images inside. I failed every single time I tried, which is the root of her anger towards me. In that moment of pure chaos and rage, I was finally able to plant myself in her mind. However, instead of making a new scenario to hurt her, or make her believe she was drowning, I was able to see into her memories as if I was there.

I found myself looking at a woman with eyes so beautiful that they shone with a different color every time the light hit them at a different angle. She was gorgeous, with long black hair and ivory skin. She wore nice, black clothes and high heels to match that clicked with every step she took. I couldn't move or talk in this state, only watch as the woman stepped forward and trail a long finger down my cheek.

"Oh, Sophia," The woman said and that's when I realized I was watching a memory happen through my instructor's eyes. "Beautiful and such a strong Mind... Yet so naive... impressionable. I would have expected any of the others to go on this journey, but definitely not you. I thought you would know better, to understand that this was a death sentence that Galen put you all on."

Sophia peeked out of the corner of her eyes, letting me see that there were others there who were all handcuffed to a pole. When I felt her move her own hands, I noticed that she was in the same predicament.

"Katherine," she spoke and I felt a rush of power surge through her body. I froze in my limbo state, knowing that this woman was the leader of the Catchers, the one the Big Six was destined to kill. "We didn't mean any harm in coming here--"

That's when all the air was cut off. Even though I was a mere observer, I felt as if I was suffocating along with Sophia. After a few seconds, the oxygen returned and she gasped out.

"Don't you dare try to use your compulsion on me," Katherine hissed. "It doesn't work, you should have known that."

"I'm sorry," she said, shaking from the post she was attached to as the leader of the Catchers stepped away. The anger dropped from Katherine's face as she scanned the others.

"Now the rest of you, I'm not quite as surprised that you're here. You're all strong, but not the ones who are in the prophecy. This mission you were sent on to spy on me is a failure, but I need to make an example of myself so your own leader doesn't mess up again." That's when several

Catchers walked in, all identifiable by their black eyes. "Eliminate these ones," Katherine said while pointing to the people on the very end. Besides Sophia, there was only one other guy who wasn't in the group that was pointed out.

One by one, the Catchers would carry the three Supernaturals out of the room while they screamed. Sophia shut her eyes, trying and failing to distract herself from the scene at hand.

"Now I only have you two," Katherine stated while standing in-between us and the boy. "A very strong Mind and her Fire boyfriend. You see, I've always loved tragic love stories. How the boy and girl fall in love, only to have it be snatched away from them."

"Please, just let her go and do whatever you want with me--" The boy said and Katherine grabbed some water out of the air, making it form into a sharp, icicle and held it up to his throat.

"Don't tell me what to do, Grant," she raged, and I felt Sophia's heartbeat grow faster. "I'm the one who calls the shots and always will."

The two stared at each other for a few moment until Katherine stepped away, walking toward us once more. She circled around and Sophia struggled to stay calm and not make a sound.

"I'm going to let you go," her voice whispered in our ear and I almost jumped in my internal state due to it being familiar, reminding me of the visions I've personally had of Katherine speaking to me through my mind. "But your boyfriend is staying here."

"What? No!" Sophia chimed in now, trying to shake out of her restraints. "Let him go!"

"You have the brains and the strength and I need the other Supernaturals to know what happened here. Grant is strong and will make an excellent addition to my team."

"No, please!" She screamed as Katherine motioned for more Catchers to come in, this time leading and pushing him out instead of planning to kill him.

"He'll be a good Catcher and maybe you'll meet again one day," Katherine winked as Grant struggled and failed to escape the grip that the others had on him. "After all, true love finds a way if it's real, right?"

"Grant!" Sophia screamed again. Her vision became blurry as tears streamed down her face.

"Get out of here!" He yelled back as they approached the door the Catchers were leading him out of. "I love you, I'll be fine--" And that's when the door shut and I found myself back at Supernatural Abilities.

The world around me was silent and I could see Sophia on her hands and knees across from me nearly hyperventilating as the others watched us.

She opened her eyes and I noticed tears, making me feel bad for intervening on what was most likely her worst memory. I had known she was the only survivor of the trip to spy on Katherine, but didn't know that her lover had gone with her, only to become a Catcher in the end

None of us said a word as Sophia got up, wiping her hands off on her knees as she stalked by me, pushing me with her shoulder. "Training's over," She muttered and disappeared through the thick forest.

Got to the early 20's on the fantasy popularity list. Good job, guys! This chapter was a bit more exciting than the one before this, but the ones coming up are going to be pretty good if I do say so myself... :)

See you all next week and thanks again for all the support!

Chapter Nineteen - The News

I felt bad that entire day and night about what I did to Sophia.

However, I knew I shouldn't have. She deserved it by egging me on and I did just as she wanted me to: I got inside her head. Granted, it wasn't the way she initially wanted me to do it, but I was still able to press deep into her most private memories to get something that definitely hurt her to relive. Right after Sophia left, the other trainers called it a day and all of us got to head off early.

So the next morning I dreaded getting up to go face my instructor again. I pulled on my usual gear, peeking at the Marking that dominated my back, and headed out for the day. It was colder than usual and being in shorts and a t-shirt, I wished I had grabbed a thin jacket to keep me a bit warmer throughout the day.

While I'm usually the late one of the bunch to training, I was surprised to find that even though I was the last of the Big Six to come in, all of the instructors were still nowhere to be found. We did our own things for a bit, stretching and light warmups, but nearly a half hour passed and still not a single one of them had arrived yet.

"What should we do?" Leona asked while in the middle of leaning down to touch her toes.

"Maybe it's a test," William suggested, his accent lining his words. "They're going to ambush us any moment because we'll be caught off guard."

All of us contemplated that for a moment before getting up and got more active just in case. While I doubt they would do that this early in training, it was always a possibility. Once over an hour had passed, one of Galen's associates walked in and handed Alex a note. The four of us gathered around him while he read it out loud.

"'No training today, but meeting at 5:30. You must be in attendance,'" he recited, his eyebrows crinkling together.

"Good going, Brain," Cole bumped my shoulder. "You scared Sophia off and the rest of the instructors as well. Now we're all screwed! But thanks for the day off."

We all headed off, Leona and William both going different ways than Alex, Cole, and I. While we get one day off per week, it's weird to have another, let alone an unexpected one. Letting a free day go to waste would be a shame, but nothing was coming to mind about what we could be doing.

"Lake?" Alex asked and Cole shook his head.

"Too cold out today. Movies in our dorm?"

Alex made a face. "I don't want to be third-wheeling the two of you."

I rolled my eyes at him and listened to the two boys throw ideas back and forth until ultimately deciding that the movie plan would be the best course of action. Alex just hoped that Claire had one of the first arena fights today so she could join us right after.

So that's how I found myself squished against Cole on his bed with Alex on his own while we had a marathon of several films. I hadn't been in the boys' room prior to today, but Cole immediately pointed to his bed when we showed up.

"Two beds, two boys," he had said. "Now, Alex is a nice fellow, you don't strike me as the type to ruin a relationship by sharing a bed it a taken boy, so you can share with me. Besides, we have already crossed the cuddling passage last time--"

He shut up when I threw a pillow at him.

We hung out there for a while and Claire eventually joined us. It was nice being in a relaxing environment with my friends, watching stupid, free movies, and just enjoying each other's company.

By the time 5:30 came around, all of us were in good spirits while we traveled to the meeting room. Once we got there, it was just like this morning: The Big Six, well, the five of us that were here, and no one else.

However, this time was different because it didn't take too long for Galen to walk in looking visibly stressed with Sophia at her side. When my instructor looked at me, her eyes immediately diverted to someone else.

They took their seats at the head of the table and Galen looked at all of us individually before sighing.

"This morning the last person in the Big Six was found and ready to be gathered," She started. "The Electric. A Seeker was notified of her position by her current caretaker."

Cole and I snuck a look at each other before he spoke up. "Any information on her?"

Galen nodded. "Her name is Mackenzie Blanchard, twelve years old. She's rather young and only came across her powers a few days before the Marking was issued." She paused for a few seconds. "Now, as said before, we plan to have two of you go on the trip and we have already chosen those individuals. We have picked Cole, for he has gone on the most pick up missions of you all."

That was expected. I know that he hates doing this, but in a circumstance such as this, he would be the most qualified person out of all of us to do it.

"And also Taylor," She continued and my eyes widened.

"What?" I asked, completely taken back about this. "Why me?"

"Her location is close to your hometown and hopefully you'll be able to find her quickly if you join Cole. However, it is crucial that no one you may know from you past life to see you."

"You'll leave tonight," Sophia continued on for Galen, still avoiding my eyes. "Everyone else should prepare because now that she has been found, we will begin having more group exercises while training."

Galen dismissed everyone but made Cole and I stay to go over the gathered information. She laid out many sheets of paper in front of us and I found my eyes skimming across the hundreds of words and numbers.

"Now this is a very tricky case. Miss Blanchard is much younger than most of the people here, but already very strong."

"How do you know that?" Cole asked while he continued to look at all the information on Mackenzie.

Galen sighed and put her fingers on her temples. "She became an orphan the day she discovered her powers. When she received her Marking, they had brought her to a local hospital, where Seeker and Nurse Valerie Watkins admitted her and immediately recognized her as one of us. Seekers were notified of the Big Six information in case anything like this happened. She did as was needed, became Mackenzie's 'foster mom' by using compulsion on the people running her orphanage and contacted us. It took a while for her to gather the Electric in her care, which is why we were not given the knowledge immediately."

Cole looked at her. "That still didn't answer my question."

Sophia now butted in. "She discovered her powers the day she became an orphan, as said. According to Watkins, she was able to read in her head that Mackenzie was the one who killed her parents."

We were quiet for a moment, taking that in. A twelve year old girl killed her people so close to her with her powers? How did that even happen?

Galen responded, sounding much more solemn than before. "According to the police report, the bodies were burned so much that they were almost unrecognizable. Not even natural lighting can have that effect on people, so this girl, despite her age, is a force to be reckoned with. You must be careful when picking her up, as you do not want any outbursts to happen."

She pulled out one of the back sheets, showing us a picture of a little girl with long brown hair but striking yellow eyes. She looked so innocent, young. There was no way this little girl could kill her parents so devastatingly.

"You leave tonight," Galen repeated what was said earlier. "Go over the information before you leave or during the trip to help formulate a game plan. Make it quick, in and out, and please be safe."

Cole nodded and looked at me. "You got all that?"

I bit my lip. "I have a few questions. You go get ready and meet me at my room."

He gave me one parting looked before leaving and I looked back at Sophia and Galen. "I understand that she is located in a familiar area to me, but wouldn't it have been better to have Alex or William tag along?" I asked, fiddling with my fingers. I never thought of myself to even be up for consideration when picking up new Supernaturals.

Galen gave me a smile while Sophia rolled her eyes and exited the room. "You're too hard on yourself," She said. "Yes, part of the reason why you were picked is due to you knowing the area. Another is because you have good chemistry with Cole from what the instructors picked up, so you two will work together well. The last part is because you're more than capable of supporting yourself during a fight."

"Even against some psycho little girl?" I joked and Galen nodded.

"Even then. Now, you need to go get ready and set off. You'll have to do whatever you can to get this girl to come with you. It might be difficult especially with her temper, but she might realize that she has nothing left there and join you. Just get there quickly, convince her to come, and leave. Try not to tell her about the Big Six. This will already be a lot of news to her so we'll tell her about that when she arrives. You'll have to make a few stops along the way for rejuvenating yourselves, but leave as soon as you're ready."

I nodded. "Thank you for this opportunity," I told her. "Cole and I will be back as soon as we can."

Galen handed me all the papers and watched me leave. Before I was completely out the door I heard her say, "I knew she wouldn't disappoint."

———————

I'm SO sorry about this being late. I know some of you saw what I posted about it on my profile (And those who commented on it are the sweetest people ever, thank you!!) but basically I had the most stressful and worst weekend ever from being really sick to bad vet visits and then Valentines day was in there too, so I was both busy and just not in a good position to write.

So here is the new chapter and while it isn't up to my standards, it's out and basically setting the stage for more chapters to come.

Thank you so much for waiting and I apologize yet again. Anything that I am late with posting, I'll definitely explain why on my profile so either fan or check there if this ever happens again!

Chapter Twenty - The Hotel

It didn't take long for me to throw some clothes and toiletries into a bag before Cole and I rushed out. We took the same car as before and I got flashbacks to when I was the one leaving my home to come here. The rushing, shock, and the fear of what is to happen was all too familiar.

Other Supernaturals watched us leave, some confused and wanting to know why we were given access to the cars. The rest probably knew what we were doing and didn't want to bother us. We drove down the long trek to the gate before beginning the drive through the woods. I was fearful last time we drove through here and I found myself in the same situation as before. However, I was scared for different reasons: The girl with already very strong powers, Catchers who could potentially find us while we were out, and anything else that could happen. Catchers sometimes hide out around here, never daring to enter the campus due to the security that roamed the outskirts. We could be ambushed anytime, but by the time we reached the freeways with no incidents, we relaxed.

"You know," Cole started. "I've never gone on one of these missions with another person before but I'm glad you're my first," he winked, making me roll his eyes at him.

"Promise that you don't nearly kill us this time?"

He laughed. "Why not, Blondie? That makes it more exciting."

I groaned and slumped down in my seat, watching his swerve around cars that were going too slow for his liking. We drove for a few hours, stopped to get some food pretty quickly, and continued forward.

We didn't talk much but unlike the time I was brought to SA, the silence was comfortable. I didn't feel as if I had to fill the silence or anything like that. It was a nice car ride, despite the waves of nausea that Cole's driving would bring me.

We finally had to stop at a hotel for the night, as we needed to be well rested in order to take this girl on. Just as before, I waited in the car while Cole made the reservation for us. It didn't take long for him to come strolling back over, a big smile on his face, while he opened my door with a swooping gesture.

"What are you so happy about?"

"Oh, nothing, missus Trainor," he winked while grabbing our bags from the back. "Our honeymoon suite is waiting for us."

My eyes widened. "You didn't."

His smirk told me otherwise. "Oh, I did. I'm quite surprised a place like this even has one of those rooms." He held out his hand for me to take but I only slapped it away. "Get ready for a night of love, Shorty."

I followed Cole up to the top floor of the hotel. When we reached the door at the very end of the floor, he whisked out a card and swiped it, letting the door unlock and open to reveal a very large, singular bed. Red rose petals were swept across the comforter, making a very floral smell fill the air. When stepping further into the room, I noticed that a bathtub was in the main room for all eyes to see.

"You've got to be kidding me," I groaned and Cole looked at me with a bright smile.

"Not at all. Only the best for my wife."

He put the bags on the ground and sprung himself onto the bed, making the flowers fly everywhere. He turned onto his back and leaned against the headboard, holding his arms out as if he wanted a hug.

"Want to join?" He asked with a singular eyebrow raised.

Crossing my arms over my chest, I shook my head. "No," I huffed out and he laughed.

"That's fine, but you might as well relax and take bath over there," he nodded to the bathtub.

I turned red and took a spot on the small chair next to a television. He looked at me expectantly while I glared back. Finally, he laughed and said, "You know I'm kidding about all this, right?"

"Of course, Cole," I ensured while reaching down and grabbing some comfortable clothes to sleep in. Despite all the jokes of tonight, we were still on a mission to pick up a girl with a one-of-a-kind ability.

I took my things into the bathroom and was disappointed to find that the 'door' to it was nothing but a screen, making whoever was behind it appear as a silhouette on the other side. The toilet was behind the world's smallest wall so there was no way to even try hiding.

"You know, I'm really liking this hotel room," Cole called over to me while I quickly changed out of my clothes. "It has a very nice view."

"Stop looking, you creep!" I shot back and shoved the so-called 'door' open again to see him sitting up on the bed facing me.

A big, goofy grin rose onto his face and he leaned back, sighing happily in bliss. "Man, I'm happy you were picked to come. You're my first choice for booking a honeymoon suite with."

I raised an eyebrow at him and sat at the very edge of the bed. "Oh, really? Not Alex?" I joked and he shook his head. "Vanessa?"

He made a face this time. "She's my last choice for anything like this. I had years of her. I like new things and experiences."

"Like me," I concluded and he smiled.

"Definitely like you," he confirmed and he got up, stretching out his limbs. "And with that, I'm going to change. Don't watch too much," he winked before grabbing some of his own items and headed into the bathroom.

That's when I began overanalyzing his words. Liking new experiences and things? Was it just me, or did that sound like a partial confession? If it was, I didn't know how to feel about that.

When I heard some humming from the bathroom, I looked up and saw the shadow of Cole shedding his shirt. I immediately turned away, feeling the blush that crept up onto my cheeks. It didn't take long for him to return and this time, he was shirtless. Just as before, I knew I was growing redder by the second as I looked away.

"Oh, what's wrong, Blondie?" He asked in a teasing voice as I felt him get on the bed. "Is it too much to look at?"

I pursed my lips. "It's nothing much," I lied, knowing very well that he was fit.

"You know that's a lie," he said while peeking around me, his dirty blonde hair flopping into his face. At this point, he was very close and instead of looking at him directly, my eyes betrayed me and snuck a look at his stomach. I immediately swore under my breath and Cole laughed.

"Fine," I said slowly. "I lied. Happy?"

He smirked, "Very."

It was this point we both realized just how close we were. His body circled around mine while I sat up on the bed. Our faces were only inches apart and when I saw him peeking down at my lips, I knew I was in deep. He slowly started leaning in and I found myself reciprocating the action, my eyes shutting.

That's when a very loud bang sounded from the hall and the two of us split apart.

My eyebrows furrowed together. "What--" Before I could continue, Cole's hand shot out and covered my mouth while the other was brought to his lips as a silent way to tell me to be quiet.

That's when I realized the predicament. It was very late, so no one should be out there, let alone at this hotel in the middle of nowhere. A Catcher could have easily figured out our whereabouts and are out there ready to kill. Cole slowly got up, making me have to take a moment to admire his physique, and held out a hand, a ball of fire quickly forming there. He tip-toed over to the door, looked out the peephole, and nodded me over.

Now I wasn't as stealthy as him, but I managed to make it over to the door in one piece. He mouthed the numbers one, two, and three before throwing the door opening and both of us stormed in the hall to find a maid facing away from us, on the ground picking up her fallen over cart. When she turned, Cole dropped the fire with a smile.

"Oh, I'm so sorry for waking the happy couple!" She apologized.

"It's very much alright," Cole answered, respect lining his words. "We just wanted to make sure you were okay."

"Definitely, sir," she smiled at him. "Now, please enjoy the rest of your night," she finished before picking up the final thing and heading back down the hall.

Cole and I headed back inside and I crossed my arms over his chest.

"A maid? Seriously? You just about gave me a heart attack!"

"Hey! I couldn't see what it was when I looked outside. Better safe than sorry?" He tried and I rolled my eyes.

We were left in an awkward silence as both of us thought back to what was about to happen before the scare.

I cleared my throat. "So, uh... Time to sleep?" I tried and he gave me a boyish smile as he scratched the back of his neck.

"Sounds good to me, I guess," he mumbled, turning away from me to organize his belongings.

And that's exactly what we did. Nothing else was said besides simple wishes goodnight before we both passed out on the ridiculous, honeymoon suite's bed that was still covered in rose petals.

We got up pretty early the next day, knowing that we needed to get back on the road. We got ready in silence and he didn't even pause to make any comments about the shadow screen while I changed. Soon enough, we were driving yet again with only the sounds of the car and some light music to keep us company.

It was weird being away from Supernatural Abilities. For weeks that campus had been my only source of scenery and seeing people, normal human beings, driving by us was interesting. They had no idea what we are and what we were sent out to do. They were going about their daily lives not knowing about the hidden war between the Supernaturals and the Catchers.

"Hey," Cole spoke up a few hours into the drive. "I'm sorry about last night."

The near kiss played back in my mind and I found myself turning red. "Oh, it's fine," I muttered, not looking up while talking.

"I just got into the moment," he admitted. "Won't happen again. I wouldn't want my friendship with my favorite Brain to be ruined."

He smiled over to me and I faked one back, wanting to hide my surprising disappointment from his words. He turned back to the road, a little grin playing on his lips, and I found myself staring for a few seconds, admiring how relaxed and good he looked. Once I realized what was going on, I turned away quickly and the inevitable realization hit me, something apparently known to everyone else but myself.

I definitely have feelings for Cole.

I just want to give you all a big thank you for all the well wishes this past week. I'm feeling better and I'm glad to feel good enough to write :)

I hope this chapter was a good one for those Caylor lovers (Which many of you are!). See you next week for the new chapter!

Chapter Twenty-One - The Electric

Our destination was a house at the top of a hill. It was old, but kept up and looked like the picture perfect grandmother's home. From reading and discussing her papers the night before, Cole and I know that Mackenzie hasn't been enrolled in school yet, due to her just recently being placed with her 'foster mom' and Seeker, Valerie Watkins. It was midday and the two of us exited the car slowly, taking in our surroundings to make sure everything was safe.

"Okay," Cole said under his breath as we approached the door. "Let me do the talking. You just sit there and look pretty."

I felt myself blush as he knocked on the door. It didn't take long for footsteps to be heard and an old woman answered the door. Her face brightened when she saw us and she ushered us inside, probably immediately recognizing us as Supernaturals due to our eyes.

"Oh, good. Galen told me you two were coming and I'm so honored to meet two of the people in the Big Six."

My friend and I snuck a peek at each other. Honored? We have been berated by our peers for so long that it's weird to have someone actually thankful for us to be there. Cole held out his hand and shook hers before she did the same to me. "I'm Cole and this is Taylor," he introduced and she nodded excitedly.

"Oh, I know. I'm Valerie Watkins. Mackenzie is just upstairs in her room. I told her she would be having visitors and she was quite excited."

"Is there anything we should be worried about?" He asked cautiously and she gave him a sweet smile.

"She has quite the past but she really is one extraordinary young girl. She is very nice, just don't get on her bad side," she winked and ushered us upstairs.

It wasn't very large up there, only three doors and one of them was a bathroom. Another was closed and the last was slightly open, a little girl's humming echoing down the hallway. Now, I'm no expert at these pick-up missions but this seems like a scene from a horror movie.

Cole and I walked forward and he knocked on the door three times, making it open just enough for us to be able to peek in and see a little girl staring at us with the brightest golden eyes. In her hands was a sketch pad but she hid it just well enough for me not to see what she was drawing.

"Hi, I'm Cole," he introduced himself to her, still standing in the doorway. "And this is Taylor. Do you mind if we talk to you for a few?"

She looked between the two of us and when her eyes fell on me, I had to stop myself from stiffening from her direct gaze. She was obviously young and her hair was longer than what it was in the picture we were given. She wore a t-shirt that was slightly too big and fell off her shoulder just enough to see the edging of the black Marking that all of us wore.

"Okay," she spoke slowly, getting up to sit on her bed while we walked in. Cole pulled up two chairs for us and faced her. I expected the same sort of speech that he gave me: Slightly sarcastic and just a bit of taunting. However, that was not the case.

"So... Mackenzie," he started, folding his hands under his chin as he gave her his undivided attention. "A couple days ago you realized you could do something weird, right?"

She was hesitant to say anything at first. She regarded him with caution as she said, "What do you mean?"

"Well, you know of superheroes, right? Those who have crazy powers and save the world?" She nodded slowly. "You're like one of them, aren't you? You have super powers just like those people in comics."

I saw the alarm on her face as panic settled in on her. I understood what she was going through. I hid my powers for years, concluding that I was some mutant being and having someone know what I could do scared me. For all I knew, Cole could've wanted to take me away for some experiments and testing.

"I'm not--I don't..." She stuttered out and despite Cole telling me to be silent, I butt in.

"We're like you, Mackenzie. We're called Supernaturals. You're not the only one capable of doing extraordinary things."

I knew she didn't believe me; it was written all over her face. That's when Cole took the initiative to spread his hands apart, creating a line of fire. Her golden eyes widened, her mouth formed incoherent words that never got out.

A little smirk spread across his face as the fire dissipated. I knew he enjoyed that initial shock he got out of us when he showed off his ability. "As said, you're definitely not the only one."

That's when he went onto explaining the concept of Supernatural Abilities, stressing the fact that she needs to go there with us to maintain her safety. I knew Cole had a little sister but I never knew how well he was at speaking to kids. He was careful with his word choice, making sure to get his point through but not enough to scare her with unneeded information. She listened intently, not speaking a single word, until he asked her about what she thought about all of this.

"It's..." she started, pursing her lips as she thought about what she had to say. "It's surprising."

"Yeah, tell me about it," I muttered and Cole elbowed me.

"I cannot stress just how much you need to come with us. If you don't, you're risking not only your life but Miss Valerie's down there as well," he told her. "You'll learn so many things there. You'll be able to control your powers and use it to help you."

She was quiet for a bit, taking in all the information that had been handed to her today. She finally looked to me, her eyes disbelieving. "Do you do anything cool?"

I resisted the urge to laugh at her question. In order to show her that I also had powers, I zeroed in on the bed she was sitting on and made it rise a few feet. A little shriek escaped her mouth and when I brought back down to the ground, she looked much more excited than before, knowing that she now knew this was all real.

"Wow!" She exclaimed, jumping up and down. "This is so cool."

"So, what do you say, Mackenzie. Will you come to Supernatural Abilities?" Cole asked and she immediately began nodding.

"Yes! You two can do some crazy things. I thought I was the only one! I mean, the fire thing was nice but lifting the bed without even touching it? Wow."

I smirked over at Cole who rolled his eyes at me. He told me just to sit there and look pretty, but I definitely was the one who won this girl over.

"Then you should get packing right now," Cole told her. "We need to leave as soon as possible."

She nodded and went to grab a small backpack that had been discarded in the corner of her room. Considering how she had just moved in her a few days ago, there was not much that needed packing. Most of her clothes were still in their bags, so she mostly needed to gather some toiletries and personal items that she had put out.

We went back downstairs where Valerie was looking anything but surprised to see that Mackenzie was coming with us. The little girl walked over to her and gave the woman a big hug.

"Thank you for taking care of me, Miss Valerie," she said into her shirt.

"Of course, dear," her caretaker responded. "Now come back and visit when you're stronger," she winked and the girl looked surprised that she had known about her power.

"Okay, let's go now," Cole urged, taking some of Mackenzie's bags and whisking us out the door before wishing Ms. Watkins a thank you and a farewell. Her things fit easily into the trunk and soon the three of us were back on the road without any issues with Catchers or crazy strong Electric powers.

Along the way, Mackenzie kept asking us a million questions much like what I did. Hers were a bit different from mine had been and more around what people could do. We didn't tell her that her power of electricity was unique as we didn't want her to feel any more of an outcast than she already did and would be once she knew of the Big Six.

Her excitement seemed to grow with every sentence we said. I know Cole made it seem more fun than completely dangerous to be a Supernatural, but I couldn't help but feel happy that someone was excited about this trip. However, we got the complaining only an hour into the drive.

"I'm hungry," Mackenzie informed us and Cole and I looked at each other.

"Can you wait a few hours? We want to put some ground behind us," Cole asked and I saw her shake her head from the corner of her eye.

"But I'm starving," she exaggerated. The two of us chose ignore her but when she kept on badgering us, we all found ourselves at a small diner per Mackenzie's choice.

We ordered and sat at our booth in the corner. We usually got fast food or something else that allowed us to stay in the car but the Electric was very adamant about going here.

"So where do people sleep?" Mackenzie asked, sitting on her hands.

"You get a roommate," Cole informed her, his hand holding up his head while his eyes searched the area. I know being out in the open, even if we were in a small town, unnerved him.

Mackenzie's eyes widened. "Like a sleepover? I've never had one of those!"

"Well, that's all there is there so you got to live with it once it gets old too," he grumbled and I kicked his leg from under the table. We needed her to be excited about this, rather than the latter. If she got too sad or scared, she could eventually blow up yet again. Everyone knows I have from time to time.

We finally got our food and ate with Mackenzie's chatter filling the silence. For a girl who had accidentally killed her parents, this is not the kid I expected to pick up on this journey. I finally had to excuse myself to the bathroom to get some peace and quiet before we set off towards Supernatural Abilities. It was pretty late now, so the sooner we left, the better.

After doing my business and washing my hands, I stepped out of the bathroom to hear some yelling coming from the outside. Because the restrooms were in a secluded corner in the diner, there was an emergency exit with a glass door. While the sun was just nearly down, i could still make out a man kicking another who was on ground. Without thinking, I stepped outside.

"Hey! Stop hurting him!" I yelled, anger flowing through my veins. Even though I fight people on a daily basis at SA, seeing someone hurt another person without reason pissed me off. When the attacker turned around, my blood turned cold. Their pitch black eyes focused on me while a large, toothy smile spread across their face.

And that's how I found myself looking into the eyes of a Catcher.

———————————

I have a favor to ask of you. Can you guys write some first and last names below, both boys and girls, for me to use for minor characters in future chapters? I have the hardest time coming up with names and I would love to have some to pick from.

As always, thank you for the support! I actually had my FIFTH wattpad anniversary this past week which is absolutely crazy!

Chapter Twenty-Two - The Catchers

- -

I just want to say thank you to all the people who submitted names! I'll be picking from last chapter whenever I need a new name for now on :) For this chapter I want to specifically thank, nataliecol159 (for the name Jack) and FaeriesAreDeadly (for the name Toby)!

"Well, would you look at that, Jack," the abuser said while his eyes were still focused on me. "There was a Supernatural around here and you're not as big of an idiot as I made you out to be."

The guy on the ground, Jack, sat up and wiped his mouth as he looked at me with a big smile. "I told ya' I wasn't lying!"

I froze as the first guy started walking around me, still several feet away. My eyes followed him while still watching Jack as much as I could. When he was behind me, he laughed.

"Jackie! You tracked yourself a member of the Big Six!" He yelled out and Jack's face brightened.

"See? I'm not an idiot, Toby!"

"Shall we bring her back to Katherine?" Toby asked the other Catcher who nodded exuberantly.

"Yep! I'm sure she'll take us more seriously then!"

When Toby smiled and stomped his foot, blocking off the emergency exit door with a huge boulder coming up from the ground, adrenaline coursed through my veins as I screamed out, "Cole!"

At this point both exits that I could go through were blocked by the two Catchers so my only option was to fight. Jack blasted some air at me, making me fly back towards Toby, who made a wall of jagged, sharp rock. Slowing down time, I could still feel the power of the air continue to force me back so I faced the wall, allowing myself to step up the spikes until I was able to reach my hand out and hit Jack with a wave of telekinesis. Time went back to normal and the two looked at me in surprise. They probably thought I was useless, especially if Katherine was able to figure out how I was doing at my training and gossiped about us to her clan of Catchers.

The wall I was disappeared, making me fall to the ground. Toby began throwing rocks at me, which I immediately responded by throwing them off track. When one came right for me, I was able to stop its course of action and throw it back to my pursuer, hitting him with a great force.

I took this brief moment of time to inspect my surroundings. In the middle of this alley, there wasn't much to work with because we were in the middle of two large buildings. The only things at my disposal were the rocks that Toby made and two large dumpsters that I didn't want to use until I was ready.

And then I was. Jack used his Air ability to cut off my oxygen intake. It took me a second to calm down and throw up my shield, giving me the ability to breathe again. Luckily, Toby was still recovering from the blow and Jack was between those two waste bins. Using telekinesis, I slammed them together and turned away before I can see the aftermath of a squashed Catcher.

Now facing the other way, I could see Cole and Mackenzie at the end where Toby was now getting up. I knew that had seen what had happened to Jack and the dumpsters because Mackenzie looked terrified. Luckily, the Catcher hadn't noticed that they had arrived and when he stood up, Cole pushed Mackenzie off to the side and blasted him with fire, burning him to a crisp.

I rushed over to them, immediately noticing that Cole looked pissed. "How the hell did you end up here?"

"I... I saw someone getting beat up and I just had to help--"

"You could've been killed!" He exclaimed. "Thank God Mackenzie mentioned that you had been gone awhile and when we went to the bathroom and saw that the emergency door was now a rock wall, we came around back. You could've been dead by now!"

I glared at him. "I'm more than capable of supporting myself, Cole. I got one--"

"Not without getting hurt," He said while grabbing my arm and holding it up to reveal blood dripping down to the crook of my elbow. "Good job, Brain. You killed one but not without the other getting you injured too."

I grabbed my arm away from him and looked down at Mackenzie who was trembling. I got down to her level, putting my good hand on her shoulder. "We have a lot to talk about," I told her and she just nodded.

"And we need to get out of here," Cole said while pulling me up and pushing us out into the open area. "You two go to the car while I finish the bodies off." He tossed me the keys. "Go there right now," He ordered, his eyes on mine to know that he was serious.

I nodded and grabbed Mackenzie's hand while the other held the arm that was hurt, trying to stop the bleeding. I walked back around to the front of the building and ran into some people who were rounding the corner.

"I'm sorry--" I started to apologize but was interrupted.

"Taylor?" I looked up and saw Ryan, my best friend from back home looking down at me in surprise. "I thought you were sent off to boarding school..."

Are you kidding me?

I know a Supernatural altered the story of my disappearance to everyone in order to make sure they were fine with me being gone. My father thought I ran away and Ryan must have been told this school story. Of all things to happen on this mission, this would have to be even worse than running into some Catchers.

When I didn't say anything, he continued on talking while his friends told him that they'd meet him 'there,' wherever that might be. "I would try to call or text you and your number had been disconnected. Your father wouldn't answer the door either. You just... disappeared."

"Why are you out here?" I finally got out, clutching Mackenzie's hand harder.

"Concert, remember?" He gave me a boyish smile. "The one you didn't want to go to."

I remembered him asking me to go to this concert while ago, when I was still living a seemingly normal life and going to high school. I declined the offer, knowing that he only wanted to go because the lead singer was attractive and the band as a whole was terrible. "Oh," was all I said, trying not to think about my past life, until he engulfed me in a hug.

"I missed you so much," He whispered into my ear. "I didn't know what to do with you gone---" When his hand reached my arm, he drew back, looking at my blood that was now on his fingertips. "You're bleeding! Why--" He looked over my shoulder and his eyes narrowed. "Why the hell is Cole here?"

I turned around and sure enough, I saw the Fire user walking up, his lips pressed in a straight line.

"Hey, Ryan," he greeted, annoyance written all over his words. "Nice to see you here."

My friend looked between us in confusion. "What is this? Are you two dating? Did you run off together?" He looked down at Mackenzie. "Is this your love child?"

Just as I was about to say no, Cole answered for me, "Definitely. She's completely smitten with me and we're in love," he deadpanned. "Now, we have to get going," he grabbed my arm and dragged me away from Ryan and to the car, while my friend yelled after me.

"What was that?" I asked.

Cole grabbed out his phone and sent out a quick message before throwing the car in reverse and getting out of here. "I'm sending out a Mind to erase the human's memories so I might as well have some fun with someone who obviously has feelings for you."

My eyebrows scrunched together. "What are you talking about?"

"Pretty obvious," he said, his jaw clenching. "He's head over heels about you. It was written all over his face."

"You don't have to sound so angry about it, Cole," I muttered. "It's not like I knew he was going to be there."

He snorted. "You should've just ignored him, or at least not hugged him."

I raised an eyebrow at him. "You sound a bit jealous there," I pointed out and he pursed his lips.

"No, I just don't need you running into Catchers and leading on a guy who you can no longer be associated with." He didn't look at me while he reached under his seat and threw a first aid kit at me. "Now fix yourself, Blondie. I don't want Galen mad that you got blood on the seat."

I began the task of cleaning up the blood while Mackenzie finally spoke up. "Taylor, are you dating that boy?" She asked and I shook my head. "Are you dating Cole then?"

"No!" The two of us said at the same time. When our eyes locked, we both stubbornly looked away.

"Oh..." She mumbled. "Sorry for asking then."

The car ride was silent then as we traveled through the night. Cole's anger seemed to subside but all of our exhaustion seemed to grow. Even Mackenzie, the chattiest pre-teen in the world, was quiet and fell asleep halfway through.

"We traveled enough for today," I finally said to Cole. "Let's stop and get a place to sleep."

He didn't say anything but pulled off to the nearest exit and pulled into the first motel we saw. He got out without a word and went in to book us a room. When he came back, he opened the back door and picked the sleeping girl up without waking her while I grabbed our bags.

"Room 119," he whispered and I nodded.

"No honeymoon suite this time?" I joked, and he shook his head without as much as a smile.

The room was small, as expected, and had two beds this time instead of one. Cole pulled down the covers of one and placed Mackenzie inside. He gently took off her shoes as she grumbled her sleep and unconsciously pulled the blankets up.

I went to the bathroom and noticed that my bandage that I had put on earlier was already soaked with blood. It came off easily and as I was cleaning it up, Cole walked in.

He looked at my injury and shook his head. "You need to be more careful."

"Sorry, I was just trying to make sure I survived," I deadpanned and put on a new band aid.

I watched as Cole sniffed his shirt, made a face, and pulled it off. When I gave him a weird look, he said, "Smells like burned flesh. Not exactly appetizing."

His words made me stop, realizing what had happened today. "Cole..." I started. "That was my first kill."

I have fought and trained with other Supernaturals and even watched Cole kill a Catcher before, but never has it been me delivering the final blow. I thought back to Jack and even though was the one who wanted me dead more and I was protecting myself, I felt sick.

Cole patted my back. "The first one is always hard. Even though they want to kill you, you still--"

"Killed another person," I finished and started examining my bandage to ensure that it was all covered. Cole watched me and before I could react, he pulled me into an embrace and rested his face in my hair.

"I'm glad you're okay," He mumbled while I hugged him back. "God knows what would have happened if you got seriously hurt today."

"An annoyed Galen and a hurt Big Six member? I tried and he laughed.

"And a very angry Cole," he added.

"Aren't you always mad at me?"

"Pretty much. You're too stubborn for your own good."

I smiled into his chest before we pulled away from each other, in much better spirits than before. "Hey," I started. "I'm sorry for the whole Ryan thing today. I really didn't know what to do and kind of froze on the spot."

Cole reached up and ruffled my blond hair, making it fall into my face. He gave me a soft smile and said, "Don't sweat it. I know it's not your fault."

"But yet you made it out like it was," I pointed out and he laughed.

"What can I say, Cutie?" He started as he began exiting the bathroom. "Jealousy reared its ugly head." And with a wink, he left me alone.

———————————

As always, thank you so much for your kind words on each and every chapter! Did you like that Cole jealousy? :)

Chapter Twenty-Three - The Reason

I just want to say thank you to WynterStars for suggesting the name Jenny Harvard, which was used in this chapter :)

The next morning we sat Mackenzie down and explained everything about the Catchers. We told her just how deadly they were and how that they're the reason why she needed to come with us. She listened to us without comment, understanding along the way and when we were done, we headed out for the rest of our journey.

Cole's words kept me up most of the night. Admitting to being jealous? 'Cutie?' I was no expert in boys, but it sounded like there were some feelings from him as well.

Our car ride was much better than the one from yesterday. Mackenzie hummed along to the music in back while Cole would peek at me from the corner of his eye, a little smile on his lips. I was able to get some sleep in along the way and we got to Supernatural Abilities late into the night.

When we arrived, the guy at the gate was surprised to see us. "I'm sorry! We didn't expect you until tomorrow afternoon. I'll page Galen while you head in," he said.

The campus at night was eerie, especially as we drove through the woods. Mackenzie had gone quiet and I knew that she must be nervous just as I was when we arrived my first time. We finally parked in our original space and got out, Cole gathering most of our bags while I got the rest. The three of us filed into the building and to Galen's office, where the doors were already open with her at the desk. For being late, I knew the gatekeeper must have had to wake her up but she looked put together as always. She rose when she saw us and held out a hand for Mackenzie, introducing herself to her.

"It's so lovely to meet you," Galen said. "Now, it's really late so we will have to chat tomorrow morning. For now, can you two show Mackenzie to her room? She'll be rooming with Jenny Harvard who will be expecting her."

Cole and I nodded and brought her to her dorm, bidding her goodbye and promising to pick her up to meet with Galen in the morning. Jenny was only two years older, but the girls immediately looked happy to be roommates, which made it easier for Cole and I to leave knowing that she would be in good hands.

As Cole and I walked to our rooms, he said, "Well, that was an exciting trip."

I laughed quietly, being mindful of the other Supernaturals sleeping. "Not what we had planned but we made it back. I don't have any complaints."

We stopped at my door and Cole patted my shoulder. "Thanks for being my partner this time, Buckley. Let's do it again sometime," he joked before parting ways.

When I opened the door, Claire was already sitting up with a bright smile on her face as I walked in. "Why are you still up?" I asked and she started jumping up and down.

"You and Cole are so close to actually being something," she exclaimed, joy radiating out of her.

I was about to ask what she was talking about until the realization hit me. "You read my mind, didn't you?"

Her smile betrayed her and she shrugged. "Alex and I took bets on if anything would happen. I said yes while Alex disagreed, saying that Cole would be too much of a wimp to make a move. I just can't believe you two were so close to kissing--"

"You're acting like a lunatic," I sat down next to her while leaning back, finally relaxing for the first time since we left. "That trip was crazy."

"And I'm glad you're back. Just please leave again and come back as Cole's girlfriend."

I smiled at my roommate, more than happy to be back at SA. In the past few weeks of me being here, this place, as crazy as it might be, has become my home. I might be in a really dangerous position right now, but at least I'm surrounded by people who support me. Well, the people who I am friends with, that is.

Claire and I went back to bed and Cole greeted me at my room bright and early by waking me up and jumping on my bed. He allowed me a whole five minutes to get ready before we picked up Mackenzie from her room and dropped her off at Galen's who wished to speak with the girl in private.

We sat down on the bench outside her office, Cole sliding closer to me so our legs touched. "What do you think they're talking about?" he asked and I shrugged.

"Everything that we didn't," I answered. "The Big Six, more about the Catchers and how we run. Stuff like that."

"And we weren't allowed in?"

"She seems to get overwhelmed easily so getting one-on-one attention might be better for her... I don't know."

He hummed in response before saying, "I wonder if they'll put her through a Placement exam. The Big Six don't train according to levels anymore, so what would be the point?"

"To access her skills?" I tried.

He smiled at me. "You know, you're really living up to your Brain nickname."

I returned the grin and thought back to our trip, a question popping up in my mind. "Um, did a Mind ever get to Ryan in time?" I asked and I immediately saw him tense up at the name.

"Yeah, they caught up to him within a few minutes. He hadn't even reached his friends again."

"So he doesn't remember what happened whatsoever."

"No, they erased all memory of us being there. Instead, they made him remember seeing a different person, so his story would match his friends' if they asked any questions. It's a shame, really. I wanted him to think that we had eloped."

I rolled my eyes at him. "As if that would ever happen, Cole. You're not even my type," I lied.

He laughed at me. "Come on, Blondie. You can't deny that you're at least a little bit attracted to me."

I thought back to his statement about being jealous the previous night and if I were to get the ball going on my whole crush issue, then I needed to get my feelings out there as well. "You're right, I can't deny that at all," I admitted and he gave me a surprised look, but didn't say anything else.

Mackenzie and Galen talked for a while and when they were done, our leader called up into her office. "She'll have her test this afternoon. She won't get a level placement but we would like to see what she can do." I shot Cole a look, letting him know that I was right in my assumptions.

Per Galen's suggestions, we then gave Mackenzie a tour of the school. People were out and about this morning and stared as we showed her around. However, they were more surprised about her being there. Supernaturals are easily identified by their eyes but all of the colors are still in a natural pigment, just enhanced to be brighter and hues that are uncommon. Mackenzie's were golden yellow, so completely unique that everyone knew that she was the last person in the Big Six and the only Electric Supernatural known. I didn't know whom they were expecting the last person to be, but I can imagine that a little girl that looked so sweet and innocent would be the last thing they fathomed.

We showed her around the same way Claire did to me on my first day here. Mackenzie was quiet, eyes down, as she noticed people staring at her. By now she knows that she's more unique than all of us, Big Six included. To have powers is one thing, but to be the only one capable of that ability is another.

When we finally made it away from the common area that was packed with Supernaturals taking advantage of their day off due to Mackenzie's placement exam later today, she would finally ask us questions about it. She wanted to know what she had to do during the test, how to hold herself up in a fight. She only came to about her powers a few weeks ago, so this is all very new. I know she knew how to use her power enough to fatally hurt someone, but maybe that was just from an influx of emotions.

After grabbing a quick and late lunch, we decided to take her to the arena a bit early in order for her to get ready without rushing. Waiting for us was some small, yellow clothing that they must have made while we were gone because Mackenzie is the only Electric out there. Adding a new color to the mix, let alone a new ability, will surely make this an exciting placement exam for everyone to watch.

We sat outside while she changed, Cole and I leaning against the building towards each other. Some Supernaturals were already arriving, taking the spots in front where it was best to see. Having never experienced watching someone else's test, I was excited too. I just hoped that Mackenzie doesn't panic too much and freak out.

"Do you think she'll do okay?" I asked.

Cole thought about it for a moment. "Yes," he concluded. "I think so, as long as she doesn't get too overwhelmed. She just got her powers, but she's also a member of the Big Six. She's strong without realizing it."

She called us back in a few moments later by sticking her head out the door and motioning us over. The clothes were a bit big for her tiny frame, but not enough to get in the way while she fought. She looked so nervous that her face was practically turning white. Above us, more voices and footsteps could be heard as more and more people arrived to watch this life changing event.

I stepped back while Cole gave her the same advice he gave me before I went in for my test. It was very helpful and I didn't want to step in and say anything that would make her more nervous than before. Finally, it was her time to go so when the wall dropped, Mackenzie slowly stepped into the arena.

"Come on," Cole said, grabbing my hand and running up to the stands the moment the door closed. The seating area was completely full, but we found Alex and Claire waving us over to where they had saved us two extra seats. Overhead, Galen was announcing the Electric to everyone else.

When it started, I watched as it went down just like mine did. One-by-one, Supernaturals would show up and fight with Mackenzie for a bit, judging how she responds to their attacks. I've seen fire, water, earth, air, and even seemingly invisible, mind powers be used, but watching lightning shoot out of a little girl's hands was incredible.

You could tell that she was uneasy on her feet and not comfortable using her ability but for being thrown into this world only days ago, she was doing alright. Her powers were different than any I've seen. Electricity of all sorts of colors would light up the arena every time she would aim it at someone and when it hit something, it would burn. She was going through the Supernaturals one by one and when Sophia arrived last, Mackenzie immediately dropped to the ground and began screaming.

Looking at my instructor now, it was written all over her face that she hated doing this but in order to see if they could overcome a mental invasion, it needed to be done. When it was obvious that Mackenzie was not able to break away, Sophia dropped her power and left the arena without another look towards the girl.

The whole thing only took less than ten minutes, which seemed much shorter than mine. Cole nodded me towards the exit, signaling that it was time to get her out of there and assess her wounds. This wasn't a placement test so Galen thanked her for her time, and called it to a close.

We rushed down to the preparation area just as the door of the arena opened, Mackenzie running out with tears streaming down her face as she fell into Cole's arms. He slowly moved her over to the bench, sitting down with her as he told her what Sophia does to people with her ability.

"She made me see my parents," she exclaimed, making Cole and I look at each other. We've been with this girl for several days and this is the first time she ever mentioned her family that she killed. "Before the accident."

"It was all ruse," Cole said to her. "None of that was real."

"Galen explained to me that you two got a lot of information on me," Mackenzie sniffled, "But you didn't get the full story. That woman made me see my parents happy, just as they acted like. She put us in our basement."

"Why was that so bad?" Cole asked slowly, not wanting to push any buttons.

She took a deep, shaky breath, wiping her nose as she continued resting against my friend. "Our house had a lot of windows and they were happy and nice when they knew people could see. When I acted up by not cleaning something right or getting a bad grade, they'd take me downstairs and hurt me."

Cole and I looked at each other, not expecting this at all. The files were supposed to be accurate but if this wasn't in it then the child abuse was never reported, not even after she had gone into foster care.

"The day I got my powers was bad. They were screaming at me, threatening all sorts of things and the moment they got too close, I... exploded. I remember letting go of all my anger, it all turning white, and then I passed out. When I woke up in the hospital, I was told there had been an accident and our house had gone up in flames for some unknown reason. I wasn't hurt too bad, only some burns that came from the fire, but my parents were gone. I knew it was my fault but I didn't feel bad. They hurt me so much all the time, that I couldn't take it anymore. I swear that I didn't want them to die, but it just happened."

Her story struck a nerve with me. While everything was good with my parents, I understand waking up to a loss. While we both had two different emotions about it, just listening to Mackenzie's story made me reimagine the day my own powers came to be.

Before I dug too deep into the memories I wanted to forget, Cole asked the girl some questions. "Why didn't you tell anyone they hurt you? How did they hide it for so long?"

"They always warmed me that if I told, I'd be sent somewhere even worse. They never hurt me enough to cause anything that would make it obvious and when the doctors helped me in the hospital, any the wounds they had given me were written off as a result the accident. To this day, no one knows. When that woman made me see that again, it scared me. You two picking me up and Miss Valerie have made me so happy these past few days that going back to that, even though I knew in the back of my mind that it wasn't real, scared me."

I understood how being angry could make your powers go out of control, especially in a situation when she knew she was going to be hurt. All of this answered a lot of questions: Why she was so small for her age, her pure innocence, her attachment to Cole, among other things. Even her talking so much is a sign that she was always censored, but now felt comfortable around Cole and I. For someone who had never experienced love from a family, we were all that she had.

"Well, you're all safe here," Cole said to her, a smile on his face. "I promise you that."

She grinned and gave us a hug. She seemed more relaxed, having finally got something so large off her chest. From over her shoulder, Cole gave me a look and I knew that she wasn't as safe here as he had promised.

————————————

Question of the chapter: Who is your favorite character and why?

As always, thank you for everything!

Chapter Twenty-Four - The Apology

I was in that everlasting darkness again, the limbo state that seemed to be between life and death itself. I was a single soul, nothing more, and I was uncomfortable and scared despite being here before.

In the silence, nothing could be heard until the voice, the now familiar speech of Katherine, the leader of the Catchers, sounded in my ear.

"I'm closer than you think."

Waking up in a fit of sweat and adrenaline, I realized that I was in my dorm room, as safe as I could be at this point. Being quiet so I wouldn't wake up my roommate, I slowly crept out of bed and was already dreading what was to come during training that day. Having had a few days off both from working out and Sophia was kind of like my own personal heaven, despite being hunted down by Catchers, running into an old friend of mine, and picking up the last person needed for the Big Six on our trip.

Following the placement exam yesterday, we walked around with Mackenzie, showing her places that we have found that were secluded and away from the swarms of other Supernaturals. I had grown attached to the girl.

I've never had any siblings and having a younger girl look up to me in admiration and support was nice.

We started practice earlier than other Supernaturals, so once I was ready, looking as worn down as ever, and quietly exiting before Claire was even awake, I was surprised to see Cole standing outside my door.

"Ready for training?" He asked. It was already warm out today so he was wearing a work out tank, which showed the outskirts of his Marking. Having been the only one who has actually revealed theirs to everyone, it was nice having someone else take the plunge and show theirs off at least a little bit. After all, they were interesting to view. It was like getting something more permanent and natural than a tattoo.

"Yeah," I said, answering his question. "Why didn't you just meet me there?"

Cole shrugged as he stuck his hands into his shorts' pockets. "I wanted some extra time with you. Is that so bad?"

I hid a little smile from him and shook my head. "Not at all."

He looked at me for a little bit, eyes traveling up and down. "You okay? You don't look too good."

I didn't want anyone to know that Katherine was basically bullying me in my dreams, so I kept it quiet just like my other vision. "You know, that's not the way to compliment a lady."

He grinned and threw his arm over my shoulders as we walked. "You should know by now that you're going to be teased more than complimented."

When we made it to our training room, I was surprised to see that Mackenzie was already there, having made it here all by herself. She looked out of place but was speaking to a new trainer, one that would most likely be helping her all that they could considering how she was the only Electric Supernatural.

I found Sophia leaning against a wall in the corner, her eyes on me. I slowly made my way over to her and once I was within a good enough range, she pointed to the ground and said, "Pushups. Now."

Sighing, I got down and started doing my normal pre-training set. It's been awhile since I starting doing these and it has become much easier as time went on. I felt my body growing stronger and my stamina increasing. I no longer felt like the weakest link by a long shot now.

When I was done with my warm up, Sophia nodded me over to where she was.

"Now," she started. "Because you managed mind manipulation, it's time to move onto something else." I thought back to invade her mind and still felt bad about it. While I didn't feel as if I could do that on command, it's also something that I hoped I wouldn't ever have to. "How do you feel about telepathy?"

I stared at her in confusion. "What?"

She sighed and gave me a look. "Reading minds," she clarified.

"Oh, I, uh..." I thought to how Claire is able to know what people were thinking and I didn't really want that responsibility. Being able to read others' thoughts would only end up with negative consequences. "I'd rather not."

"Understandable. Then let's work on illusion manipulation."

According to her, illusion manipulation is changing your outwards appearance to match someone else's. This could come in handy when we go to battle Katherine, as I'll be able to look like a Catcher or something equivalent. While Sophia didn't know that ability, she had called in another trainer who did and I was pleased to see that they were much calmer and patient than she would ever be.

In the few hours before lunch, I wasn't able to grasp it as expected. When Sophia called training to a close, I grabbed my water bottle and started to head out of the door.

"Hey, Brain! Wait a minute!" Cole called out while he was still training. Rolling my eyes, I did as he asked and I leaned against the wall as I watched him finish up. At this point, everyone else had already headed out except for us and our trainers.

Of all the abilities, Fire was the most interesting to me to watch. For something that seems so uncontrollable, it's amazing to see how well Cole is able to manipulate it. I watched as he formed a ball of fire in his hands, making it slowly grow until it was the size of basketball. Concentration formed on his face while he aimed and threw it at a large steel plate several feet in front of him. It hit the metal and spluttered out, making Cole look unhappy about it and swear under his breath. His instructor analyzed the damage and shook his head.

"Very close, Cole. Increase your distance and power and you'll get it."

He ran a hand through his hair and headed over to me. "You ready?" He asked and I nodded. "Then let's go eat."

We walked quietly at first before he put his arm over my shoulder and I jumped back when an unexpected heat hit me. "You're hot!"

A confident smirk grew on his face. "So I've been told."

I rolled my eyes and pushed him away. "You know what I mean."

He laughed as we trekked on. We were kind of late to lunch, so there weren't many people to be seen during the walk through the forested areas. To fill the silence, Cole asked, "So what'd you do during training?"

I shrugged. "Talked about reading minds--"

"Really?" He interrupted. When I looked at him, he had an uneasy expression on his face. "Any, uh, progress on that?"

A little grin rose onto my face as I stopped to look at him. "Why are you so nervous about that, Cole? Do you have any secrets that you're hiding?"

Apparently he didn't take too kindly to teasing because his nervous expression dropped and turned into the flirty Cole that is so common for him. He backed me up into a tree and leaned towards me, his hand pressing against the trunk above my head.

"You know... I'm sure we're both hiding something from each other. Might as well be the time to start confessing."

His expression told me everything. He knew and now I knew about him as well. I guess my so-called hidden feelings were obvious enough that he knew exactly what was going on. I felt myself turning red but judging from his expression, he wanted me to be the one to admit to it first. His smirk and body language told me that.

But I wasn't going to do what he wanted. He's someone who seems to have people fawning over him and professing their love, but I wasn't about to be another one of those girls. If he truly had feelings, he was going to be the one who showed it first. Not me.

So I decided to play this little game. Holding a hand up, I scooted him away with an unseen telekinetic force and walked past him, a little smile lifting my lips. He looked surprised, maybe even a little impressed at my confidence, and didn't try to stop me.

"I have no idea what you're talking about, buddy," I teased. "And, by the way, I said no to learning how to read minds. Digging into your deep, private thoughts is the last thing I would want to do."

I heard him laugh as I kept walking. I wasn't even a few yards forward when someone jumped out from behind a tree, making me let out a little scream.

"Allyson?" I asked, once I realized that this was someone I knew. I felt my face turning red from what she might have heard between Cole and I, who now stepped forward to be next to me. "What are you--"

"Can we talk?" She asked, her voice seeming even younger than it usually is. "I have a few questions and concerns."

I snuck a peek at Cole who looked suspiciously at the other girl. Having not have really seen her since the night of the Marking, I was confused as to why she would want to speak to me now, weeks later. I finally gave into my questions and nodded. She immediately grabbed my arm and led me away from Cole, deeper into the forest.

"What's going on?" I asked. "What do you want to talk about?"

She turned around, her very unusual eyes sparkling. She seemed very wound up and uneasy, almost as if she was anticipating something awful happening because she kept looking over her shoulder.

"How was your trip?" She asked and that's when I got even more confused than before. Did she really just drag me away from making progress with Cole for some small talk?"

"Fine..." I dragged out. "Why did you bring me out here?"

She took a deep breath as if to calm herself. "I just wanted to say that I'm sorry for how I acted the day of your party," she admitted, instantly calming down from her freak-out mode. "I'm just trying to be a really good

Supernatural and you're one of the best here, especially now that you're one of the Big Six. I really look up to you."

I blinked once, twice. Is that it? All this fuss about an apology? "Uh, it's fine, Allyson. Don't sweat it."

"Really?" Her eyes shone with disbelief. "I felt like I ruined our friendship with my nosiness! Oh, thank you, Taylor! I'll make it up to you, I promise!"

She then threw her arms around me for a hug and while I was definitely short for my age and gender, this girl was several inches under me. I felt like I was being embraced by Mackenzie all over again. I awkwardly patted her back, not really knowing what to do, before she stepped away with a grin.

"Want to go to lunch together?" She asked with hope lining her words and I sighed, giving in.

"Sure," I started leading the way, wanting nothing more than to leave. "Let's go."

The whole incident with Cole and Allyson took up most of my lunch time and by the time I had gathered my food and sat down with the girl next to me, the others were already long finished with theirs. Cole gave me a questioning gaze, as if asking what all that was about, but I shook my head enough for only him to notice and let him know that I wouldn't be talking about it now.

In addition to him, Claire was looking between Cole and I suspiciously and judging by the look of concentration on her face, she was digging into our minds.

What happened to privacy, Claire?

She looked down, a smile rising onto her face, letting me know that she heard my telepathic message. She peeked up at me with a shrugging, wagging her eyebrows the slightest bit to show me that she had already gotten all the information she needed from us.

The amount of unspoken communication between this table right now was ridiculous.

Finally, lunch drew to a close and Allyson gave me a parting smile before she left. When she was out of earshot, I groaned and rested my head on the table.

"What was that about?" Cole asked, scooting his chair closer to mine.

"What was what?" Alex chimed in, completely oblivious to everything going on.

"Allyson snuck up on Blondie and I as we walked here, then stole her away from me."

"Really now? Did she come in at a bad moment?" Alex teased, making Claire laugh as Cole and I snuck a look at each other.

"She walked in on something rather entertaining," my roommate mumbled, a smile on her lips.

"Claire!"

She looked at me unapologetically, plopping a grape from my lunch into her mouth. "What? I was just answering a question."

Looking at Cole, he didn't look embarrassed whatsoever and shrugged when he caught my eyes, making our friends laugh. Leave it to him to never be humiliated once in his life.

But the thought of Claire's telepathy crossed my mind. "Hey, is there any way you can read Allyson's mind?" I asked her.

She nodded. "Of course I can. Why?"

"She's just acting weird..." I mumbled, remembering her skittish behavior. "I want to know if she's hiding something from us."

"I'll look into it next time she's around. I didn't get any off feelings from her, but I'll still do it."

"Thanks," I mumbled, getting up to throw my stuff away. While I've talked to Allyson before and I know she's friends with these guys, there had to be something she wasn't telling us. No normal person would ask a million private questions to someone they just met and then apologize as if it was some idolization thing.

But honestly, of all the things to happen here, this was probably the most normal.

Sorry for it being late! Finals really screwed up my writing schedule.

But, as always, thank you for reading and everything that you do! We got to NUMBER SIX on the fantasy charts this week and I couldn't be happier! All your comments and votes but not seem like much to you, but for an author on here, they're everything :)

So, Question of the chapter: what do you all think about this Taylor/Cole nonsense? Want them together? Want them to stay friends? Want things to happen now or later?

I have the timeline of things in my head and none of your answers will change my mind, but I'm always curious as to what you think about them

:) Some people hate it, some people love it. But I'm the only one with the final say in things!

Chapter Twenty-Five – The Vision

Today wasn't an arena day for us, thankfully Cole and I missed that during our few days off, but we were doing something different. In some ways, it was worse.

"Why do we have to fight each other again? Isn't injuring someone in the Big Six something we want to avoid?" I asked-slash-complained to Sophia who wasn't taking any of it.

Today's exercise would be combat, of course. However, it was against each other, as if that will prove anything other than the fact that I'm one of the weakest people here. I didn't know who I was going to be facing, but I hoped it would either be Will or Leona, the ones I barely knew, so I wouldn't be humiliated if one of my friends beat me.

"You guys need to learn how each other work," Sophia told me. "By fighting, you learn each other's weaknesses so hopefully you'll learn to cover each other during a real battle."

"So who will I be against?" I asked, praying that it wasn't Cole.

She grinned, "Alex."

Not my first choice, but I'll take it over the blonde, cocky, Fire Supernatural any day. Looking over at my opponent who was talking to his own instructor, his eyes found mine and waved like a madman once he realized I was staring at him. Rolling my eyes, I turned back to Sophia who was already more annoyed than before.

"I know you have no chance in winning, but please go out there and try to put on a good show at least," she requested, making me purse my lips together.

"Of course," I replied through gritted teeth. "Anything to please my supportive trainer."

She didn't respond to my sarcastic comment and made me continue stretching. Looking around at the other Supernaturals, it was interesting to see how each person warmed up. William would jump up and down, hovering just the slightest bit while using his power. Leona did her yoga, relaxing more than doing. Cole and Alex mostly messed around with each other, probably not having to worry too much about this because they're the two strongest people in the Big Six. And Mackenzie? Well, she looked terrified and lost. I didn't blame her. I would be too if I was barely trained and at least five years younger than the closest age here.

While this was a very informal training practice by fighting each other, it was still intimidating. Even though I was going up against my friend, he was obviously much stronger than me and I knew I was going to lose and hopefully when I do, I don't get made fun of too much for it.

I was going second so thankfully I wouldn't have to be the first one to face a loss. While the first group, Cole and Will, got ready, Alex came and sat down next to me with a big smile.

"Ready to fight, Taylor?" He asked, excitement lighting his face.

I held back a groan and gave him a look. "Please spare me, I'm begging you to go easy."

He started laughing and bumped my shoulder with his. "Come on, it'll be a good fight! I know you haven't been here too long, but you've definitely improved from what I can tell. Besides, if I even hurt you to the point of doing some serious damage, Cole would never let me live it down."

I raised an eyebrow at him. "Really? Why?"

Alex shrugged, his blue eyes leaving mine and focusing on his best friend who was rolling out his wrists. "He's a big softy when it comes to you. The kid gets his panties in a twist every time I tease him about feelings and such."

I held back a smile and turned my attention towards the area in front of us while William and Cole spread out from each other. We weren't in an official arena for fighting or anything, but rather a vacant space in the forest to make it more realistic. To initiate the fight, one of the instructors blew a whistle and the two boys began doing their thing.

While I am familiar with Cole's style of fighting, it was interesting analyzing what William did using his Air ability. Many times I'd find him with his eyes shut, judging the change in wind and air to know where Cole and his attacks were coming from. After several minutes of going back and forth, it was obvious that Cole had the upper hand and was able to disable Will, making it come to a close.

Cole walked out of the arena reserved for our battles and gave me a cocky grin as he sat down next to me on the grass. "You're up, Sport. Knock 'em dead!"

Alex leaned around me to glare at his best friend. "Hey! Aren't you going to give me any encouragements?"

Cole turned faux-serious and point a finger at his roommate, his eyes narrowing on the boy. "Don't you hurt my Blondie."

Rolling my eyes, I stepped up with Alex trailing next to me. He wished me luck before heading over to his side, preparing for our fight. Taking a deep breath and calming myself, I began thinking of my course of action.

Just keep on throwing stuff at him to make him go off course and prolong your inevitable loss. Make it seem like you know what you're doing and it won't be too bad--

And there went the whistle.

I can honestly say it started off well. I would use my shield, telekinesis, and time manipulation to dodge and block his attacks as well as send over my own attempts of doing some damage. While Alex did have an advantage over me, it wasn't as big as I anticipated.

Then things took a turn for the worse when I found myself falling into the dark world created by Katherine.

I was a person this time. An actual being in this separate state of being. I wasn't able to move, but the feeling of having a body instead of just a mind was definitely there. Around me, I heard the sound of a sinister laugh, making the blood run cold through my veins.

From out of the darkness walked Katherine. It was funny, after being here several times before and having this Marking, I had never yet seen her in my own head, but rather only in Sophia's. However, in that invasion of her privacy, I was only able to see her through her eyes, making me unable to control what I would focus on. Being able to control my own sight, I was able to focus on details of Katherine that I hadn't seen before.

What was most enticing was her eyes. Normal Supernaturals have irises depending on their ability while Catchers' go completely black once they turn. Katherine's was a rainbow, an array of all of the colors that are seen around here. However, of all the blues, greens, black, and even blends of them all, there were two things I noticed: There was no yellow signaling the Electric ability in her features and the most prominent color was gray.

She went straight for me, a dark smile lighting her face. She didn't stop until she was right in my face. "Oh, Miss Taylor... How nice is it to see you today! I hope you're doing well."

Unlike other visions, I discovered I had a voice. "It's going great," I answered sarcastically, wanting nothing more than to break away and run from this woman. "May I ask why you've brought me here?"

Her face formed a pout, as if I had insulted her. "What? Am I not allowed to see my favorite person in the Big Six? I won't take it personally, my dear, you look like you're in a compromising situation back in the real world."

"Then why don't you send me back? I'm sure they're missing my joyful presence there."

She hummed in response, as if contemplating it. "I guess I should since I don't have anything important to say, really. I also can't keep you from your training, can I? But don't you forget, Miss Taylor... I'm always watching... Preparing... and waiting. I suggest you do the same if you want even a sliver of a chance of beating me."

I blinked and I was back to normal, now looking at Cole who stared down at me with a concerned expression as he held my arm. The darkness was gone as quickly as it came and I found myself gasping for breath. "What happened?"

"I--" I croaked out, not even realizing that I was crying, which was impacting my speech. Shaking my head and pulling away from him, I denied everything. "Nothing, I just--"

"That wasn't nothing," Sophia stepped in now. Looking around, I saw everyone in the Big Six and our instructors watching me with similar expressions as Cole, who now made me sit down. "You don't just stop in the middle of a fight, go blank in the face, and start screaming."

I shook my head, definitely feeling that embarrassment I aimed to avoid earlier. However, this was for a different reason. I would much rather take the heat of getting beaten than from having people find out that I'm having horrible visions. "It's fine--"

"You..." Cole started but then froze, realization hitting all his features. "You had a vision."

I felt myself turning red as I forced myself to look away from him. "No, it's just--"

He grabbed my chin and forced me to face him. "Taylor..." He warned.

I looked around and began to panic as everyone stared and watched. None of them had to deal with Katherine invading their dreams and now even in my waking moments. From Katherine's conversation, it must be only me, especially since I'm the only Mind and, therefore, the only person able to get visions like this.

I knew there was no way around this and everyone could tell I was lying. With my head low, I slowly nodded. "Yeah, it was a vision."

Before anything else could be said, Sophia pulled me up and began dragging me away. I struggled in her grip, but she was surprisingly very strong.

"Where are we going?" I asked while the others watched us leave in confusion.

"Galen. You're going to show her what you saw." She finally turned around while walking, looking back at the group and called out to Cole. "Lover boy! You're coming with us. Obviously she won't confess anything with me so you might be of some help. Maybe even calm her down with your sweet, sweet words."

Cole caught up to us while we continued on. I didn't even feel the embarrassment from Sophia's words about Cole, but rather fearful of what our leader would say about this. Halfway through, Sophia realized I wasn't fighting her anymore and let me go, just making sure that I was still following. Cole was silent, which made me believe that he too was intimidated by my instructor.

Luckily, training was still going on for the rest of the Supernaturals so no one saw our walk of shame to our leader's office. When we finally arrived, she almost looked surprised to see us here until her expression changed, probably because she read one of our minds.

"You had a vision, Taylor?" She asked me immediately, making me bite my lip in uneasiness.

"Look," I tried. "I can't help them... Katherine is getting in my head--

"Katherine?" Galen asked, now confused at my words. "I saw the one with the smoke... I didn't see anything with her."

I thought back to my last actual vision, the one where I wasn't in the darkness but rather seeing something that will supposedly happen. If Galen was able to see that one, why wasn't she able to know that Katherine was talking to me too?

"She is getting into my head in the same way, giving me visions..." I muttered, wanting nothing more than I fade away at this very moment. Not only am I physically weak, but I'm also unable to keep someone out of my mind. "I can't stop it--"

"Wait... Visions? Cole reiterated, an unreadable expression on his face. "As in more than one?"

Galen ignored his commentary and leaned forward on her desk, her gray eyes focused intently on me. I looked around awkwardly, not knowing what I should be doing until she swore under her breath.

"I can't reach into those. Katherine must have set up a block in your mind so no one can read them."

"But why me?" I asked, now almost panicking. "She talks to me a lot... Sending me into this weird, dark place and says all these things... Why can't it be one of the others?"

"You're a Mind," Sophia cut in now. "And so was she."

Cole and I looked at each other, now confused at her words while Galen rubbed at her temples.

"According to the legends and books from the time Katherine began her rule, she first came in touch with her Mind ability. Shortly after, the others began to arrive, but she still had the basis and understanding of that first. Because you're also a Mind, she is probably most connected to you, making it easier for her to reach in."

I thought back to what she said today about how I was her favorite in the Big Six. The fact that we were the 'closest,' per se, scared me. I could barely hold myself together with just the training and Big Six stuff, let alone this too. I could deal with getting weird, random visions about future events but having to hold a conversation with the number one person trying to murder me was another.

And I still totally hated small talk.

"What should I do?" I asked, now desperate and in need of help. "Please, these are too much."

Galen sighed, an almost pained look on her face as if she felt sorry for me. Now, turning to my instructor, she said, "Sophia, go over shields and blocks for her mind rather than her body next training session. Make sure she gets it." Her next sentences were directly towards me. "Until you do, you must report every incident of a vision or something similar to one of us. We're all in this together, Taylor, and we need you to be on board and trust us as well. You got that?"

The eyes of Sophia, Galen, and Cole all rested on me and I sighed, nodding. "Yes. I'm sorry I kept it a secret."

"Okay then. If this is all settled, feel free to take the rest of the day off. I hope for your sake that you learn blocking quickly. I know Katherine is very good at pulling some mind games," She concluded, sneaking a peek at Sophia.

I nodded, thanked her for her time, and rushed out of her office, Cole trailing behind. When he finally caught up to me in the middle of an expanse of trees, he spun me around with an angry expression on his face.

"Why didn't you tell me?" He asked, the irritation clear in his words. "I thought you trusted me."

"I do, but--"

"But you still chose to hide this, something huge, from me. Hell, if you were struggling so much with her in your head, you need to tell me."

I looked away from him, avoiding his dark eyes. "It's not like you could have helped any--"

"But you're going to be getting help now!" He countered, sweeping his arm out the way we came to show me what he meant. "You need to talk to people! Whether it's me, Sophia, Claire, or even Mackenzie, you need to tell someone when Katherine and Catchers are involved. This war is not just between you and her, it's with all of us, and if you don't realize that soon then we're all screwed."

I felt the tears well up in my eyes at the same time he noticed, his expression quickly changed from livid to apologetic. He immediately scooped me up for a hug, a swear word coming off of his lips.

"I'm sorry..." He mumbled into my hair. "But it needed to be said. You can't do this alone. Even if you don't want me involved, please tell someone before you go crazy, okay?"

"I'm the one who should be sorry," I blubbered. "I just... there's so many other things going on and I'm trying really hard with my training that telling people that Katherine is mind-bullying me would make me come off as weak. It was selfish and I'm sorry... I promise to go to someone if anything else happens."

He pulled away from the hug, now look happier at my words as he pushed a piece of hair behind my ear. "Good. The last thing I like seeing is this little Shorty all worked up," he joked, making me laugh as I wiped at my eyes from my most recent breakdown.

We began walking back to our dorms, occasionally bumping arms and smiling at each other along the way.

"Hey, thank for being such a great guy," I told him and he gave me a cheeky grin.

"Anything for you, Blondie," he winked. "Just as long as you start being honest about those things."

I nodded. "Of course--"

"And in turn I'll continue blessing you with my lovely presence and quirky banter."

Rolling my eyes and shaking my head I gave him a look. "Of course, Cole. That's everything a girl could want.

———————————

So sorry about the late upload! Just a series of no wifi, time, ect. BUT it's currently 3:30 in the morning, I just finished editing it, and I have to be up real early for work so I hope you all like this one!

QUESTION OF THE CHAPTER: Who has read the original version?

I'm seeing some comments of people spoiling stuff for others, so please refrain from doing that if you already read it. Things are changed, obviously, but major plot points will still stay the same. If you haven't read the original version, please DON'T! I would much rather you experience this story and all the joys of it in this version rather than the others, especially since they might confuse you as a reader.

As always, thank you for your amazing words and votes. PLEASE don't be a silent reader! I did the math and less than TEN PERCENT of you vote on each chapter. Please do me a solid and toss a little love my way to show that you enjoyed it.

OH! And happy Easter if you celebrate! See you all next week :)

Chapter Twenty-Six - The Break

Sophia's trainings on putting up a barrier in my mind were much better than the other ones I've had. For one, she was actually patient and gave me time to try to learn how to do it instead of insulting me when I couldn't figure it out. Within a few days I was able to put up that block, keeping it up with little to no thought of constantly maintaining it, and there has been no additional word from Katherine in return. It was like breathing, something so basic and simple that it required no additional energy or power to keep it up.

And today would be a good day. Why? It was one of our day offs, giving me an entire day free of fighting, getting hurt, and having to use any powers whatsoever. I planned to sleep in and only get up for the bathroom and when I would eventually need to eat. Alex had already picked Claire up for some date, or whatever else people in relationships do together, so I had the entire room to myself.

Well, until the devil himself ruined it.

"Hey, Princess!" Cole announced as he let himself into my room and turned on the light.

Groaning at the sudden brightness, I threw a pillow over my head and then asked, "How did you get in here?"

"I stole Alex's key so I could get your little butt up for a day off!" He chirped and I heard him open up the blinds.

"And why does Alex have a key for here?"

"When you weren't here and Claire didn't have a roommate. he would sneak in at night and--"

"Enough!" I interrupted him, sitting up down and squinting as the sun hit my eyes. He was perched at the end of my bed in a position that would only mean that he was preparing to jump on me. He gave me a sheepish grin and sat down next to me, trying to seem innocent. "It's like nine in the morning, why are you even here?"

He gave me a weird look. "First of all, it's noon." I shrugged, completely indifferent about that. I wasn't Leona or any of the other Earths who wake up at the crack of dawn. "Second of all, aren't I allowed to want to see you and possibly even hang out?"

"And do what?"

"Train?"

I groaned again and threw myself back against my bed. "Seriously?" I asked, bewildered that he even wanted to do such a thing. "You want to train on our day off?"

He rubbed at the back of his neck. "Well... There's some stuff that I just can't seem to get and would like your help with practicing them.'

"I don't want to get burned."

"Do you really think I'd do that?"

I blinked at him. "Yes?"

"I wouldn't," he put, crossing his arms over his chest. "Now I'm not taking no for an answer. Get dressed and if you're a good sport today, we can go to the lake after."

I have to admit that that seemed fun. We haven't been there in a while mostly because we're just all too busy with training, Big Six stuff, Mackenzie, and other things. I reluctantly agreed and tossed on some light clothing that could easily be shed to go swimming in and after doing basic bathroom necessities, the two of us were off.

As Cole led the way, the wandering Supernaturals also taking advantage of their day off would peek at us, some whispering to their friends unknown words as they watched us pass. While I wish I would say that I was used to it, I wasn't. Wearing the shirt that I was now, most of my Marking was clearly visible. However, Cole's was as well.

We finally made it out of the groups of people and headed into the forest.

"Is this where you kill me?" I joked and Cole turned around to show that he was rolling his eyes at me.

"Funny," he deadpanned. "Just like the first time you said that when you first came here. Get more jokes, Clown."

I laughed, now remembering that I did say the exact same thing before, while we continued on until we were pretty deep within the foliage. Around us, the only sounds that could be heard were from the branches moving with the light breeze and the faint chirping of some birds.

Finally, he turned around and raised an eyebrow. "You ready?"

I was about to reply until his hand formed a ball of fire and he shot it straight for me.

"Hey!" I yelled as I jumped out of the way just in time for it to fly by me. "That could've hit me!"

He gave me a grin, "Maybe you should pay more attention next time."

Instead of being a gentleman and asking if I was okay, he fired one at me again. This time I was ready and countered with a force of power hitting him in his back. We continued like that, each taking turns with an offensive and the other defending it. I noticed that he was incorporating new moves that his instructor must have been teaching him. This was all in good fun, but soon his attacks became more persistent as he stepped closer and closer to me. He would toss light-hearted insults about how I needed to try harder, but nothing like what Sophia did to me the day I got into her head.

Finally, one of his moves caught me off guard and I jumped out of the way to dodge it, tripped over some debris, and fell to the ground. Cole took advantage of that and stepped forward, throwing his body over mine, seized control of my arms by lightly pressing them down with his knees, and held up two hands of fire menacingly, a smirk resting on his face.

"I win," he grins and I pouted.

"Of course you do," I rolled my eyes at him. This was to be expected, as he had more experience than I did. "Now, can you get up?"

He shook his head and dropped the fire, looking down at from where he was on top of me. "I'm liking this a lot."

I was about to respond until I realized that this fight wasn't over just yet. He expected to win and was just messing around. An idea popped into my head and using my best acting skills, I made a confused face at him. "Wait, what did you just say?"

He crinkled his eyebrows together. "I said that I liked the position that we're in?"

I shook my head once, twice, before making my eyes widen in fake-surprise. "Cole, I think I just read your mind--"

His happy expression immediately dropped and he began to grow red in the face. "Please tell me you didn't--"

I took the moment of his surprise and threw him off me using telekinesis, pushing and holding him against the tree and walking forward so my body was pressed against his.

"I think I won," I whispered and he gave me an impressed look.

"Deception..." He nodded in approval. "Hot."

I stepped back and dropped my hold on Cole, making him relax as he brushed himself off. He gave me a smile once he was done and said, "I'm impressed. Didn't think you had it in you to trick me like that..." He paused and peeked up at me from under his lashes, his black eyes displaying a slight hint of anxiety. "You did trick me, right?"

I laughed and nodded. "Trust me. I'm sure I'd react much more disgusted if I was in your head."

"Nah, it isn't that bad in there."

"Oh, really? Is that why you're so relieved that I was just messing with you?"

He gave a sheepish smile and rubbed the back of his neck. "Some things aren't meant to get out just yet."

I rolled my eyes at him. "I thought you said you wouldn't ever lie to me."

"It's not lying if I'm keeping something personal to myself," he pointed out. "You'll find out eventually, unless Claire decides to dish out the details of everyone's mind to all of us."

I made a face. "God, I hope not."

He started to laugh but then went quiet, his eyes tracing the bushes and trees around us. When I opened my mouth to speak, he immediately covered it, rolling his eyes at me. He then eyed the trunk of a large oak, holding up his hand to it.

"Get out of that tree is coming down on you," he warned and I was instantly confused. Was there someone watching us? He was just a Fire, not some guy with unnatural hearing... or was he? I didn't know what was going on in this place or even if that was a power one of us could possess.

He looked ready to strike but the person then revealed themselves. I expected some random Supernatural or at least Allyson because the girl is always in random places that I am, but I didn't think it would be Mackenzie. Her little form was shaking as she held up her hands in an innocent posture.

"I'm sorry," she mumbled. "I was trying to practice to be like you all but then I heard you guys. I came over to say hi but I, uh... You guys looked... busy and I didn't know how to leave without bothering you."

I felt myself turning red when the girl told us that she saw us, probably meaning the proximity that we experienced with our fight. I shook my head at her and motioned her over. "It's fine, just don't sneak up on us like that. You almost gave us a heart attack because you could've been a Catcher."

"Us?" Cole asked, a smile on his lips. "You might be a Mind, but you didn't hear anything, Miss Oblivious."

"Well, maybe if you weren't laughing so loud, I would've heard."

"Or if you opened your ears--"

"Are you sure you two aren't dating?" Mackenzie asked, a smile on her lips as she watched us. "You two act like you are."

"Not you too," I mumbled, running a hand through my hair. I already had Claire and Alex asking if we were, so I didn't need her to be doing the same thing. Quickly deciding on a subject change, I thought back to what she was previously saying. "So what were you practicing?"

She turned red, "Just the stuff my instructor had gone over with me. All of you in the Big Six are much older and better than me and I want to be like you guys."

In some ways Mackenzie was like a little version of me. The nervousness of coming here, the anxiety of being the weakest link, both of us having family issues.... Albeit, my problems with my dad were not being nearly as awful as hers were. I understood her, and I'm pretty sure if she also knew my thoughts and background, she would feel the same way.

"You're the only Electric out here," Cole told her. "Even if you're the worst Supernatural ever, which you're not, you would have that upper hand on us. There are plenty of our abilities to go around, while you're one of a kind. Does that make you feel better about it?"

She nodded and looked down. "I know and while it's pretty cool that I'm the only one, I still want to be good and practice."

"Then let's do it," Cole said, wrapping his arm over his shoulder. "I'll help you train right now."

So that's how I found myself leaning against a tree watching the two of them run exercises and practice. I wasn't much help for her considering that my ability wasn't physical like theirs were. The other powers, Fire, Water, Earth, Electric and Air, all come from using the world's elements while mine comes from my brain. It was interesting watching Cole instruct Mackenzie on how to channel her power and seeing them do similar techniques that produced drastically different results. I haven't seen much of the girl's powers, but watching the electricity radiates off her body, I saw a very powerful, yet adorable, twelve year old Supernatural.

They practiced for quite some time and I could slowly see Mackenzie's confidence growing. Cole was patient and kind, explaining things to her in ways that she could understand. I found myself wishing that he could be my instructor because Sophia was everything but that. As the sky began darkening, the three of us decided to call it quits and head back to the buildings. She seemed much happier than I've seen her since she arrived, a little spring in every step she took. Cole and I brought her to her dorm and she engulfed us in a giant hug.

"Thanks for everything you've done for me," she said, grinning up at the both of us. "You two have helped so much!"

"Of course, Mack," Cole replied, a smile of his own resting on his face as he ruffled her hair. "Whenever you want help, just ask us."

She looked at him with a confused expression. "Mack?"

"Oh, you don't like nicknames?" He slightly panicked, most likely because he didn't want to strike a nerve knowing her background. "Sorry, I didn't know--"

"No!" She interrupted before looking down in embarrassment. "I just haven't had a nice nickname before. I like it."

He relaxed and nodded. "Then I'll continue calling you that. Just ask this girl right here," Cole nudged me. "All she gets is nicknames."

I made a face. "At least hers is cute."

"Hey! I called you Princess today!"

"As you woke me up--"

"Are you sure you're not dating?" Mackenzie asked, a joyful look on her face while she watched our interactions.

"We're sure!" I exclaimed before the girl laughed, thanked us again, and headed inside her room. Cole and I then headed in the direction of my room, calling it quits for the night and not bothering to go to the lake this late in the day.

"You two are cute together," I commented, bumping hips with him. "She basically worships you."

A little smile rose onto his lips while he shrugged it off. "She reminds me of my little sister back home. I haven't seen or talked to her in years, but Mackenzie reminds me so much of what I remember of her."

The mention of our past lives and families hit something deep in me. While it wasn't constantly on my mind, I wondered what my father would be doing right now. I'm sure nothing has changed for him, but seeing how Ryan reacted when he saw me made me realize that he still misses me. After this war is over and if I survive it, I will have to go back and explain everything to him. Make him understand that I just didn't get up and leave to some random boarding school and cut off all ties with him, but rather it was against my will and everyone was safer without me around.

"What are you thinking about?" Cole asked, interrupting my thoughts.

"Back home..." I mumbled. "About what they're doing without me."

"Ryan's probably sobbing in his bed right now, thinking about his love for you."

I pushed him lightly away and stopped in front of my door, pulling out my key to get ready to go in. "Enough with the jealousy, Cole. It's not a good look for anyone."

I opened the door to my room, giving him a farewell smile and leaving him there, running his hands through his hair with a sweet look on his face.

––––––––––––––––

A little late on a Friday (It's 11:00 on the west coast!) but still technically on time!

I hope you like this chapter, kind of a filler but soon we'll be reading the climax of this story!! Dun dun dunnnnnnnnnnnn. And then I'll finish this one up and start on the next.

So question of the chapter: If you had to choose an ability (Water, Fire, Earth, Air, Electric, or Mind), what would you want to be?

Please don't be a silent reader! I love hearing from each and every one of you :)

Chapter Twenty-Seven – The Jealousy

"Project!" Sophia was telling me. "You need to release your power for things to actually happen!"

The next day brought on more training. Sophia was back to illusion manipulation, changing your outwards appearance to match someone else's. The extra trainer was back due to the fact that Sophia is unable to do this and was sitting back watching while my own instructor laid down the law.

"Haven't you thought that maybe, just maybe, I'm not able to do everything a Mind is capable of?" I asked, plopping down on the ground in defeat. "This is hard stuff, Sophia. I'm just able to touch on getting into someone's mind, but changing my look? This is even worse than that."

"Stop complaining," she snapped. "You're just wasting everyone's time by not being able to do this."

Groaning, I ignored her and put my forehead on my knees, wanting nothing more than to be in my bed, watching some of the free television sitcoms we got, and eating something fattening. When I looked back up, I found myself looking directly into the eyes of Cole.

Confused, I sat up a little straighter. "Aren't you supposed to be training--"

"Come on, Taylor," He spoke, a little smirk resting on his lips. "Let's practice--"

I rolled my eyes at him, pushing him away knowing right off the bat that this was the trainer trying to trick me. Besides, the real Cole has only ever called me by my first name once and I'm pretty sure he's not ready to drop all the nicknames.

"You'll have to try harder than that," I told them while the trainer transformed back to their real being. From behind me, Sophia groaned.

"Isn't Cole motivation to you?" She asked. "Your little puppy love for each other should be enough to get you to focus and want to do the task--"

"It's not puppy love," I butted in, feeling a wave of flush creep onto my cheeks. Observing the others training, I saw Cole throwing some fire punches against a bag that his own instructor held. I'm not one to lie, so I can honestly say he looked really good. He took a break and wiped his forehead off before peeking over at me, realizing that I had been watching. He winked and went back to training.

"You guys are ridiculous," Sophia muttered under her breath, looking down at the floor. "Let's get back to practicing before I abandon all hope on this too."

For a trainer, Sophia was pretty much awful. How did she expect me to be able to do all these things when I barely had a grasp on the underlying beginning concepts? Being a Mind Supernatural is hard, as everything is mental and there are so many different things that could be taught. The physical abilities--Water, Fire, Earth, Air, and now Electric--seemed easy to build on. As long as you know how to use your power, you're already halfway there as everything stems off of the basics.

Sophia worked me well into my lunch time. Everyone else had left except for the instructors before she finally let me leave, annoyance clear in her voice. I grabbed my water bottle, feeling the hunger pains in my stomach, and began to rush out before a trainer stopped me.

"Hey, can you bring this to Mackenzie?" She asked, handing me a sketchbook. "I know she likes to draw during her lunch so I'm sure she's missing it."

I nodded and took it before rushing out once more. As I began the walk to cafeteria, I looked down at the book in my hands, faintly remembering it from when we picked Mackenzie up. She was drawing when we walked in, and immediately blocked her artwork from us.

I know it was wrong, but I couldn't help being curious. Looking around to make sure I was alone, I leaned against a tree and began to skim through the colorful pages that the girl had drawn on.

The beginnings ones were nice--pictures of kids, assumedly her friends from school back home, and different sceneries. The dates at the bottom were from several months ago, before she even knew she was a Supernatural.

Then came the date where Katherine officially made us a part of the Big Six. Her drawings were now rough sketches, no color to be seen in the following pages. I saw the familiar lines and detail of a Marking, hers being different than mine. I found hands with a ball of light in the middle, a lightning bolt across a room. Then there were pictures of the Catchers we encountered, their pitch black eyes denoting their kind. I don't know when she drew it, either in the car or when she got here, but this says that she was really affected by their attack.

Amongst the newest ones were some happier sketches: The school, the familiar layout of a dorm room. Even Cole and I sprawled out on the bed asleep.

But the worst would be the obvious self-portraits. She always wore angry or hurt expressions, clothes tattered or wounds lining her body. For a girl so young and innocent, she's experienced a lot of negative things that will continue on hurting her if she doesn't get help.

She was quite the actress. Here I was thinking that she was beginning to get used to being here, the lifestyle, and even the pressures we have to face. However, it was all faked. These drawings, the dozens of them in this book, were what she truly felt. I've held stuff in and it always ends in a total breakdown. For me, it's not all that bad as I have had my powers for years and know how to control them. For Mackenzie? Her history said it all. Even the slights panic attack could be detrimental to us, her, and anyone around.

And with that, I needed to find Cole. He seems to be the one who she really adores around here and I had to get to him before lunch was over.

I was about to set off, until I heard a noise within the woods. Jumping back, I immediately closed the sketchbook and searched my surroundings. Sure enough, Allyson emerged from between some bushes with a big smile on her face.

"Hey, Taylor!" She chirped as if it were completely normal to see someone in the middle of a forest. "How are you?"

"I'm good, thanks for asking..." I mumbled, still not trusting her behavior around me. She was too sketchy, showing up at just the right moments. I straightened up and held the book closer to my chest. "I'm sorry, but I really need to go--"

"Want to hang out after training today?" She asked, hope within her gray eyes. "I'd love to see what you've been learning with the others."

"I really need to go, Allyson--"

"Have you been doing well?" She continued on as if I wasn't speaking. "You're just so talented so you have to--"

"Enough!" I cut in, already beginning my trip to the cafeteria. "I can't do this right now. I need to be somewhere!"

I didn't look back at the girl as I continued on. Mackenzie obviously needed help dealing with her past regrets before she'd be able to grow. Cole can help her with that and if she sees that she has a supportive group behind her, maybe she can be happy again and not held down by what happened in the weeks, months, and even years before she arrived here.

The trip didn't take too long and practically ran into the lunch room to see Claire and Alex in their blissful, gooey relationship form. I even had to clear my throat before either of them perked up and realized I was standing there.

"Hey!" Claire exclaimed. "You're late."

"Sophia," I replied, that one word being enough of an answer to them. "Do you know where Cole's at?"

The couple shared a grin. "Why?" Alex asked. "Are you missing a secret make out session right now? I'm sure he won't be too mad about it--"

"Where is he?" I interrupted, not wanting to waste any more time with small talk.

"Caylor must be fighting..." Alex muttered to his girlfriend who held back a laugh.

"Caylor?" I asked, not understanding what he was saying.

Alex grinned, looking nothing but proud of himself. "It's you and Cole's couple name. Nice, huh? I came up with it myself with no help from Claire."

"You did not mash our names together-"

"To answer your question," Claire interrupted me, seeming entertained by me and Alex's conversation. "I saw Cole head outside with Vanessa," She finally answered me. "I don't know what it was about, but it didn't seem too important."

The mention of his ex's name struck something in me, making my impatience turn into displeasure. My body went still, no longer fidgeting in place, and I crossed my arms over my chest. Why would he be talking to her? As far as I knew, their last conversation included me ending up in the medical ward and them breaking up.

"Oh?" I asked, cocking an eyebrow up. "Did you see which way he went?"

Claire shook her head and started gathering up her garbage. "I just saw them go outside, that's all."

"Thanks," I mumbled, turning on my heel to go the way I came in.

Before I left completely, I heard Alex sing to Claire, "Someone's jealous."

Not knowing where to look, I headed to the outside training grounds where we would be doing partner practices today. Being the first one here, I sat down and began stretching, thinking about why Cole was with Vanessa.

They ended on bad terms, but he has said that they were best friends even before their relationship began. Could one stay that close after a bad breakup, let alone for a one-sided relationship? Cole was a nice guy, but

I didn't like how Vanessa made him act. He was angry all the time, and I liked this funny, sweet version of him more.

But who was I to say anything? We weren't together. Even though he'd flirt up a storm and even, almost, admit to some sort of feelings, we were not anything official. He was free to do whatever he wanted, even if it concerned his ex.

I just didn't like not knowing what that was.

The normal Supernaturals started arriving at their end of the field, but I was still the only member of the Big Six at our meeting point. Soon enough, the man of the hour showed up, Vanessa by his side as they walked over laughing.

"See you later," He said to her while taking a spot next to me. His ex continued walking, not even bothering to take a single look in my direction, and went over to where the other Supernaturals were gathering across the way. When she was out of earshot, Cole turned to me with a smile. "Hey, Blondie. How's it going?"

I clenched my jaw and reached down to touch my toes. "Just dandy..." I muttered. "I was looking for you, y'know."

"Sorry," he rubbed at the back of his neck. "I was catching up with Vanessa for a bit--"

"Oh, really?" I played dumb. "Hope you had fun."

Cole kept looking at me with suspicion in his eyes. "Why are you acting like that?"

"Like what?"

"That."

I raised a single eyebrow at him, shook my head, and continued on with my stretches until he snapped his fingers. "I got it!"

"Got what?" I mumbled. I'm sure he got a lot of things out of that conversation with Vanessa, but it didn't mean I would say them out loud.

A huge grin spread across his face as he leaned down closer to me, humor in his eyes. "You're jealous."

I felt myself turning red as I looked away from his pointed gaze. "What? Don't flatter yourself--"

"You're cute when you're jealous," He pointed out, forcing himself into my line of view. "But don't worry, we were just talking. She was asking how training was going and all that."

Wanting nothing more than to change the topic away from my embarrassment, I remembered my true reason for needing to find Cole. My eyes landed on the notebook next to me and I leaned closer to him so that anyone passing by wouldn't hear.

"Look... I found something today. Do you remember back to picking up--"

"Is that my sketchpad?" Mackenzie suddenly appeared. "I was wondering where I left it! Thanks for bringing it with you, Taylor!"

She gave me a little smile and reached down, hugging it to her chest before putting it into the backpack she always carries around here. When I studied her closer, I found that her cheerful expression never reached her eyes, proving even more that she was hiding and tucking in all her past feelings and guilt.

"Will you continue now?" Cole's question brought me back and I shook my head just the slightest amount.

"Later... In private," I mumbled and a smirk played on his lips.

"I like the sound of that--"

He shut up when I hit him.

It didn't take long for the rest of the Big Six and our respected trainers to get there. Alex even had the nerve to wag his eyebrows at us when he arrived, proving more and more that he was a fan of us getting together. I couldn't deal with my so-called 'jealousy' or even my friends right now. What I needed to focus on getting help for Mackenzie and that's it.

I was so lost in my thoughts that I hadn't realized that Leona's instructor was laying out the guidelines for our partner training today. I didn't even have time to look around for a person to work with until Cole was dragging me over to an empty part of the field.

"We will begin sparring in a few moments," the instructor announced. Cole looked me straight in the eye while mine narrowed on him.

"What are you thinking about?" I asked, suspicion clear in my voice.

He gave me a mischievous smile. "Just about how jealous you are."

I frowned. "Cole-"

"Begin!"

I had to admit it, I was envious of Vanessa's past relationship with him and if they were rekindling their feelings and relationship, it would definitely hurt. They were together for a long time and even though Cole never truly liked her all that much, there must have been at least something there besides guilt to get him through that relationship without saying something. Taking it all that emotion and confusion about my feelings, I threw everything I had into the training session with Cole. He obviously noticed and looked surprised, but expertly dodged everything I had coming for him.

Soon enough, the two of us were in close combat, him blocking while I trying to land a mark on him.

"Still jealous, Shorty?" He asked, a smile written all over his face while he continued to maneuver away from everything I tried to get him with.

Gritting my teeth, I slowed down time and continued with my pursuit. I would finally land marks, never anything to leave a lot of damage because this was just a training exercise, but I was able to actually hit him with something.

"I can honestly say we just talked," Cole told me until that oh-so stupid smirk came up once again once I made time go back to normal. "We did have one slip up... We might've--"

Not wanting to hear anymore, I packed a lot of unseen force into my next punch into his right peck, making him slip and fall to the ground. Taking the advantage of this, I went forward, placed my foot on his chest, and threatened him with a looming medicine ball over his body. My chest rose up and down while I tried to control my breathing from the training session. From below me, Cole looked really impressed and didn't hide it as Sophia came over and assessed the situation.

"Hmm," she hummed while she looked at us. "So, that's how it works, huh? Get the girl jealous and she'll fight..." My trainer nodded to herself. "Duly noted."

Huffing out, I threw the weight onto the ground and held out a hand to help Cole up. He gave me a cheeky grin and began brushing off.

"Strong, hot, and cute while jealous?" He whistled. "You're a catch--"

I pulled him closer to me and while he looked surprised at first at this blatant sign of affection, it was so I could whisper in his ear as his standing height towered over me. "Mackenzie's on the edge of a total breakdown," I told him. "We need to do something."

When I pulled back, all traces of flirting and amusement were gone and now replaced with worry for the girl. Looking over to her now, it was obvious to see her struggling with the practices and probably even internally panicking. She covers her emotions well in situations like this, most likely a skill she learned from her family life, but that's nothing but dangerous here. One outburst from her and we could end up like her parents.

"Explain later... we'll talk to her after training."

I nodded and went to grab my water bottle but he grabbed my wrist.

"To be honest, Vanessa was asking for tips. She has her Final exam coming up soon, the one that lets her out of this place and into the real world, and wanted any advice I could give her. You're fun to mess with and I took the opportunity to do so. Sorry for getting you all worked up, but it was really cute to see that feeling come out of you."

I hid my smile from him, feeling better about both him and my feelings I held. "Thanks, Cole."

"But maybe I'll hang out with her some more if it means you get all jealous--"

I moved a tree branch right in front of his feet, making him trip and fall flat on his face. After that, he didn't make any more of those jokes.

I hope you guys all love me because this chapter is longer than average. I've been into writing this SO much this past week because of all your comments last week! Definitely the most I've gotten for this story in seven days. I loved hearing about which ability you'd all like to have! It's so interesting to hear of all your different reasonings to it all.

I've been so enthusiastic about writing that I even plotted out each chapter until the end of this story. We're looking at around ten more for here, and then I'll begin the next book in the series. Hopefully all you guys will stick around for that and the next chapters, but I'm so excited to write them.

And here's the question of the chapter for this week:

Are there any characters you'd like to see more of? While I tried to develop the main characters the most for this story, all the minor ones will definitely be having a larger role in the next book, but who would you like to learn about the most?

I'm nearing both 100,000 views on this story (AHH) and 5,000 followers (WOO). I'm thinking about doing a Q&A for that, so if you have any questions about this story, any of my others, or even myself, feel free to ask them!

Chapter Twenty-Eight - The Sketchbook

What is this?? An update on a Tuesday?? Please read the author's note at the end of the chapter :)

———

After training, Cole pulled me away from everyone else and went a little into the woods so that we wouldn't be bothered.

"Okay, what's going on?"

I explained everything about the sketchbook to him, the pictures of the Catchers, her family, and even herself. He sat there silently, taking in every word before he finally spoke up again.

"I know she's probably depressed, but why are you so urgent about it? There are therapists and people all around that can help her."

I sat there, just staring at him for a few moments before speaking. "How did she kill her parents, Cole?"

"By electrocuting them to death?"

I raised an eyebrow at him, moving my hands in a motioning pattern to urge him to say more. "And?"

He blinked once, twice, before he finally realized that I was getting at. His once confused expression turned into slight panic. "She blew up on them... Which is what she'll probably do again if she continues holding everything in."

"Bingo."

"We need to do something, calm her down or anything else that could possibly work. She can't do that here--"

"Well, well, well..." A booming voice announced as I saw Claire and Alex parading through the trees. Alex had a large grin on his face, looking in between the two of us, before speaking again, "Sneaking away already, aren't you?"

"Alex," Cole gave him a serious look. "We need time alone right now--"

"Or time to make out..." he trailed off when Claire nudged him, her eyes focused on Cole with the familiar sign of her reading his thoughts. Alex immediately understood and gave us a sheepish look. "Sorry, guys. Just thought you two were finally making progress. We'll just be going now." And sure enough, he grabbed his girlfriend's hand and ran off with her out of sight.

Cole took a deep breath and looked back to me. "So what can we do?"

While biting my lip in concentration, I realized I hadn't gotten to that point yet. My whole plan revolved around Cole helping her, but what exactly could he do? "I think you're her best bet. She worships the ground you walk on. Just like when we picked her up, you need to do the talking. Make her realize that she has a supportive backing now, that she's not alone and not at fault for anything she did in the past. She needs to get help, professional help. You need to convince her to do so."

"You know, Buckley... You're putting me in a pretty difficult position."

"I'm sure you'll figure it out."

He gave me a desperate look, pulling in a deep but slightly shaky breath as he ran his fingers through his hair. "Will you be there though? I would like your moral support."

I patted his arm. "Of course, bud. Anything to help."

We began heading out to where Mackenzie's dorm was so that we would be able to talk to her. "Bud?" Cole repeated me, making a disgusted face. "As if."

I raised an eyebrow at him, "What do you mean?"

"Way to put me in the friend zone," he joked, a smile lining his lips. In an act of pure humor he put his hand to his heart and pouted. "I thought we had something special. I thought that we're Caylor!"

The mention of our couple name forced a groan out of my throat. "Not you too!"

"What? I like it a lot!"

"We're not even a couple!"

"Well, we'll never be if you keep denying your feelings and putting me in the friend zone!" He shook his head incredulously. "Bud, my ass."

"Is that a confession I hear?"

"You're not getting anything out of me, Brain."

I hid a smile from him, shaking my head in disbelief at this conversation. "Okay, maybe bud was a bad term."

Cole laughed, throwing his arm over my shoulder as the dorm building came into view. "You think?"

We didn't say much else as we climbed the steps to the floor that Mackenzie lived on. Nerves began circling in my stomach because there could be some really bad consequences if this conversation went wrong. I know she would never purposely hurt us in any way besides our training, but with a new Supernatural, a young and unstable one at that with the background that she has, there is no telling what she could do on accident.

"So, how do you think I should approach this?"

"Make her see that she's not alone in all this. If you get far where she is actually getting what you're saying, recommend her to the therapist here. She really needs to use her past as building opportunities instead of letting it drag her down or she'll never last in a fight with a Catcher."

Cole nodded and we stopped in front of the door we had dropped her off when we first arrived with her. After taking a deep breath, I knocked three times on her door and after a bit of scuffling, Mackenzie appeared when it opened. A smile appeared on her face when she saw the two of us standing there.

"Hi! Why are you guys here?" She asked. Her golden yellow eyes traced the two of us, confusion and wonder lining her innocent features.

Cole cleared his throat before speaking, "Could the three of us talk for a bit?"

She must not have thought of it as anything bad, because she nodded exuberantly. "Of course!" She answered and opened the door wide enough for us to pile in. "Jenny is still at training so we're alone for now."

Mackenzie plopped down on her bed and a noticed she was drawing on a new page now. The outskirts of a face were just beginning but when she saw me looking, she immediately closed it and put it aside.

Cole and I took the other side of the bed, sitting down awkwardly without a word. When we were in the midst of silence, I bumped his arm as a motion for him to start talking.

"So, uh, how's it going here, Mackenzie?" He asked and I had to hold back from face palming. Really? Is that really how you're going to approach this? But, I guess, if I gave him the responsibility of talking to her, he gets to choose how he starts.

The girl looked confused for a split second before saying, "I'm doing fine. Is that all you wanted to talk about?"

Cole took a deep breath and looked her in the eyes. "We know that that's a lie, Mack. We know you're not okay."

She looked surprised, but didn't deny what he said. "What... How do you--"

"Taylor saw your drawings." Great, thanks for throwing me under the bus. "What happened in your past doesn't matter here. You're strong, much stronger mentally and physically than most of the people here, but that's not going to matter if you can't grow from your past. You need to take everything that happened to you and make it into a learning experience. None of that was your fault and seeing you hold it in and only project your emotions into your artwork isn't helping you or anyone else. You have a lot of support behind you. There's us, your roommate, instructors, everyone in the Big Six.... We all want to help you and make sure you're okay but we can't do that if you hold everything in."

Her breathing increased and stared blinking back tears. "I--I... It's hard."

Cole held out his arms for a hug and the little girl crawled into them, her cries now making their way forward. "I know, Mackenzie. But you need to let us help you or you won't be able to be the best Supernatural you can be."

"I'm sorry," she blubbered out, making it really difficult to even understand her. "I can't help feeling like this. Everything that happened is my fault. If I just kept my mouth shut--"

"You got magical, electric powers. It's not your fault that you couldn't control them and one incident set you off. All of us have had our fair share of breakdowns both before coming here and after. Just ask Taylor--"

"She doesn't need to know that," I huffed at him, making the girl crack a tiny smile at our dispute.

"Maybe not, but it's always entertaining to make fun of you."

Mackenzie giggled as she wiped away some of the tears on her face. She finally turned to Cole, her voice turning small. "What should I do?"

"Talk. Speak up when you need help with anything. You're not alone and you won't be as long as you're here."

She took a deep breath and did just as Cole said: she talked. She explained the guilt of killing her parents, that she only saw a monster when she looked in the mirror. She told us that she hated using her powers because of what she did and training only made her panic. Her words came out in a jumbled mess, as if she had been holding them in for such a long time and they all rushed to get out at the same time.

"I like it here and I like everyone I meet, but I hate doing what I have to do," she huffed out, slamming her fists on her lap. Immediately, a strike of electricity left her hands, bouncing off the reflective surfaces until it landed on a book, immediately lighting it on fire. Cole hardly reacted and with a wave of his hand, it was extinguished. Mackenzie sniffled and held her face in her hands. "See? I can't control it!"

"But you will once you forgive yourself for everything. You need to focus on training, rather than what can't be changed," Cole told her. "I think you should go talk to some professionals on campus. They can really help you with everything."

She peeked out from behind her hands. "You think?" She asked.

"I know. I've been there before and they can really help."

His words made me furrow my brows. He's talked to some of the therapists on campus before? Could it be because of the Catcher who attacked him and Vanessa on campus or some other reason?

He caught my expression and gave him a confused look. He mouthed the word 'later' to me and went back to consoling Mackenzie. He told her where to go and that she should swing by as soon as possible. After the long talk, she seemed in better spirits and gave the two of us big hugs as a token of her appreciation.

"Thank you," she muttered. "I'll get help."

"And if you have anything you want to tell us, don't be afraid to say it, okay?" Cole told her. "Even at three in the morning you can go wake up the Mind here and she'll help."

I rolled my eyes at him volunteering to do the night shift, but I honestly didn't mind. I'd rather miss out on sleep than have her do something drastic. And with that, more promises of her talking with someone, and a million more thank you's, Cole and I left Mackenzie's room.

The two of us walked together, now stepping around and through the crowds of people who just got done with their own training. We started separating through the swarm, so Cole grabbed my hand and led me out the door to where we had more space and less noise.

"So," He started, still not letting go of my hand. "You want to know what I meant back there?"

I nodded, but added on with a, "But only if you want to tell me."

He considered that and began leading me the familiar way to the lake. Hopefully Alex and Claire weren't there, because privacy with Cole was always an interesting time. "Please," He started, moving away a branch so I could easy pass by it. "I know a lot about you because of all your paperwork, so I think it's time for me to talk a bit about my past."

"Anything as exciting as mine?" I asked and he laughed.

"I don't think so, but there's some stuff that you might be surprised about."

We finally arrived at the lake, alone as anticipated. Cole immediately shed his shirt and jumped into the water. When he came up, he spurted out water with a smile, motioning for me to join him. Because it was a warm, humid day, I took him up on that offer. Soon enough, the two of us were swimming around together.

He finally leaned against a rock and I joined, looking at him expectantly.

"So, you gonna tell me?" I asked and he nodded.

He took a deep breath and gave me a look. "I came here when I was seventeen," he started. "Before all the training and everything, I wasn't like this."

"What, you weren't a jerk?" I teased.

He laughed and made a face at me. "You wouldn't be talking to me right now if you really thought that," he pointed out before continuing on with his story. "But no, I was weak. A total mama's boy, to be honest. I really missed my family. I was having troubles focusing and even tried to leave Supernatural Abilities."

"Let me guess... You got caught?"

He tossed me a cheeky grin, "Didn't even make it close to the fence."

"Knew it."

"But anyways... I was really having a hard time. I wasn't like you and Mackenzie. I had a great relationship with my family. I'm not bragging about that or anything, but you two easily came here because you had nothing to lose. Well, you had Ryan but let's not talk about that." That flash of jealousy came onto his face and I patted his shoulder. "I was heartbroken leaving my family and having to write the letter saying goodbye. To this day, I hope they think I'm at some military school so they know I'm not purposely avoiding them. Coming here just made it worse and in order for me to succeed at my ability, they put me into counseling. It helped a lot, which is why Mackenzie needs to go there. We might have two different pasts, but they'll be able to help her push that aside for her to grow."

"And eventually she'll turn into a macho, tough guy like you?" I teased.

"Please. There can only be one of those around here and that's--"

"William?"

He was about to push me away but I put up my shield. Instead of meeting skin, his hand collided with an unseen barrier, taking him by surprised, as a groan of pain escaped his mouth.

"You're the worst," He grumbled as I laughed harder than I have in a long time. "You're lucky you're cute."

We didn't speak much about the past after that, and continued on swimming around until we became too tired to continue on. It was been a long, exhausting day, both mentally and physically, so the two of us collapsed on the ground, happy and tired.

"Hey, Cole?" I asked while looking up to the sky. The sun was just beginning to set, creating a wave of beautiful colors above us. The air was still warm, heating our bodies as we lay there.

"Yeah?"

"Can you tell me about how you discovered your powers?" I asked, mid-yawn.

He chuckled, pulling my body closer to his as we continued to lay there. "I can't spill all my secrets in one day, Shorty. That story will be for another day."

I didn't remember much after that, as the familiar dozing feeling of sleep washed over me. While it felt like five minutes, I woke up to complete darkness and Cole shaking me awake.

"What are you doing?" I yawned, leaning on my elbows. "You couldn't have just carried me to my room like a gentleman--"

I stopped when I finally heard the sirens, growing louder and louder with each passing second. Cole pulled me to my feet, grabbed our clothes that we shed for swimming in one fist, and my own hand in his other.

"We have to go--"

"What's going on?" I asked while we ran, still groggy from our nap earlier. As we headed closer to the main buildings, the alarm continued to grow even louder than before.

"The sirens," Cole said during his puffs of air. "That means there's a Catch-er on campus."

———————————————

YES! I updated early! Why? Because we hit 100K READS AND 5K FOL-LOWERS! WOO!!

Thank you so much for the love and support all of you bring me and this story! I couldn't have gotten here (And even reached the #5 spot for Fantasy!) without all of you! As a token of my appreciation, I hope you liked this very early update, and I'll try to have the next one out as usual, meaning Friday, or possibly Saturday depending on my schedule.

And as another present, my question of the chapter to you is... What are your questions for me? I have been asked so many of the same questions so if you have something you've been wondering about me, this story, Wattpad, or anything else in general, please ask it below! I'll either add a FAQ section to the next chapter(s) or make a video answering them if I get a lot of different ones.

And going back to the question of the chapter last week, a lot of you guys mentioned wanting to see more of Leona and Will but DON'T WORRY! They'll be very big figures in the next two books and their outcast-ness (not a word, but please go with it) will be addressed later on :)

As always, thank you so much for everything you do! I hope you enjoyed this, and see you in a few days :)

Chapter Twenty-Nine - The Sirens

I UPDATE THIS STORY ON FRIDAYS (Usually around 4 PM, PST). I live on the west coast of the US, so please look into what time that is for your location.

PLEASE DO NOT COMMENT SAYING TO UPDATE OR SOMETHING ALONG THOSE LINES! I update Fridays, unless otherwise stated. Demanding an update will not change that.

(okay, rant over. Now time for the chapter!)

We continued running through the woods, both of us keeping an eye out on our surroundings while we did. It had to be past curfew, so luckily everyone else would be inside. Besides us, there would only be the security Supernaturals roaming the outskirts, but how could a Catcher get through them?

Luckily, we made it too our building but all the doors were locked. Inside, the lights were off, just like the average lockdown procedure you could find in schools. Cole immediately began pounding on the doors, yelling at them to let us in. Sure enough, someone must have either heard, seen, or read our minds to know that we were out here and opened the door, ushering us inside, before locking it again.

"Go to your dorm," they ordered. "Lights off, remain quiet. We don't have any information about the break in."

In all the time that I've been here, the dorm hallways have never been this quiet and vacant. Cole and I remained on high alert as we traveled as quietly as possible before landing in front of my door. Before I could even fetch my key, it opened and Claire pulled the two of us inside.

"Are you crazy?!" She whisper-screamed at us. "You two had to go on some romantic rendezvous the day we have a Catcher get through! Could your timing be any more horrible--"

"Sorry, mom," Cole rolled his eyes at our friend. "We accidentally fell asleep. I'll be home before the sun goes down next time."

She looked us up and down, as if just now taking in our appearance. Having swam and then fell asleep, we were still dressed for the water instead of normal activities in public. "And you're naked? Are you serious?"

Cole shrugged, taking a spot on my bed as if he owned the place. "What can I say? She couldn't keep her hands to herself--"

"Cole!" I interrupted him, already turning bright red from their words. To any other person, this would've looked way worse than what actually happened. Luckily Claire was a Mind and could, and most likely already did, read our minds to see what happened.

She shook her head at the two of us before sitting down, staring intently at the wall. "Alex is probably worried sick about you so I'll send a message out to him."

As we sat there waiting for the clear, Cole explained to me that they frequently had drills that happened just like this. However, they were always notified about them ahead of time so this wasn't one of those instances. When a Catcher does make it past the fence, all of our instructors go on a hunt for it, or them if there's more than one, to track it down. It isn't very common because even though the Catchers and Katherine know we're here, there are a lot of us in one place. They rarely try to make it past and when they do, they're killed.

Between the three of us, Claire was the most shaken about this experience. I didn't understand at first, but then I realized that she, and most of the others here, probably hadn't even seen a real Catcher in person before. Me and Mackenzie's pick up missions were peculiar in that aspect, meaning that we did run into our enemies, but that is usually very rare. I'm sure it has to do with our Big Six reputation and even though the times I have encountered them were terrifying, it did give me an edge to my peers.

This was Supernatural Abilities though. This was the place for people like us to go to train and eventually go out and fight who is threatening us. Compared to every other place in the world, we're all much safer here even without constant security roaming the woods.

Looking at the clock we had on our TV stand, it read that it was around ten at night. Not super late, but definitely past our curfew time. Cole and I were definitely going to get it from Galen once she finds out that we were out tonight.

But in our defense, we fell asleep... Okay?

Claire rambled on for a long time about how unsafe we were and how we could've gotten hurt out there. I was only half listening and more focusing on Cole messing with the tips of my hair in boredom.

"I mean, if you guys need a night to yourselves, just let me know and I can spend the night with Alex. God knows I don't want to be in the room with you two if you ever--"

"The campus is clear," A voice sounded throughout our room. "Please resume your normal schedule."

"Oh, thank goodness," I mumbled, so grateful that they were able to interrupt Claire's lecture.

"Big Six Supernaturals must report to Galen tomorrow morning at eight. Thank you for your cooperation and have a nice night," the voice concluded before sounding off.

Cole slapped his knees and stood up, stretching out his limbs with a yawn escaping his lips. "With that, I'm heading off to bed. Not that I didn't sleep well before this whole thing," he winked at me. "See you tomorrow, guys."

When he exited our room, Claire began shaking her head at me. I gave her a confused look and asked, "What?"

"You two are so ridiculous," She muttered, a little smile on her lips. "Cute, but ridiculous."

"I thought you didn't like intruding in people's heads, Claire?" I accused and she held up her hands in defense.

"Hey! When your boyfriend demands to know all the dirt on 'Caylor' and you two are too stubborn to admit anything, I kind of have to snoop around. Besides, once you two are finally together, I'll stop."

"And who's to say that we will even end up together?"

She shrugged. "I don't know, maybe everyone including you? Taylor, I've been living with you long enough to know that you really have feelings for him. It's written all over your face and body language.

I huffed out and avoided her accusatory stare. "Fine... Maybe a little--"

"Ha! Like I said, the two most stubborn people in the world. We'll have to wait and see how this all plays out. I'll try not to dig in too much."

I smiled and changed into some comfier clothes for bed. When I climbed in and turned off the lights, I almost immediately began falling asleep until Claire began talking yet again.

"Hey..." She started, pausing her sentence for a few moments before continuing on. "I know I can go through your mind for the answer, but I don't like doing that with you. I have a question that I would like you to answer out loud for me."

"Yeah?"

"Do you really like Cole?" She asked. "And I don't want any of this 'maybe' nonsense. I want a clear-cut answer."

I didn't hesitate at all and said, "Obviously."

She laughed under her breath and I heard her turning over in her bed, probably preparing herself more for sleep now that she got an answer. "Good," she mumbled. "Caylor must happen."

––––––––––––––

The next morning I found myself in Galen's office bright and early. When I arrived, Leona was already there with her beautiful, glowing self while I looked more like a gremlin than anything else.

Honestly? Screw morning people. It's eight in the morning and I wasn't about to get up and look good for anyone.

Our leader's eyes narrowed on me when I walked in. Ducking my head, I took a spot and began waiting for the others to arrive. Soon enough,

William and Mackenzie came in and we were only waiting for Cole and Alex.

"You are so stupid!" We heard before their faces emerged.

"We fell asleep!" I heard Cole defending himself to his best friend. "Believe it or not, humans have basic needs that need attending to!"

"I don't see any beds in the woods--"

Alex stopped mid-sentence when they finally walked in, seeing everyone stare at them. Cole gave us all a cheeky grin before the two of them took their spots at the table. Galen cleared her throat as Sophia silently closed the door behind them.

"As you all know, a Catcher was able to break through our line of defenses late last night," our leader began. "While their motives are unknown and there seemed to be only one intruder that was easily eradicated, we mustn't let this go easily. Katherine might have been sending a signal to us, or the Catcher was eager to make his mark and try to hurt one of you six. Whatever it was, the campus is on high alert until you all are ready for battle.

"In the event that this happens again, please make your way to the safe room under the dormitories. Do not engage and do not fight. Everyone here is dedicated to ensuring that you are all safe first. You can bring others, but there are other safety measures intact for the rest of the Supernaturals. Due to your standings in this war, we must provide even stronger defenses for you six in the event of an attack."

"So where is this safe room?" Leona asked. "I've been around the entire building and I've never--"

"There's an old cellar door that leads to a stronger one. Your fingerprints are already in the system, so only few people are able to get in," Sophia told her.

"Please be alert while you are walking around, as well," Galen told us. "That means obeying curfew, the rules, and paying attention to your surroundings." At the mention of the curfew, she looked pointedly at Cole and I. "We have a lot of things going on this time of year. The final tests are right around the corner and--"

"Wait," Alex interjected now. "The tests where people can move up in levels or go out in the real world?"

"Yes..." She answered slowly, looking confused by his question. "I thought you of all people would have known considering that Claire is in the position to move up a level."

Judging by the look on his face, Claire did not mention that. The boy muttered something under his breath before slumping his seat. I don't think she purposely kept it from any of us, but rather just didn't think it was important enough to mention. Claire might love meddling in our heads, but she's not one to hold anything in either.

But I guess we should've realized it. I remember Cole telling me that these tests happen seasonally and those who are qualified have the chance to move up in levels or take the final exam to go out into the real world. Vanessa did ask Cole for tips for hers just yesterday, but I didn't realize that they were so soon. Since I had just missed the last one when I arrived, this set of finals would be my first to watch and I was interested in seeing how they would go.

"Now please," Galen's words brought me out of my thoughts. "We're a very fragile union, so please stay safe. You are now free to go to training now."

When we all started getting up, her eyes landed on Cole and I. "You two need to stay for a few extra minutes."

I immediately felt like I was going to the principal's office as everyone but Cole, Galen, and I stayed put. She looked between the two of us with judgment in her eyes.

"Now... I know the full story, but you two are aware of the curfew, correct?"

I felt myself turning bright red, knowing that she went through our minds to discover that we were out at the time the Catcher broke through.

"Of course," Cole answered, looking as relaxed as could be. "We just fell asleep and didn't wake up until the sirens came on. It won't happen again, we promise."

"It shouldn't have happened in the first place," she reprimanded. "You two have a high standing at this facility and for our kind. You must take that into account first before you make decisions for yourself."

Her words didn't resonate well with me. I was forced into this life--the powers, Supernatural Abilities, Big Six, all of it--but I was also supposed to put my whole life, feelings, and everything else aside for this? I was only seventeen, eighteen very soon. I shouldn't have to already be locked down by something when I still need to grow and mature in ways unrelated to being a Supernatural.

Galen raised an eyebrow, her eyes now resting on me. I immediately looked away, knowing that she had to have heard all of that through her telepathy. Not only am I forced into this whole lifestyle, but I also have no privacy whatsoever.

"Just..." Our leader started again, pinching the bridge of her nose. "Please keep in mind that people are looking up to you two and the rest of you. Every decision you make from now on will affect someone or something else, so please ensure that you are making choices with positive outcomes. That's all I need to say, so you can also head off to training now."

Cole nodded and got up, the two of us heading over to the door. We were about to leave when Galen called out my name.

"You go on," I muttered to him as he continued walking.

"Good luck!"

I turned around, still in the doorway while Galen looked at me solemnly.

"You know, Taylor..." She started. "I have a lot of faith in you, probably more in you than anyone else in the Big Six. I know you haven't been here too long, but you have so much potential and growth waiting for you along the road. However, that won't happen if you have certain distractions holding you back... Please consider that."

I nodded and turned back around, heading to training just as I always did now.

———————————

All of you guys are Claire and Alex, just wishing for Caylor to finally happen. even though it might not, hahaha.

Thank you so much for everything as always! I got some pretty interesting questions last week that I'll be answering soon! Until then, feel free to ask more questions below! Unless I get a lot, I probably won't be making a video out of them so I'll just attach it to the end of next week's chapter.

Hope you enjoyed, and DID YOU ALL SEE THE SNAPCHAT FILTER THAT MAKES YOU LOOK LIKE A CATCHER?? I was so excited about it, haha. See you all next week!

FAQ + Cast List

<hr>

AN: As many of you already figured out, I took down the original version of SA and CTC as of yesterday, 4/20. I have had many people getting angry about that series not being continued despite them explaining that this new version will cover the entire series into much more detail. While I know many of you loved those books, I feel like they misrepresent me as a writer and don't want those to potentially hold me back once I get into the processing of attempting to publish. Not only that, I don't want them holding back other readers from enjoying the new version, as many people are getting them confused or refusing to even read the new ones because they insist they'll only like the original. Say what you will, but they were honestly very badly written, hahaha. They are currently unpublished, so they could always be put up again but I do not plan to do that anytime soon. I'm sorry to any fans of them, but it was time for them to go.

ALSO, when I was doing this, wattpad decided to unpublish and republish some other stories, including SA. Having to go back and fix everything was a total hassle and gave all of you a ton of notifications, saying that I posted 30 chapters in one day. SO, I'm so sorry about that!! I'll make it up by posting two chapters next week :)

And onto the questions!!

"Which element would you like to be?" @grizlycody

I've been asked this question before and I've actually answered it in the comments! But I would be a Mind. This is also why Taylor is one because I cannot write a character that I don't relate with. She was actually going to be a Water originally but after a few chapters, I had to change her entire character because I just couldn't do it.

"Are you one if the characters in this book? What power would you choose? Why did you decide to write this book? Who made the characters?" @herokaty

(This question is also answered before: "what inspired you to write this book?" @mysterysoulstealer and "Where did you get the idea for this story?" @riflegirl597)

I wouldn't say that I'm a character in the book, but, as said above, I relate with Taylor quite a lot. I'm the one who made my characters, but many of them are based off of people in my normal everyday life. One of the main things is that Taylor and Cole's relationship (Caylor!!) is TOTALLY based off of my own relationship with my boyfriend. So all you guys begging them to be together was basically our friends a few years ago, haha.

I decided to write this book because I've always been infatuated with elemental powers and really wanted to make a book that explored that. As many of you know, I began writing this series when I was thirteen and my original vision only included one book with the 'school' aspect in mind. However, now you can see that I had definitely expanded that concept to include Catchers, the Big Six, Katherine, and more training than actually schooling, especially in this version. This whole series started off as some little idea but I was able to create a whole world within a few months. This is the main reason why I wanted to rewrite the series. I didn't have enough planning the first time, or writing experience, so everything was really choppy! I'm liking this version a whole lot more :)

"How different is this revised version compared to the original?" @honeyH4

Let's just put it this way.... By this chapter in the original book, Cole and Taylor had already done the dirty. 0-100 REAL QUICK.

This book is much more detailed. The other one is just bam bam bam, plot hole here and plot hole there, something that makes no sense everywhere. I didn't give myself a chance to build up the characters and Taylor and Cole basically got together within a week of knowing each other and an hour after Cole broke up with Vanessa. I just wrote to produce a response out of people, which is not the way to go. Besides main plot points, everything else is written much better and just makes sense in the new version. I was thirteen at the time, THIRTEEN. I know many of you guys are that age, but being nearly twenty now, I have undergo so much writing and personal growth since then. The original is much more of a romance than a fantasy/adventure, but I have no idea how people were able to believe that considering that I was young, never kissed a single person, or even dated anyone, hahahaha. Overall, I just think this version of the series is better and there's even more growth to come :)

I know many of you loved the original, but this is just my opinion. I do hope anyone who has read both versions likes this one more though :)

"How many chapters is there going to be?" @Bershka127

I THINK it's going to be 34 chapters (maybe more??) and then an epilogue. So very soon!! However, don't fret because there's still two more books of this trilogy :)

(and psst... Chapter 32 is pretty good in my opinion... just remember that)

"Who is your favorite ship? Will there be one for Mack?" @Awesomecords2

I'm definitely a fan of Caylor and Clalex (Claire and Alex). However, don't get any ideas about that because I can also disappoint myself by not getting them together!

And for Mackenzie... I don't think so, but who knows? I think she needs to figure out herself first before letting anyone in. Besides, she's only twelve. She doesn't need any man until she's at least thirty ;)

"When does Taylor turn 18? What kind of abilities does electric have?" @riflegirl597

Taylor turns 18 VERY soon. Not this upcoming chapter, but the next will say when!

And the Electric ability is very interesting, as Mackenzie is the only one to have it. She's the only one able to figure out how much she can manifest and control, so while I can't reveal the extent of her powers just yet, just know that you'll find that out soon!

When do you usually update? (Very commonly asked!!)

Fridays! Works best with my schedule and I know that it's easier for most of you guys to read it at the end of the week when there's no school for many of you. It's usually around 4 PM PST, so that might be considered Saturday for many of you.

Non SA related:

"How do you motivate yourself to keep writing and get past writer's block?" @EarthlyRain

This is a question that I don't have a good answer for because if you followed any of my teen-fic books, you would know that I STRUGGLED with writer's block with basically every chapter. However, with SA I don't have any problems with writing. I think what's helping me get through it is having a plan for every chapter and knowing what will happen. There's no guessing or anything, it's all right there in front of me. Along with that, writing something you truly love and in a genre you enjoy really makes a difference. I never really liked writing in the teenfic section, so I struggled with it.

Any advice for someone going into their freshman year of high school next year? @gamedays

Let me give you the lovely wisdom of a college student~~~

Long story short: high school is not the movies. As long as you stick to yourself and your friends, no one will bother you. Upperclassmen are not rude unless you're being obnoxious. PLEASE do not stop in the middle of the hallways to talk to friends or anything, that is what people get angry at the most. Other than that, enjoy your last four years of basic schooling. Enjoy your friends because after HS, you probably won't talk to them much or even at all. Go to football games, dances, and school functions because you'll regret it when you're older. I don't suggest dating in HS, boys are immature and lame, college is a good time to get into all that (but this is a total personal preference).

Just don't waste these four years because after this, you have to be an adult and do adult things which sucks.

And the MOST asked question ever:

Are Taylor and Cole ever going to get together?

Is Caylor ever going to happen?

When will my ship sail?

And the answer for that is... you just have to wait and see :)

I've also had requests to upload pictures of the cast list! So here's what I have come up with... While these people don't fit my characters exactly, I can't figure out who else could fit their spots. If you have any ideas, let me know!

Cast list:

Taylor Buckley (Taylor Momsen)

Cole Trainor (Alex Pettyfer):

Claire Richardson (Sarah Hyland):

Alex Carpenter (Matthew Daddario):

Mackenzie Blanchard (Emma Engle):

And this is what I have right now! They're subject to change and add on other important characters once I have people figured out for them. If you have any suggestions, comment them below!

As always, thank you so much for all your support! You guys have really made my life SO much better with all your kind words and encouragements :) I'm sorry for the fiasco this week, but I know you'll enjoy the last few chapters of SA!

If you have any additional questions, you can include them below and I'll try to answer them!

As always, I'll see you Friday (tomorrow)!

Chapter Thirty - The Power

HUGE thank you to drosostalida for the amazing cover up top!!

AN: If you didn't see my FAQ/Cast List I posted yesterday, then let me apologize and say that I'm SO sorry about the millions of notifications I might have given you a few days ago. This story was unpublished for some reason and in order to put it back up, each chapter needed to be republished, which means a million notifications for everyone!

As an apology, I'll be uploading TWO chapters next week :) So updates will be on both Tuesday and Friday!

"Can you watch out?!" I exclaimed as I ducked from yet another Supernatural walking by carrying a slab of wood or something else for all the exams happening in only a few days.

The campus was a mess of people building and preparing for these tests. While the main, final exams which Vanessa will be taking will be happening in the main arena, the level-tests, like what Claire is going to do, happened in a field so they must transport and build new stands for people to watch.

And, of course, that field just so happened to be the one that the Big Six trained on.

"I don't get why we can't just move," I mumbled to Sophia, rubbing at my shoulder that had been hit with a slab of metal earlier. "This is hurting my training."

"Oh, cry me a river," She muttered, inspecting her nails while she leaned against a tree. "Not like you were getting any further with your body manipulation."

I furrowed my eyebrows together in agitation. "Yes I was! I feel it happening!"

"Oh, really? Let me see it now."

"It doesn't work like that yet," I mumbled. "I'm still working on it--"

Sophia snorted, rolling her eyes at me. "See?"

"I can't see you being able to do it," I pointed out, making her glare at me. "So I'm one step ahead of you on this."

"Yet I can do many other things that you can't, kid." When I was about to counter, she snapped her fingers at me. "Try it again."

Sighing, I asked, "What should I try to look like?"

Sophia looked around, her eyes searching the others who were training. I have been trying to become the instructor who has been helping me get this down, but continuously failed. Finally, she motioned William over who was cooling down to come over and help.

"Change into him," she ordered once he got here. "Study his features and project yourself into the power."

I took a deep breath and focused on William's look. From his caramel skin to his ultra-light gray eyes, I studied each feature more than I will ever do again. He looked pretty awkward to be put in this position, but still compliant. After trying for five minutes, I finally groaned and looked away.

"Nope, can't do it."

William patted me on the back with a smile, "You'll get it eventually, Taylor," he said with his accent lining his words. "Let me know if you need my help again."

After giving him a thank you, he headed over to continue with his training. Sophia looked as annoyed as ever, and whispered something to the instructor. Within the time I blinked, I found myself once staring at them to now seeing my old best friend Ryan right in front of me.

"Maybe you need a familiar face," Sophia tried while I stared at this not-Ryan in front of me. "Try it now."

It's been weeks since I've seen Ryan and even though this isn't him, I wanted nothing more than to give him a hug and tell him how sorry I was about leaving. I wanted to tell the real him the truth about my powers, Big Six, everything but I know it would do more harm than good.

Despite this being a manipulation, I was surprised by how much detail it had. The instructor has most likely never seen him, so Sophia had to have sent them a mental picture that she could have received with my files. There was even the little freckle that rested on his upper lip.

I was so focused on this fake-Ryan, that when I felt the power surge through me, I knew I had changed. I was able to hold it for only a moment before I felt it leave, transforming me back to the average Taylor Buckley that I am.

Sophia swore under her breath in surprise, her eyes wide. "I can't believe that actually worked! You actually did something for once!"

"Congratulations, Taylor," The instructor as Ryan said to me. "I knew you could do it"

I was so excited about finally doing something that I bombarded them with a hug. "Thank you, thank you, thank you!" I yelled and right before I was about to pull away, my eyes caught Cole's who was staring intently on us, a certain emotion touching his features.

"That's a hard skill to manage," They told me, now becoming themselves again. "So good job at getting a touch on it. Continue practicing and you'll get really good at it."

The instructor then had to leave to help out with the final exam set up as well, leaving me in the hands of the lovely Sophia.

"I have to say..." she started out. "I'm pretty impressed that you were finally able to pull it off. I'll let you cool down and we can start up with this again tomorrow."

And, in that moment, I swear I saw a hint of a smile on her face before she left to probably go help out with the final exam preparation as well.

As I did my basic relaxation techniques, I looked out onto the field to where they were assembling several large stands. Apparently they change fields every season so that those who are being tested don't know what to expect. Lucky for them, this terrain was mostly flat and had a good expanse of trees around it that they could use to their advantage.

It's been different here following the Catcher's break in. There were more guards and supervision occurring at all times of the day. Curfew was now strictly enforced, as opposed to being able to slowly walk back to your dorm around that time. At least the finals broke the rigidness of this place right now, but I'm sure it will be back like this after they're all done.

But despite those kinds of things, I found myself wondering about Galen's words.

She mentioned a distraction that was potentially holding me back. Did she mean my past? Was I focusing too much on what I had and not the present?

My eyes wandered to the others in the Big Six also cooling down, except for Cole. His eyes found mine and that same emotion from earlier was spread throughout his entire body. He seemed angry as he trained with his instructor, even making him fall to the ground following a blast of fire to his chest. Thankfully, his trainer was flame retardant, as are all Fires, and didn't feel any heat.

I bit my lip as I looked away, not wanting to deal with that right now and went back to Galen's words, a question rising in my mind.

What if she meant my fixation with Cole?

Whatever it was, hopefully with word that I've learned body manipulation she'll think better of me.

As I got up and began heading out, I decided to wait until Cole got done with his own training to see what was going on with him. After fifteen or so minutes, he finally finished up and stomped by me as he began towards the common area.

"Whoa!" I called out to him before running to catch up. His mouth was taut, and his eyes were set straight forward. "What's going on?"

"You seemed pretty happy back there," he said in a deep monotone voice. "You know, seeing Ryan and all."

I had to hold back a laugh knowing that if I released it, I would only make him angrier. "Relax," I told him. "It was to help me get the body manipulation which I did!"

"By using the boy who's in love with you."

"By using my best friend," I corrected. "It wasn't even him so I don't know why you're freaking out over this."

"Could've used me," he muttered under his breath, running his hand through his hair in agitation.

"I don't know you as well as I know Ryan and it's not like I asked for him. Sophia thought it would be a good idea and it worked. You can stop your jealous attitude--"

"Jealous? Me?" he scoffed, turning a little red in the cheeks. "I'm not--"

"Cole," I stopped him, raising an eyebrow. His eyes dropped to the ground and a little, boyish smile rose onto his lips.

"Okay... I might be a little jealous..." he admitted, making me laugh at his ridiculousness. "That guy just sets me off, okay? I know you don't have feelings for him but he definitely does, even now that you're away. It was really obvious when we ran into them at the diner."

"Well, you have nothing to worry about," I told him. "It's not like I'll be seeing him anytime soon so until them, I'm stuck with you."

He ruffled my hair. "And that's just how I like it, Brain. I don't think I could go without your wit and charm."

We began walking again, now in better spirits now that Cole's inner jealous monster was taken account of. As we cleared the forest, I noticed a figure sitting on one of the benches right outside our dorm building. As we approached, I recognized them and swore under my breath.

"Taylor!" Allyson yelled, jumping up. "Can we please talk? I'm so sorry!"

Cole looked confused as his eyes jumped between us. "I'll just let you two talk..." he muttered and escaped through the building doors.

Gee, thanks for throwing me to the wolf.

"Allyson...." I started in exasperation. I didn't like this girl and being around her just creeped me out. "I'm sorry about being rude to you the other day but I was really busy--"

"I shouldn't have bothered you, Taylor," she exclaimed, making me think back to the last time I saw her. It was when I was trying to find Cole and tell him about Mackenzie's sketchbook. "I just would love to train with you one day and see what you can do. You're my role model and I have my test coming up to move to level four--"

"Sure," I interjected, knowing that she would only continue to ask until I gave in. A bright smile appeared on her face and she grabbed my arm and pulled me away. We walked far away from the main area and further than I've ever gone before. When we finally got to where she wanted, she let go of me.

"Here is good!" She announced before dropping her bag and stretched out her hands. "I just want to see how you do your skills and how I can enhance mine."

"What do you want to start with?"

She thought about it for a moment, her finger even rising to her chin. "Telekinesis?"

I sighed and began showing her what I could do and then judged her own ability. While I've never really been around a level three, I was surprised by how, for lack of better word, bad she was. The girl could barely pick up a small boulder that had to be around five pounds. I would expect that from one of the lowest levels, but definitely not from someone in the middle with the potential to move up.

Regardless, she seemed excited that she was able to even that much and in the hour that we 'trained,' she kept thanking me for helping her and telling me how good I was. If she wasn't so creepy, I would actually like the compliments but they only seemed to be forced coming from her.

When I finally was able to go, the small girl gave me a strong hug, a little too tight if I'm honest, and said to me, "Thank you so much, Taylor! You're a total inspiration to me, especially since you've fought so many Catchers already--"

"How do you know about that?" I asked, suspicion in my voice. Her joyous expression faltered the slightest bit before she jumped back to normal.

"Claire told me! You're so heroic. I wish I could be just like you!"

She finally gave me one more hug before running off to do whatever, leaving me alone in the middle of the woods. Something was off with her and I didn't quite believe her story about Claire telling her that. While it might have been true, her expression when I called her out on it told me otherwise.

I don't know much about this Allyson girl, but I was definitely had to find out what was going on.

———————————

So there's only a few more chapters left, guys! But don't worry, there's still two more books of this trilogy! All the action will be coming up in the next few chapters and I must say... chapter 32 is my favorite :)

Question of the chapter: Who will be reading the sequel to this? Just curious.

As always, thank you for everything and I cannot stress how amazing you all are! See you on Tuesday for that extra chapter! :)

Chapter Thirty-One - The Exams

T hank you to @Mage0412 for the name Trevor Kent that was used in this chapter!

The campus was crazy today with people running around every which way while I, and the others in the Big Six, hung back in relaxation. Why? Because it was the day of the final exams and we didn't have to train.

"I wonder if we can crash a party," Cole wondered out loud. "Usually every level has one following the exams but since we're kind of secluded from everyone now, where would we go?"

"We should have ourselves one!" Alex announced while the five of us looked at him. "Come on, it would be fun!"

"Definitely," Cole added sarcastically. "A party is always fun with a twelve year old and a guy who can't stop bugging me about a girl who mocks my every move."

"Hey!" Alex, Mackenzie, and I exclaimed, all obviously taking offense to his jab.

Cole flashed us a big smile and slapped his hand on William's shoulder. "Don't worry, the rest of us will have fun."

I rolled my eyes at them and relaxed in my spot on the bleachers. We had to be here much earlier than everyone else for these final exams that would go on for an hour or so before the lower levels had theirs. So here we were relaxing with everyone else running around like chickens with their heads chopped off while we discussed our party plans.

"But we could have a lot of fun--"

"Alex, please," Cole interjected. "Of everyone here, we're definitely the misfits. We're like the parents of this place who can't have any fun because of responsibilities."

Leona made a face. "Gross."

"I agree."

Alex didn't and continued bickering with his best friend. "It's also Taylor's birthday tomorrow. She's turning eighteen! She deserves to have a night of fun--"

"We'll celebrate that tomorrow."

"Okay, fine," Alex slumped in his seat. "You all stay in for the night while I have a party of one in my bedroom."

Cole snorted. "Please, we all know what you'll be doing at your party--"

"Enough!" I stopped the two boys, peeking at Mackenzie to make sure she didn't catch on to the sexual joke that was about to be made. William looked like he was about to burst out laughing while Alex blasted his best friend in the face with some water.

The two continued with their dispute while I tuned it out the best I could. After an hour of sitting here, people began piling in as the final exam for the level fives were about to start. There were only two people participating in these, Vanessa being one of them. From what Leona was telling me, these tests were much harder than the placement exam as it is to test you to see if you are capable of supporting yourself beyond SA.

Soon enough, the stands were packed as we all waited for this to start.

"Welcome!" Galen's voice boomed over the loudspeaker. "Today we will be testing the abilities of two individuals and their quest to pursue their life's path of being fully trained Supernaturals. Today we will begin with Vanessa Page and finish with Trevor Kent. They have both exhibited immense power and control during their time here and today will determine if they stay or go forth with their paths."

"This speech seems like something out of a video game," I mumbled to Cole who held back a laugh.

"Or maybe something from the gladiator era," he returned, making me hide a smile.

"Now, we welcome Vanessa to the arena. Please begin on the buzzer."

The girl entered the arena, wearing her head high and usual Fire attire. She oozed confidence as she took a deep breath just as the sound went off.

It was similar to the placement exam, meaning the instructors were the ones fighting them. However, it wasn't just one-on-one, but rather many trainers, anywhere from three to ten of them, fighting her at once. I recognized some of them as our own Big Six instructors, but many had to be from the normal Supernaturals' training. Regardless, it was ridiculously difficult to see where Vanessa began and they all started as the arena looked more like a blend of all the elements.

There was no question that she was very powerful and seeing how she navigated through instructor and instructor proved that. Fire was a very unruly ability to have and seeing her control it like she did was incredible and quite a sight to see.

I watched as Sophia came out, focusing on Vanessa while she was mid-fight and least expecting it. I knew she was doing what she did best by implanting some hurtful or completely believable scene in her head because the Fire girl immediately dropped to the ground, clutching her skull. The instructors immediately seized up on their actions and watching, waiting to see if she was able to get out of it.

Sure enough, Vanessa broke out of Sophia control after a little bit of time, shakily stood up, and began fighting yet again. She seemed mentally exhausted now, but still capable of doing some damage out there.

"Damn," Cole whistled. When I looked at him with an eyebrow raised, he just shrugged. "I didn't mean that in a bad way. I'm just saying she's good and that was impressive. I am happy to see that she's using my tips too."

And eventually, all the trainers were beaten and Vanessa stood victoriously in the middle, very clear battle wounds lining her body while her chest heaved up and down as she struggled to regain her breath.

"Vanessa Page," Galen finally came back on. "You have shown great power and we are very happy to announce your graduation from Supernatural Abilities. Please come down and we'll discuss details."

The whole crowd around me screamed and cheered for the girl who looked so incredibly proud of herself that I couldn't help but smile. Despite her hatred for me, she is really someone to look up to when it comes to her ability.

We watched her leave the arena and waited a few minutes for the next guy to begin his own test before we all transferred to the field where the lower levels would be doing their own. There were more of them, obviously, and these were not going to be as difficult or constructed as the final. They go in descending level order so Claire would be one of the first people to go.

The setup was different here than that of the arena as we were working with a field rather than an arena. The bleachers were lined on either side and at one end of the pool held a long table where Galen and the other judges would watch. Cole, Alex, and I were able to get a spot together while the rest of them were a few rows ahead.

They announced these events in a similar way, but didn't do the whole spiel about moving forward with life or anything like that. They brought in each person and once they were finished, they would say if they moved up in levels or not. Some did and some didn't and by the time Claire's turn came around, it was clear that she was nervous.

"If she doesn't pass this then we're breaking up," Alex joked and when I gave him a judging look, he raised his hands in innocence. "Hey. You know I'm kidding!"

She walked out onto the field and Galen announced, "Claire Richardson, your level five exam will begin with the buzzer."

And when it went off, trainers jumped from the surrounding trees and immediately went after Claire. They made each test different so that those taking them didn't know what to expect. My roommate immediately went into action and I saw the familiar look of her reading their minds to know which moves they were to make next. She was able to know ahead of time, effectively blocking and returning the attack to give her the upper hand. It was much simpler than the placement or final exams, but I guess being able to take this test was half the challenge. You had to be approved by several instructors before even being considered to do this.

And as I watched Claire fight, I noticed some mistakes and hits she'd take, making Alex wince next to me. But sure enough, it was soon over and she stood in the middle, awaiting her result.

"Claire, you have passed," Galen came on a few minutes later, following their deliberations. "We will see you in level five training tomorrow."

She jumped up and down and was taken to the side by an instructor who would tell her the information about it. Alex whooped and hollered, Cole doing the same right. I took the easier route and cheered much more calmly for my friend.

Finally, another person was called up and we continued watching. Towards the end, I could see Allyson's turn approaching and I quickly looked away when she caught my eye and started waving.

"Your biggest fan?" Cole teased and I hit his arm.

"More like my biggest stalker," I muttered, covering my face to avoid her stare.

And sure enough, it was time for her to go. The girl practically tripped onto the field, causing a few of the people around us to snicker.

"Allyson Humphrey, your level four exam will begin with the buzzer," Galen announced, and sure enough, it was sounded and some instructors came in from all sides.

She began very shakily, getting hit more times than she made a mark. Despite not liking the girl, I couldn't help but feel secondhand embarrassment from how she was performing in front of everyone.

Well, until it all changed.

The confused expression left her face as a fierce, fighter emerged from her. All at once, she was everywhere, fighting better than I've ever seen someone do before. The crowd had gone silent as Allyson kept hitting and even sometimes hurting the trainers she was up against more than necessary, performing moves that I, let alone Sophia, had no idea how to do.

Within five minutes, much shorter than everyone else's test, she 'eliminated' the last of them and stood up straight and tall, not even gasping for breath as a big smirk rose onto her face.

Everyone was quiet and didn't dare to make a move. There weren't many people at this place so I'm sure everyone knew that Allyson wasn't the best fighter... or so we all thought. Even Galen and the others at the judging table didn't know what to do.

"What just happened?" Cole whispered to me.

I shook my head, my eyes narrowing on the girl. There was something wrong with her, something that wasn't quite right. I've known it all along, but since she never showed it in front of other people, no one believed me. They just thought she was my own personal fan girl, not some creep in disguise.

"I don't know," I muttered to him. "But something isn't right here."

I looked over at Galen to see her scribbling on a piece of paper, her eyes still set on the girl. It was the face of someone reading minds, but judging by the confused look on her face, she didn't get anything out of it. "Miss Humphrey..." She finally started. "We will have your results by the end of the day, please go to the holding rooms in the main arena and we'll speak to you following the conclusion of the last exam."

Allyson nodded exuberantly and hopped off. When she caught my eyes, she gave me a wink before heading off. I needed to get to the bottom of this right now, but when I got up to go follow her, one of the instructors standing along the edge of the field immediately noticed.

"Buckley!" They barked. "Please remain seated. No one is allowed to leave until everyone has gone."

"But--"

"I don't care who you are," They argued, not even letting me get a single word in. "Sit."

I slumped back down, making the guys laugh from besides me. "Good job," Cole joked. "You got in trouble."

"You might be in the Big Six but you still have to sit like everyone else," Alex teased.

I didn't even fight them on it because they didn't see the big picture. I knew something was wrong and the more time they kept me from finding out what that was, the more things Allyson could do. No one was taking this girl serious, not even now when she's obviously been fooling everyone with her strength. She was already playing dumb with her ability, but for what reason?

The rest of the exams continued on as planned but seemed to go much slower than the how they were going before. When Galen finally called them to a close I immediately jumped up but Cole grabbed my wrist to stop me.

"I need to go now!" I tried but he laughed.

"Why? To talk to Allyson? You won't even be able to get to her because Galen and the others were going to go there first," he pointed out and I saw that they were already gone when I looked at their table. "Relax for a bit and then go. All the parties are starting soon and I'm sure someone will let us in." His words make sense and when he saw me starting to turn him down, he pouted. "Please?"

I groaned. "Fine, but only for thirty minutes and then I'm off to look for her."

"Deal," he grinned and grabbed my hand, pulling me through the crowds of excited Supernaturals who were all making their way to their parties. Everyone had already forgotten about Allyson and was more focused on having their seasonal night of fun.

It was getting to be the point of sunset but there was still enough light to make it easy to pass through the trees. Alex followed us, still mentioning that having a Big Six party would be more enjoyable than crashing one, but Cole shushed him enough to make him stop.

"We'll go to the fives," he told us. "We were all there before, so why wouldn't they let us come in?"

When we arrived at a clearing near the main common area, there were already many familiar faces there, including Claire who immediately ran into Alex's arms with a big smile.

"I'm so proud of you!" He yelled while he hugged his girlfriend as tightly as he could.

Cole rolled his eyes and nodded his head over to some guys that were setting up some food. "Are we good to be here?" He asked and they nodded.

"Of course, man! Make yourselves at home."

The thirty minutes I had to be there dragged on. Cole explained to me that this one of the only nights of the year where our curfew was set at midnight. While the instructors didn't approve of underage drinking or anything like that, they all seemed to go to sleep at ten o'clock anyways so at that point on, they turn into actual parties. Everyone was happy and truly enjoying themselves. If I wasn't so hung up on Allyson, I'm sure I would also welcome the fun for a change, but my mind was otherwise occupied.

Finally, I was able to break away from Cole only after promising that I'd be back after I found her. I immediately began running through the woods towards the holding areas in the main arena, hoping that she would still be there or just leaving. When I arrived, the arena was closed off, signaling that anyone who had been there was now gone, and I hit the wall in anger.

Most of the parties seemed to be stationed at various areas close to the commons, so I decided to start there. I began running through the woods again as it slowly began getting darker and darker as the sun finally decided to set. I was around halfway there when I heard her familiar voice.

"Hey, Taylor!" Allyson chirped from behind me. I turned around and stared at her up and down. She looked fine, not a single mark on her despite her rocky start. Her cheerful grin and expression told me that she didn't have a single care in the world right now, as if nothing could hold her back or be wrong.

"What the hell was that back there?" I asked her. The anger in my voice did nothing to faze her.

"What do you mean?"

"Don't you dare play dumb with me. I know you're hiding something from all of us."

"I have no idea what you're talking about, Miss Taylor Buckley," she sang, even doing a little dance. "I'm just an-- Oh!" I went to grab her but the second I reached my hand out, she disappeared. I immediately felt a tapping on my shoulder and when I turned around, she was right there, giggling like a schoolgirl. "That wasn't too kind of you."

"Well, I'm not trying to play nice anymore. Tell me what you're hiding!"

"I'm hiding a lot, Taylor, but you're not all that innocent either. You hide your feelings from Cole, you visions from everyone, your powers from your old life. You hide and never reveal your secrets to anyone. For once, that's going to bite you in the back and unlike you, I'm ready to finally tell everyone what I've been holding in. Get ready for an exciting night, Taylor."

She winked at me and when her eye opened again, their unusual gray color was now replaced with pitch black eyes. Before I could react, she disappeared.

A million thoughts were running through my head while I stood there in complete shock.

Allyson was a Catcher.

She's about to do something, most likely dangerous.

I needed to get to Galen, Sophia, anyone.

I began running through the woods faster than I've ever gone before. In my head, I was internally thanking Sophia for the countless hours of conditioning, making this journey much easier on my stamina than it would have been when I first arrived. However, with the darkness of the woods, I found myself getting lost. Each tree looked the same and after five minutes of going at a full blown sprint, I paused to take a break.

Seriously, Taylor? You finally get the truth out of this thing and you get lost. You finally do something good and you're already turning out to be an idiot.

Then I heard a frog croak. Looking around, I was able to make out a slight glistening through some thick foliage and when I pulled it back, I saw the familiar view of the lake we've spent so much time in. From there, I knew exactly where to go to get back to the common area.

The second I took a step, the sirens went off just like the other night.

Either someone knew Allyson was a Catcher or another had broken in.

———————

DUN DUN DUNNNN

AND HERE WE ARE, FOLKS. The climax of the story is now happening! Chapter 32, the one that is my favorite, will be out this Friday, so prepare for that :)

So question of the chapter: Thoughts on Allyson? Thoughts in the chapter? I know a lot of you called it and there's still more to come with this story :)

As usual, thank you SO much for all the support! We're at a constant #6 spot, (WHICH IS SO AMAZING) so if you guys want to do me a solid and push that star button, that'd be great. I'd love to make it higher in those charts before this book is finished and sharing your love for this story through voting/commenting/reading helps so much. If you REALLY want to make me happy, you'd drop a comment (or more if you roll that way) below!

See you THIS Friday for the next chapter!

Chapter Thirty-Two - The Invasion

I f you can't see chapter 31, please log out and it should show up!

I followed the familiar route to the school but I heard the fighting before I saw anything. Screams were now beginning to echo through the dark woods, making me jump from any sound that seemed too close to me. But I never stopped, I continued trekking forward, making sure to move anything out of my way before I reached it, and sprinted on.

When I made it through the last of the trees, now in the common area with the surrounding campus lights, I stopped dead in my tracks. I was frozen, completely shocked by what was happening.

Around me there were Supernaturals, my peers who I lived and trained next to, fighting dozens of Catchers. There was blood, pain, and all the elements being thrown around. I resisted the urge to pinch myself, wishing that this was some sort of vision or, better yet, a nightmare, but I knew it wasn't. I didn't know what to do, what to even think, besides the feeling of raw hatred run through my veins for Allyson.

Suddenly, an explosion went off to my right, throwing me to the ground as a cloud of dirt covered the air.

My vision. The one I had a few weeks ago, this was it.

I should've told someone, anyone, but no one could have thought this was going to happen.

I got up, not bothering to brush anything off of me or check for injuries. There was screaming all around me, but I couldn't see any faces through the dense smoke and dust. It was a mess of all the elements, fighting while I stood in the middle doing absolutely nothing. Completely frozen, in shock.

"Taylor!" I heard a familiar voice yell at me. "Get the hell out of there!"

Cole came bursting through the smoke just before blasting some fire at a Catcher that had immediately appeared to my right. I didn't even realized that he finally used my true name as I snapped out of my daze and held the thing still, making it easy for Cole to kill it off.

"Are you crazy?!" He yelled at me once it dropped to the ground. There was dirt covering his face, a growing red spot on his right side of his shirt. Other than that, he looked okay and didn't seem like it fazed him. "You could've gotten yourself killed!"

"I don't--"

He ignored me and the smoke cleared just as several other Catchers made their way on us. One of them, a Water, tried to nail me with strong jet but I put my shield up just in time. After stepping out of the stream, I held my hand out, and forced them back at an incredibly fast speed until they hit the side of the building, falling down to the ground either unconscious to dead. I couldn't check, there wasn't time or a care left in me.

I was able to sneak a peek at the rest of the field of battle, seeing the bodies of both our enemies and my own kind of the ground. I felt sick as many of these people were kids taken from their lives to train and control their powers. We were all forced into this world, being told that our families were in danger if we were to stay, but it turned out that we were the ones truly at risk of dying, even here at a place of so-called refuge. Everyone, with the exception of the instructors whom I also saw on the battle lines, wasn't fully trained. It was like releasing a professional on a middle school wrestler: Someone stronger and obviously more trained. Catchers were stronger and faster and if they had been preparing for this, which I knew they were, Katherine had to have them skilled as well.

And, of course, Allyson helped them pick the perfect moment. Her whole facade of being a poor, innocent girl worked well and she was able to deliver information to Katherine. They chose this day and time because everyone was out and happy, having a relaxing time that was so rare around here. She picked the time she knew would hurt us the most and we were all too dumb and late in realizing her true motive here. She hid herself well, even fooling Galen, but how?

When Cole and I finished off the last of the Catchers actively pursuing us, he grabbed my arm, "We gotta go!" He yelled. "The cellar, like Galen said!"

My first instinct was to pull against his grip, but I failed miserably as he continued dragging me. "What? We can't just leave them to fight! They need our help!"

"Galen said--"

"Galen never anticipated this, Cole! We have to fight!"

He didn't listen to me and even used the precaution to surround me in a veil of fire so I wouldn't get away easily. When we finally arrived at the cellar door, he threw it open, making sure no Catchers saw, and pushed me in. Further in was the more secure door, just as Sophia said, and Cole's fingerprint easily let us inside. He bolted everything shut when we got in as I realized we were the first ones here.

I sprung forward the moment he relaxed, trying to get past him and out the door to go help everyone else, but he grabbed me by the hands. I struggled to get out of his hold on me, but he was too strong. Above, I could hear the sounds of fighting, of Supernaturals losing their lives up there, but I couldn't help. I had to sit back and listen to it all happen while I was safe down here all due to my standing in this war.

"Let me go, Cole," I glared at him, still trying to shake him off of me. "This isn't right. They need our help!"

"I can't let you do that," he answered, his jaw set as he looked at me. His arms still held mine tight to my sides, keeping me in place while I continued to attempt to get away. With every shake, his grip would tighten to the point where it hurt, but got the job done.

"So you're just going to sit back then?" I seethed, my blood boiling in my veins. "Hang out down here like a coward and listen to our people die because of us? I know we're in the Big Six and dying out there would result in an automatic and easy win for Katherine, but I can't just be down here while they're fighting. We're supposed to be protecting them, not the other way around!"

Cole looked defeated and deep down I knew he wanted nothing more than to go up there and fight as well but he was following the orders of Galen. However, she must have only anticipated one or two Catchers breaking in, not a full blown invasion at one of the easiest pickings of the year. "Taylor..." He started. The usage of my name surprised me but the emotion and pain in his voice concluded that this was not a time for all those nicknames. "You have to remain safe."

"Safe?" I ranted on. "I'm the last thing from safe here. Am I not strong enough? Too weak to even support myself in a fight? I'm sorry I'm not like you and I haven't killed tons of Catchers and won dozens of fights, but I need you to let me do this!"

I was pulling every move I could: The weak link, the Big Six, everything that could potentially get him to let me go, but nothing was working. He took out a shaky breath, his arms struggling to keep me still. I continued to fight because even if I couldn't be out on the battlegrounds now, I would keep on trying until I was. He knew me too well and positioned my hands in a way that prevented me from using my power to get away. When he started losing his grip on me, he pushed me against the wall, holding my hands there with the extra leverage. He finally looked me in the eye and quavered, "I can't let you go up there."

I was so angry, furious even, at them breaking in, at Allyson's stab in the back, at them coming at the time where everyone was out. It was a good day, a rare thing around here, and this ambush had to ruin it. In my only form of release from this awful emotion, I took it out on him. "You're a coward, Cole," I spat and I saw anger flash across his face.

"Taylor..." He warned. I could see the rage in him growing with each passing second and struggle of mine.

"You're weak. A sad excuse for a Supernatural. You can't let these people fight this war for you. Let me go up there!"

"I can't do that," he replied through clenched teeth.

"And why not--"

He cut me off with a kiss.

To say I was surprised would be the understatement of the year. Immediately, all thoughts of resolve and war left my head and I was consumed by the kiss, by Cole and his lips. Throughout the months of me being here, time seemed to go by much faster than it did before Supernatural Abilities. There was a tension between us that was waiting to burst and in this moment of fear, need, and the unexpected, all of our held in emotions exploded. His hands left my wrists to trail down the sides of my body before grabbing my waist, pulling me closer to him while I kissed him back. My hands made their way to his hair, mingling with the strands, while our lips moved in synchronization. He was everywhere, everything, and in that moment, despite all the pain and anger of the situation, I only thought of him.

And when he pulled away, his forehead still rested against mine as we caught our breath. My heart was beating rapidly in my chest while I looked into his dark eyes that held nothing but longing.

"Does that answer your question?" He finally whispered, breathing deeply as his fingers squeezed my waist where he still held himself close to me.

"I--I..."

The cellar door opened, making the two of us jump apart while Claire and Alex came stumbling in. Immediately, reality washed over me.

Of course I'd be the girl making out with an incredibly attractive boy in a cellar while we were under attack.

Damn sexual tension.

"Thank God you're okay," Claire ran over, engulfing me in a hug. "We were with Cole when it started but he broke away from us to look for you. I, just... I don't know what to think right now. This is all too much."

"I know what caused this all," I muttered, pulling away from her embrace. "I'll explain once when everyone gets here."

Claire nodded and looked between the two of us. If she was reading our minds, she didn't do anything to reveal the fact that she knew about our kiss just seconds ago. Instead, her eyes focused in on Cole's growing wound and she jumped over to his side. To be honest, I had completely forgotten that he was hurt and it's not like he acted like he was when we were fighting earlier.

"We really can't have you injured right now," She told him. "Shirt off, let me heal you."

There were no sexual innuendos, no jokes about stripping, and he did just as she said. Alex and I hung off to the side in silence, the weight of the situation digging into all of us. Besides a few scratches along his body, he was otherwise okay. I didn't know my condition, I was too worked up to check right now as I heard the screams continuing from above.

I didn't try to escape out now with three people on one because there was no use. I wouldn't win and I'd just hurt everyone in the process. I was stuck down here listening to everyone be hurt or murdered in this all out massacre.

They knew what they were doing, the Catchers, Katherine, and Allyson. They used our weaknesses against us. I don't know what their goal was today, either to kill those in the Big Six now or later, I don't know, but it involved hurting dozens of people along the way. My only hope now was that as many teammates as possible would come running through that door.

And sure enough, Will was the next one to come, followed by Mackenzie and her roommate, Jenny. The girl immediately ran over to Cole who was undergoing a slow but sure healing process from Claire. Apparently he was hit in the side by a rock that a Catcher had thrown at him, creating a large gash. When he caught my eye, I immediately turned away with a light blush spreading across my cheeks, thinking about what had happened earlier.

Leona eventually made her way into the cellar alone, wielding her own share of battle wounds as she came piling in. Now that everyone in the Big Six was accounted for, we were only missing Galen, Sophia, and whoever else had clearance to this room.

And sure enough, as the cries from above quieted down, Sophia and a few others came storming in. Despite our mutual hatred of working together, I was happy to see she was okay. I didn't want to know what it looked like up there.

Of the faces Sophia brought with her, they were all familiar; two instructors, Leona and Mackenzie's, and very surprisingly, Vanessa. For someone who was so victorious with her final exam today, it's awful to see how the excitement all ended.

And then I heard some cries from behind the instructors. Peeking around, my blood ran cold when I realized who it was.

"You," I seethed and sprung towards Allyson. Before I could lay finger on her, Cole grabbed my waist, forcing me away.

"What the hell, Taylor?" Claire exclaimed, rushing towards Allyson to swing an arm over her shoulder in comfort. "It's been a hard day as is. There's no reason to freak out on her--"

"She's a Catcher!" I growled. "She's the reason why all of this happened! She's a mole who used our weakest time of the year against us!"

Everyone around me looked at me like I was crazy, but when my eyes caught Sophia's, she was looking suspiciously at the traitor. She stepped forward, inspecting the girl. I noticed the familiar glint of her getting into her mind before a great power radiated off of Allyson, blasting everyone at least ten feet away.

Then she began laughing, a sickly sinister cackle. "You two are smart," she grinned at my instructor and I. "But you caught on too late."

I rubbed at my head where it had pounded into the wall. Because Cole had been holding me the time she hit us with her power, he took most of damage and groaned from beside me.

"What's going on?" Mackenzie asked, her yellow eyes scanning Allyson up and down, as she shakily got up.

"She's a Catcher," I repeated my words from earlier, standing up to prepare to fight. "She's been pretending to be one of us, finding out all of our information to report to Katherine. I saw her eyes, they were all black. That's how she did so well during her test today. She has that extra strength."

Allyson began laughing again, her eyes focusing on me. Their unusual gray color made sense now as it hit me: It was all a mask. Their true color was hidden underneath a manipulation.

"Oh, Taylor..." She started. "How you wish to be right, but you're not."

That's when her eyes changed again, but not to the black. Instead, it went to the rainbow of colors that I knew so well. I froze, immediately losing all sense of fight in me as I watch the girl whom I had known for months now grow, her hair becoming longer and darker, her skin developing into a pale, ivory shade.

"You were right about me pretending, but I'm not some Catcher..." She told us all, confidence radiating off of her being as my breath hitched in my throat and true fear settled in. "I'm Katherine."

DUN DUN DUNNNNN

Again, so many people called it, but it's finally out!! I'm so happy with how this chapter turned out and I've actually had certain parts written up for weeks now.

So I'll cut you a deal: Next week I'm going to be very busy preparing for a trip I am going on soon. If this chapter gets to 200 votes and 150 comments by Tuesday (My time, PST) I will post the next chapter early again! If it doesn't, which it might not because it's a pretty good goal to hit in a few days (it usually hits that in about a week or so), then I'll post on Friday as usual. I know so many of you hate cliffhangers, but this is an easy way to get the next chapter early, right? It'll help me and it would hopefully make you guys happy as well :)

So question of the chapter: WHAT DID YOU THINK OF THAT CAYLOR KISS? OF KATHERINE? THE INVASION? I'm going to be real with you, I am so proud of that kiss scene and I hope you enjoyed it as much as I did writing it! A couple of you guys didn't want them to happen, but let's be real... That chemistry was there from the first chapter and I won't let it override the actual plot.

Thank you all for everything and I hope you enjoyed this chapter as well :)

Chapter Thirty-Three - The Leader

Guys.... GUYS. YOU WENT ABOVE AND BEYOND WITH THE COMMENTS LAST CHAPTER! I cannot stress how thankful I am for each and every one of you so as a token of my appreciation and as promised, this chapter is early for all of you :)

Even more than the Catcher facade, this made sense. Her shifty eyes, her desire to know about my training techniques... everything screamed Katherine and despite seeing her through visions and in Sophia head, it was nothing like being in person.

Just her presence oozed power and control. Her stance was strong, as if she was looking down at some ants. I didn't know what to do and looking at the others, they felt the same way. As her eyes scanned the room, they only stopped when they found mine, narrowing in on me with a little smirk rising onto her lips.

I'm closer than you think.

My vision from a few weeks ago echoed in my mind as I gulped. Indeed, she was.

I expected her to fight and kill us immediately in that instance but instead, she leaned against the wall and began inspecting her nails as if she couldn't be more relaxed. "I've been pretending to be Allyson for months now, a little, tender girl."

"Was she even a real person?" I found myself asking as I struggled to keep my voice from trembling. "Or was she just some person you thought would be great to make up?"

"Who knows?" She winked while sarcasm was obvious in her voice. "Maybe she is, or maybe she isn't. I achieved her look through—"

"Body manipulation," Sophia finished, her gray eyes focused on the enemy. Of all of us, she's definitely had the most contact with her as she even broke into her home. "The greatest usage I've ever seen of it. You block out everything from us, your thoughts, voice, everything. You basically created a whole new person with a fake family and background and no one caught on."

"Oh, Sophia," Katherine drawled. "How I've missed your intelligence. I can't say that Grant feels the same way because he is now keeping me company."

The mention of her lover made Sophia grit her teeth together in anger. I remember Grant from when I got into her head, he was the Fire turned Catcher. When she jumped out to lay a mark on the Catcher's leader, Katherine held her up using telekinesis bringing her close to her face.

"Smart, but naive," She whispered to my trainer before throwing her against the wall in a heap.

"Why did you do this?" Leona asked, horror written all over her face and voice as she looked at Sophia. None of us dared to make a move toward her, knowing that we would most likely end up the same way. A collective release of a held in breath sounded through the room as she slowly began sitting up. "We're safe from the invasion but here you are, taunting us. If you were going to kill us, you would've already done it."

"To take out your line of allies," she answered as if it was nothing. "I enjoy this game, so you're right and I'm not going to kill you now. You must come to my home and challenge me, home advantage you see, instead of me pursuing all of you. After today it's obvious that you are all incompetent and even though it would be easy right now, I enjoy a challenge and I want one when our fight commences."

"So until then you're just going to mock us?" Cole huffed. "Belittle us however you want?"

Katherine shrugged. "I've had been doing it to Taylor for weeks before she learned how to block me out. It was fun watching her scramble around. When I couldn't do it as myself, I did it as Allyson. I even tricked her by 'showing' her I was a Catcher," she giggled as if it was the most hilarious thing ever. "Funny, right? I made you think I was one thing, but it turns out that I am way worse than any ordinary Catcher!"

I stared at her incredulously. I know this woman was hundreds of years old, but how did all this bring her joy? This wasn't some little prank. This was a full blown war where people were currently fighting for their lives right above us. This lady, this thing, thinks it's all a game.

"Well, Taylor?" She asked, raising an eyebrow at me. "Were you surprised?"

My anger got the best of me and despite knowing how stupid of a move it was, I did the same thing as Sophia and charged. Katherine only laughed, but actually went along with it and blocked my every move. She was very strategic, her rainbow eyes following and darting across my every move. But I continued fighting, giving it my all but I knew it wasn't enough. She had me beat to everything before I even had the chance to make it. Within a few seconds of me trying to land a move on her, she gave me an evil smirk and grabbed my hand, twisting it back, making me drop to the ground in pain.

"Tsk, tsk...." Katherine hummed, getting down at my level as she continued with her grip on me. "You need to make smarter choices, Taylor, or this will be all too easy."

With a single blow of air towards me, I found myself flying across the floor, hitting the wall just as Sophia did early. Lucky for me, my head was spared and my butt took most of the impact. Cole came rushing over, checking to see if I was alright. When he realized I wasn't seriously injured, he began charging at Katherine.

"No!" I cried out and grabbed his hand just in time to stop him, even projecting my power into the grip to help hold him back. Katherine looked at us in amusement, her tongue running across her teeth in thought.

"Interesting..." She mused, stepping forward. Cole was fuming as his glare was focused on our enemy. Not once in my time of knowing him did I ever see so much hate written all over his face. When her eyes landed on me, Cole stepped in front, blocking me from her view.

"Don't you dare touch her again," he warned her. My hand tightened on his wrist and I hoped that he wouldn't do anything stupid. If he was able to stop me from pursuing the fight above, I was going to prevent him down here from a battle that he would surely lose.

Her eyes scanned him up and down, a little smile tugging on her lips. "I wouldn't dream of it," she affirmed. "I see both of us take an interest in Miss Taylor Buckley over here, but perhaps in different ways."

Cole didn't say anything as his body still stood protectively in front of me, as I was still on the floor from when Katherine threw me down. She continued scoping the room, but not one person made a move to attack knowing what she could easily do to us. We were not ready for a fight and, thankfully, she seemed true to her word that she was giving us time. She was so cocky in this situation that anything we seemed to do just made her even more confident in herself.

"Now..." Katherine finally started, standing up straighter and wiping her hands off. "Now that this whole thing ended on the perfect note, so I'll be seeing you six around," She gave us a sinister smile and she disappeared into thin air faster than any of us could react.

The period after Katherine left was silent and tense, the sounds of the fights going on above us finally stopped. She must have gathered her ranks before she left, taking them all back to wherever they resided. Claire got up and rushed to Sophia's side, starting to heal a head wound that she just got from when Katherine hit her. The rest of us got up, but didn't dare leave this place not knowing if the fighting was actually done and what awaited us there.

My body ached with the blows that both Katherine and the Catchers had landed on me, but I didn't ask Claire for any help with it all. She needed to focus on the bigger injuries at hand before I was treated. Instead, I moved slowly, but eventually rose to my feet with Cole's help.

"We'll go back up in the morning," Mackenzie's instructor announced to us. Thankfully there was a clock on the wall, signaling that it was nearly midnight. "Rest up now because we might be in for it tomorrow."

The inside of the cellar was equipped with more than enough sleeping bags for all of us to create our own make-shift beds. Nonperishable food and water was passed around along with an elaborate first aid kit for any minor wounds. Claire was able to use her healing powers to help ease anything major, but she wasn't a fully qualified healer and couldn't do the entire job. Besides her, the only other person capable of doing that was Sophia who was still struggling with her own injuries.

Cole gathered our things and took it all to a secluded corner. However, in a place like this, nothing was ever really private. That included the toilet, only half a wall blocking it from the rest of everyone's view. People would take turns doing their business and changing into the clothing that was supplied here. They really did think of everything when this place was set up.

"We need to set up a guard schedule," Sophia muttered while Claire wrapped her head. "Two of us on at once, incase anything tries to break in."

And so went the schedule. It started with Mackenzie and her instructor, Will and Leona, Cole and I, Claire and Alex, Sophia and Jenny, and then the last instructor and Vanessa. The shifts would go for an hour and a half before the next couple would be woken up.

No one said anything as we all settled in. There was a sniffling in the room, signaling at least one person was crying. Me? I felt numb. This whole day was a nightmare and there was no telling what we would be waking up to tomorrow.

I pulled the sleeping bag higher up on my body, squeezing it in anger. I now understood why Cole wouldn't let me go fight, but it still didn't erase the fact that all the people up there had risked their lives or even died for us.

When I drew a shaky breath, Cole immediately picked up on it and pulled me to his body. I immediately turned red and was thankful for the dark room, besides the few lanterns surrounding those on watch.

"Thanks," I mumbled just loud enough for his ears only.

I felt his lips in my hair, kissing me where I had hit it. It was tender, but nothing unmanageable. "Of course, Taylor."

Of the months he has used nicknames ranging from Blondie to Sweaty, it was weird hearing him say my name now. I liked it a lot and it seems to have become some sort of sentiment to only be used in serious situations.

I didn't even realize that I had fallen asleep until Cole was shaking me awake. Blinking, I saw Leona and Will making their way to their own sleeping arrangements. Slowly getting up and stretching, Cole and I took watch by sitting on the bench resting against a wall. It was around three o'clock now and thankfully everyone had managed to make it to bed during a time like this. It was nice from escape reality, even if only for a few hours.

We were quiet at first, bored even. I caught myself looking at Cole quite a few times, his face illuminated by the lantern we had. When he would catch me staring, he'd only give me a little smile but wouldn't say anything.

"What do you think is up there waiting for us?" I whispered, not wanting to wake anyone.

"Bodies," he answered gravely. "A lot of hurt people, unless they don't make it through the night. I'm sure at least some Catchers are hanging back and waiting for us, but hopefully they'll leave tonight."

"This has been a mess..." I mumbled, my fists clenching. "If only I figured out that Allyson... Katherine, whatever, was one of our enemies, none of this would've happened."

"I don't agree with that. I think Katherine would've made this happen no matter what. She has the power to teleport and probably had Catchers staking out this place for weeks in case she was caught early. With one word, any of those things could've jumped in. Yes, she did pick the absolute worst time, but there would have been major casualties regardless."

I sighed, resting my face in my hands. "I just feel like I failed them. We're supposed to be the protectors, the ones who save everyone, but instead we probably have dozens of dead Supernaturals waiting for us up there."

"You know we had to come down here. This wasn't to start the battle, but to set us back--"

"I know, I know... Galen's rules and such, we need to be safe so that we can eventually win, I know. You kind of made me realize that when you--"

I stopped myself, now thinking back to our kiss. I felt myself turning bright red as I snuck a peek at his dumb, smirking face.

"When I what?" He challenged.

"Shut up, Cole."

"Done talking, Blondie? Funny, you also couldn't speak right after I kissed you--"

"Stop!" I had to stop myself from getting too loud and risk waking everyone up.

He chuckled under his breath, smiling at me. "It's still fun messing with you..." he mumbled. "But we'll have to talk about that eventually."

I ignored my stomach dropping as I immediately looked away, trying to make it seem like I was watching the area. Instead, I was hiding the look of pure disappointment of my face. He hated it. It was a mistake. It shouldn't have happened. All those same thoughts that occurred and were said by him following our almost-kiss back in the hotel room weeks ago.

"Hey." When I didn't respond, he bumped my shoulder. "Taylor..." he warned. When I continued ignoring him, he grabbed me by my shoulders and forced me to face him. "I didn't mean it like that."

"Like what?" I mumbled, playing dumb.

He gave me a little smile, his eyes focusing intently on mine. "I liked it. A lot. I've been waiting to do that for months now, but there are many things that we need to talk about before anything continues. That conversation will be for another day, when we're able to focus on it and not be distracted by this war that we're in."

I breathed out the air that I hadn't realized I had been holding in, feeling more than relieved that he actually enjoyed it as much as I did. "That makes sense," I replied to him and he nodded, putting his arm around my waist and pulling my body closer to his.

"I'm glad you can agree, Shorty. I knew that brain of yours was good for something more than just your powers."

I rolled my eyes at him because, despite being in a serious conversation, he still had to make fun of me somehow. But his words made me remember something. "Cole?" I asked.

"Yeah?"

"Why did you all of a sudden start calling me Taylor?"

"You know... I do realize that you have a name," he pointed out, sarcasm lining his every word. "I obviously saw it on your papers, right next to the part with your br--"

"But why don't you say it more often or before all this?" I interrupted him, not wanting to hear anything else about those God damn papers.

He thought about it for a second or two before shrugged. "Everyone calls you by your name, so all the nicknames I give you are special. Besides, we made a deal. I'll write you a book of everything I call you by the time we leave here. Now, that s a bit skewed with our positions now... so how about when we're free? When this war is over, you'll have a huge, long and loving list of all my adoring nicknames for you."

I held back a laugh, not wanting him to know that I thought it was actually pretty cute. "Oh, I totally can't wait."

"Your sarcasm isn't as endearing as you are but I'll let it go because it's your special day," he eyed something behind me and when his eyes caught mine again, he gave me a smile. "Happy birthday, Blondie."

Confused, I looked up at the clock to see the exact time of my birth. A year ago I was on the phone with Ryan, listening to him count down the seconds to this time over the phone as I laughed at how excited he was about it. Not once did I ever think that I'd be spending my eighteenth birthday down in a cellar, waiting out an attack from our enemies.

"Those papers do come in handy sometimes," He mumbled. "At least I was the first one to say it."

"You know... this isn't exactly how I wanted to celebrate."

"Me neither. I actually had a whole thing arranged," he rubbed the back of his neck. "I know you don't like parties, but I was going to come jump on your bed and--"

I stopped what I knew would become rambling by putting my hand over his mouth. "Even if that couldn't happen, I'm glad that I'm at least with someone I care about."

"Oh?" He replied after I pulled away. "Is that a confession, Brain?"

"In your dreams, Trainor."

The rest our guard shift was spent in silence, a few words being said here and there. It was nice just to be around him, in his company, because despite everything that had happened today, we were still here along with everyone else in the Big Six. We still had a chance in this war and Katherine wasn't going to win. There's no more messing around, complaining to Sophia, or anything. This means war.

"Time's up," he muttered once the clock ticked over to the next hour, signalling that our shift was over. Exhaustion sounded extra heavily in his voice as he yawned. "Let's wake up Claire and Alex."

When I got up, Cole didn't follow, but rather sat there blinking back sleep. "Need a kiss to wake you up?" I joked and he immediately perked up. Laughing, I shook my head and headed towards where our friends were sleeping. "I was kidding. You already got one today, so no need to be greedy."

When I reached down to shake my roommate up, I found that she was already awake, her eyes shining with happiness. From that one look, I knew she had heard our conversation about the kiss.

"Don't worry," she muttered. "I'll let Cole tell Alex when he's ready, but I'm glad at least one thing came out of today."

I gave her a smile of my appreciation and watched her get up, slowly pushing Alex so he could wake up as well. Cole and I said goodnight, and returned to our sleeping bags to get at least a few more hours of sleep in before our rude reality woke us up in the morning.

WE GOT TO THE #4 SPOT, WOO!! LET'S TRY FOR #3, YEAH??

If you guys didn't know, I'm actually going to start sending out query letters to some publishers/literary agents as soon as this story is finished! Maybe, just maybe, someone will like it enough to pick it up because publishing has been my dream since I was in elementary school. So, with that... question of the chapter: If this were to get published (which will probably not happen, but who knows?), who would pick up a copy?

IMPORTANT AND COMMONLY ASKED NOTE: I've officially finished this story and have barely begun writing the sequel which will be called, Catching the Catchers (same as before). SA will have 35 total chapters, plus an epilogue. The prologue of second book will be posted the same day the epilogue of Supernatural Abilities comes out, so you won't have to wait around for it to be posted!

And one more note: The next chapter will be posted on Friday as usual, but it might be a little bit later because I'm going out of town but it WILL BE POSTED!

Chapter Thirty-Four - The Aftermath

T he next chapter will be posted in one week, so next Friday/Saturday depending on your timezone. I'm super busy right now, so I can't do two uploads in one week :)

(PS: this isn't edited very well, so I'll go back and fix the mistakes when I have time!)

And thank you to @karenj345 for the name Colin Kroeker!

Everyone was woken up early the next morning. It was silent above us and throughout our group as we got everything packed up. Claire tended to more wounds now that she was better rested and Sophia was even able to help out as well. I was the only other Mind, but I hadn't even had the chance to try healing just yet.

None of us knew what we would be opening the doors to. I expected a lifeless battlefield, but hopefully there were some survivors that we could help out. If not that, then maybe others had gotten away. Above all, I hoped that Galen was around somewhere.

"Listen..." Sophia called out to us, motioning us to gather around once everyone was ready. "I don't know what's out there, but stick together. Be in groups at all times and stay alert. There is a good chance that there are Catchers still hanging around. Our goal is to find any survivors and then we'll decide what to do from there. We will split into three groups of four and search different areas. After an hour, we'll meet at the doors to the dormitories. Colin, can you pick the groups?"

Colin, Mackenzie's instructor and an Air, stepped forward and eyed all of us. "Group one will have Alexander, myself, Vanessa, and Jenny. Group two will have Taylor, Sophia, Leona, and Mackenzie. The last one will have the rest of you, Dakota, Claire, Cole, and Will. Any questions?"

Cole immediately stepped forward, "I--"

"This is no time for your boyfriend duties," Sophia eyed him. "You and Taylor are in separate groups, deal with it."

Cole didn't argue and stepped down, his lips pressed in a firm line. All of us began heading towards the exit, but he grabbed my arm to make me end up towards the back of the group.

"Be safe, okay? We don't know what's out there," he muttered to me, anxiety written all over his words and face.

"Same to you," I mumbled as Sophia opened the doors exiting the cellar, allowing a vast amount of light to enter.

Once we stepped out and after the sun had momentarily blinded us all, our surroundings were anything but welcoming. While I had personally been preparing all night for what awaited us, there was nothing that I could've done that would've made this moment easier. Around us were bodies, of friends and neighbors all marring the fatal wounds of battle. Dozens of them, all taken way too young. Granted, there were also the bodies of Catchers. Maybe even more of those than our own kind, but the loss of Supernatural lives still weighed heavily on all of us.

Mackenzie eventually made her way back to Cole and I and stayed closed, probably as a form of comfort. He never once questioned her pressing against his side as we continued forward.

"We'll take the arenas," Sophia muttered, pain clear in her words as she kept her head down. "Alex's group should focus on the woods, while Will's can stick around the common area. There doesn't look like there are any survivors, but please make sure."

Mackenzie then made her way to my side as she was in my group and had to leave Cole. She didn't say anything as we walked away with Leona and Sophia through the woods, making our way towards the arenas. We were quiet as we ambled on, sometimes passing by bodies which we would inspect before casting off as another fatality.

"In the past people would sneak out of the parties and do whatever they pleased at the arenas. I don't suspect many people to be down here, but since it's a ways away, it'll take us a while to check it all out and head back," Sophia told us, her eyes scanning the forest for any potential threats.

I looked down at Mackenzie and despite her need for comfort through being at our side, she was holding it together well. Her face seemed empty, as if slowly taking everything in, but there were no tears. I felt the same way. I hadn't completely digested all of this, but I knew it would all hit me soon.

We first started out at the basic training arenas, the one with four arranged in a square- like formation. There were the bodies of several Catchers, but luckily no Supernaturals around. Whoever had fought these monsters had gotten away and was hopefully on the run or hiding, rather than dead.

When we finally arrived to the main arena with no issues, the four of us began inspecting the area. The bleachers and the locker rooms were all clear with no bodies to be found. The last door was the one leading to a meeting room. When I opened it, my heart immediately dropped.

"S-Sophia..." my voice called out, as my hands began to shake.

My instructor came over and looked in, her breath immediately hitching in her throat as she overlooked the destruction that Katherine must have caused following her exam. They had met over here and despite the meeting they had planned, it ended in a massacre.

The faces of those who judged my placement exam lay before me, eyes open and empty. I hadn't personally known them, only knew of their standings and places at Supernatural Abilities. Well, all except one.

"Galen..." Sophia whispered, running forward and falling to her knees to clutch her leader's lifeless hand. "How could this happen? She can't be dead! She's the strongest one out of all of us!"

I initially felt remorse, tears welling in my eyes at the woman who had made me feel at home and important here. Similar reactions were settling on Mackenzie and Leona's faces as Sophia began bawling. The only other time I have seen a reaction like this from her was when I got in her head. Then, she lost her love. Today, she lost another important figure to her.

But my sadness then turned to anger. It was a boiling, red hot fury as my hand that wasn't by Mackenzie clenched into a ball, my nails digging into my skin.

"This shouldn't have happened," I hissed. "If it's a war Katherine wants, it's a war she's going to get. There's no time for messing around anymore. She's playing this like it's a game, and she needs to realize that we're a force to be reckoned with."

"Taylor..." Sophia's voice broke. I've never heard her sound so defeated before. "She's killed our leader. I don't know what we can even do-"

"You'll have to be in charge now," Leona answered while wiping away her tears. "

"But I--"

"There's no buts now," I replied, stepping forward to her. "Katherine has taken Grant and Galen from you. The only way to get her back is by leading us and making sure we're all trained enough for her. You're the only one with memory of her home and how she operated. Show us. Tell us what to do. Above all, train me."

"What do you think I've been doing this entire time, Taylor?" I could tell my words were getting to her.

"Not trying hard enough," I answered, my instructor getting up as the two of us faced each other head on. "Neither of us were. If you want us to kill Katherine, then we need to get along. You need to train me harder than you ever have before. Make me hurt, make me beg to stop. Train me like the Mind Big Six that I need to be because Katherine cannot get away with something like this again. She hit us where it hurts and now it's her turn to feel the same way."

Sophia look at me, her eyes still glistening with tears but much like my own emotions, anger at this situation now overtook everything. She gave me a proud look and held out her hand, which I returned with a shake. "Now, that's the kind of attitude that I want."

I nodded, grateful to now be, hopefully, taken more seriously and vice versa. In order for us to win, all of those in the Big Six needed intense training before Katherine makes another strike at us. I didn't know what we would be doing after this but with Sophia now in charge, we might have to make decisions as we go.

After concluding that everyone in the room was dead, we slowly left the arenas and slowly began our walk back to the dorms. Mackenzie had jumped ahead with Leona, while Sophia and I trailed only a few feet behind.

"You know, Galen was like family to me," she muttered to me. "I was never close to my real mom or anything and I've been here since I was a teenager. She thought I was talented and was even a trainer of mine who would take extra hours with me before she got the leader position that she was just in. She originally didn't want me to go spy on Katherine because we were so close, but I begged her just like you did to me. I don't think I'll ever be able to fill her shoes, but I do know that there's a lot hidden in her office that might help us out."

"We'll start there then," I concluded. "You don't have to take on the role all by yourself. We're all stuck with each other now and we can all help."

She nodded as we continued on in silence. We didn't pass anyone or anything new as we walked up to the common area. I found Claire trying to help out some people in very critical condition yet still alive, but I knew that that was beyond her healing capabilities. It wasn't like we could go strolling into the hospital either. Not only is nearest one dozens of miles away, but I don't think telling that this was done by a mutant breed of Supernaturals who invaded our home would go over well. Whoever was alive here either needed to be healed from Sophia or Claire's abilities or have to die.

The other group, Alex's, comes walking in front out of the woods. In his arms was an injured girl, battered and bruised, and Sophia immediately rushed over to help her.

The amount of bodies around us didn't come close to the amount of people at Supernatural Abilities, so I only hoped that they were able to get away. Where they would go, I have no idea, but with Supernaturals comes our abilities. Not only are they useful in fights with Catchers, but can also be helpful in terms of survival. Hopefully they realized that and are able to make it through before finding civilization.

"Claire's been trying on several people," Cole said, now coming up to me. "But they're too hurt to be fixed by us. They need a real healer Supernatural, one that specializes in it. She's good, yeah, but not a professional.

Many of the instructors were with Galen when they died, all victims of Katherine. The healers who resided in our hospital were either still locked away somewhere, not found by us and dead, hiding, or among the rest of the bodies out here. I've seen enough death today to not want to go out of my way and search for more.

I wish Sophia had taught me how to heal, rather than just offensive techniques. Illusion manipulation was a good tool to have, just look at what Katherine/Allyson did with it, but it's not very useful in a time like this. In the event that we're fighting together, I need to be able to heal my teammates in a time of need rather than sit back and watch like I'm doing now and have been doing all night.

Finally, Claire huffed out in anger and gave up. Will stepped forward and was able to give them an easy, painless death that took them out of their misery. Sophia was continuing to heal the other girl, who was in much better condition than anyone else here. Stepping forward, I didn't recognize her, but she was making painful noises as my instructor continued to do all she could to help her. After an hour or so of healing, she had done everything she could do and let the girl begin healing on her own. Many of her larger wounds were treated so she would survive, but would definitely be in pain for a while or until we can find someone who can help her even more.

The rest of us helped move her back down to the cellar where we would be having the meeting.

"We only found her in the woods," Alex nodded over to the girl who was now sleeping on a group of sleeping bags. "Vanessa said she recognized her, but she was quiet and didn't know her name. Other than her, there were only bodies around where the parties were. No other survivors."

Claire continued next. "Five were alive, but too hurt to be helped. Maybe Galen--"

"Galen's dead," Sophia continued, her voice dark and monotone. "We found her and the other officials where they were meeting Allyson after her exam. They were probably the first ones to go last night."

No one said anything as the realization that our leader, the one who has been helping us this entire time and had all the answers, was gone. It hurt and put us at a huge disadvantage, but hopefully there were some answers lying in Galen's desk, something to put us back on the right track.

"We need to go through her things. There's dozens of old documents and scrolls, those even talking about the Big Six. She never let me see them, but I know they're in her office somewhere," She announced to everyone. "Then we need to be on the road. We can't stay here anymore. There's nothing left of Supernatural Abilities besides us and whoever else is running."

"So what do you need us to do right now?" Alex asked.

Everyone's eyes were on Sophia as she realized that now we're all looking to her. I'm obviously not the only one who realized that she is fit to be our leader and right now would be her first form of action.

"Taylor and I will go to her office, the rest of you gather up as much food, supplies, and personal belongings as practical and we'll head out before sunset. Stay in groups, as usual."

Without a word, everyonefollowed her action as she nodded towards me with a look of determination.

WE GOT TO #3!!!! WOOOOOOOOOO

One more chapter (posted in one week, sorry!) and an epilogue and then it's onto the next. As said, I'm very busy this week, so it might take me awhile to answer any messages/comments.

Question of the chapter: Opinions on the chapter? Galen's death? Taylor's demand for better training? Sophia stepping up to take the leadership position?

As always, thank you so much for the support and I hope you enjoyed :)

Chapter Thirty-Five - The Safe

Sorry for this being late! I've been on vacation for the past week and came home to a long workday and an awful sickness, so I was too exhausted to edit yesterday. But here you go!

Sophia didn't allow me to do anything before she grabbed my arm, dragging me through the cellar door and to the outside. Like before, I avoided all the bodies as we headed inside the main building that held the office of Patricia Galen.

"Why'd you pick me?" I asked while Sophia forced the doors open using her power. "I know we just had a heart-to-heart but I'm sure you're still not a fan--"

"Besides me, Galen trusted you the most. She had so much faith in you and would get mad at how I was teaching you everything. Granted, she didn't know how much of a complainer you are--"

"Thanks for the compliment," I muttered and began pulling out some of the drawers of the desk. Sophia immediately went for the filing cabinets, gathering everything into a box.

"These are all the files for everyone," She told me. "Better to have them rather than throw them away."

I nodded, agreeing with her. I know it's the wrong moment to think about it, but I hoped I would be able to grab ahold of Cole's information so I could tease him about his just like he does with mine.

I found basic diagrams, training schedules, and a million other things, but nothing that would be of use to us. We searched for over an hour, through each and every cranny there and found nothing but information that would be useless to us at this point. Sophia groaned and collapsed in Galen's chair, putting her face in her hands.

"I just don't know where to go from here," she told me. "You all aren't ready to fight Katherine, but we can't continue staying here."

I climbed up on the desk and took a seat. "Has Galen ever mentioned any emergency policies or anything like that? Someone must have had been planning in case something like this ever happened."

"If they were, she never told me."

I huffed out, stumped and not sure what to do. It's not like we could waltz around just anywhere, flashing our handy powers out in public. We needed somewhere secluded, but also stable enough to support us in the middle of nowhere.

"They have to be here somewhere..." she muttered, her eyes scanning the office. "Something... Anything. She would always plan. It has to be in the same place that holds all the old artifacts about Katherine and the Big Six. She wouldn't let her plans stick around for anyone to find."

"Okay," I said as I started to get up. "Where should we look--"

When my feet hit the ground, a clanking, hallow noise was heard. The two of us looked at each other for a split second before we were both on our hands and knees, pulling back the rug that lined her desk. Sure enough, there was a small safe embedded into the ground.

However, this wasn't some ordinary safe. Instead of a lock, there were two handprints. Sophia looked at it in confusion and hummed, "Okay... this seems easy enough," she thought out loud and placed both her palms on the surface. After a few seconds, it beeped and showed a red light, signaling that it didn't work. Her eyebrows furrowed together in frustration. "Huh. There must be something around here that we can use."

She got up and began searching around while I stayed at the safe. For some reason, I felt like the answer was right there. If Galen was to hide hundreds of years in a safe, she wouldn't make just anyone get in. She would make it accessible to someone she knew was going to be here after a situation like this happened, someone that she could trust. Sophia, while she was Galen's second in command, wasn't guaranteed to survive following an attack. However, everyone in the Big Six would be and if we didn't, anything in this safe would be useless.

So when I put my hands on the scanner, I awaited the moment it would unlock, showing that the power of this war was truly in the hands of the Big Six--

Beep beep... red light.

I slumped down in defeat. I guess having a huge, internal monologue didn't solve every problem in the world.

That's when I looked closer at it and saw very tiny, minuscule holes that lined the marks where one's hands would be. Galen's words began echoing in my head. All the comments that she's say every time I talked to her.

Every compliment she gave me revolved around my power and how I was stronger than I gave myself credit for.

And when I put my hands back on the scanner and projected my power into it, I wasn't even surprised to see that the light showed green and unlocked.

I didn't waste any time in opening it. On top, there was a letter labeled clearly with my name on it. Confused, I snatched it right up and saw that there were others all written with the names of the others in the Big Six.

"You opened it?" Sophia asked, now taking notice that the door to the safe was now unlocked. "How?"

"Had to use my power," I mumbled as she began pulling everything out.

"I have to hand it to you," she started. "You might not be the most focused in training, but you're really starting to step it up and impress me lately."

"Gee, thanks."

She ignored me and rummaged through the countless documents. She carefully pulled out a box and opened it, showing me the inside which contained several old, wrinkled scrolls.

"These are the artifacts that called upon the Big Six and Katherine," She told me.

So these were the pieces of paper that determined my fate. "Can we burn them and act like they never happened?"

She gave me a look and gently closed the box, putting up on the desk for protection. "Funny, but no." She continued going through the papers, until she reached the bottom, where a single letter with the word, 'Emergency' written in thick, black letters. Sophia gently opened it and began reading it. Judging from her facial expressions, she was surprised by what was written.

"What does it say to do?" I asked gently once she put it down.

She didn't say anything and grabbed the landline phone that was on the desk, immediately dialing a number that was written on the letter. The call was answered within seconds.

Sophia didn't introduce herself or say anything besides a string of letters and numbers. "Code SA318DM." She was silent for a few moments before someone must have answered on the other line again. This time, she actually spoke normal words. "I'm Sophia Harley with Supernatural Abilities. Our leader, Patricia Galen, is dead following a massive invasion by the Catchers and their leader. Dozens of our kind and theirs is killed, with the prediction that some have ran away. On campus, there are thirteen survivors, including everyone in the Big Six. Anyone else within our grounds has been confirmed dead."

She was silent for a moment, the person on the other line talking. When her eyes widened, I raised my eyebrow, wanting information behind this conversation. Who was she talking to? What Supernatural would Galen send us to?

"Are you sure, sir?" Sophia asked now, her voice shaky. "Yes, we have enough cars to transport and I'm sure the cards have money on them. We can be there in a few days and we'll try to stay out of the public's eye. Thank you."

She hung up and took a deep breath, her hands trembling. "What happened?" I asked, my curiosity taking over.

"Turns out Galen was hiding another secret from all of us," She mumbled. "She's had this prepared for years. We're not the only ones who know about our kind."

My eyebrows crinkled together in confusion. "What do you mean?"

"The government knows about us and has for years. We have to go to DC where they have a special training area for us in case something like this happened. Galen's been working with them, so they know each and every single one of us by name. I've always wondered where all those files come from, but Galen would never tell me. I guessed it was from the police department or intense mind manipulation, but instead they've been keeping tabs on anyone under suspicious of having powers."

"So we're leaving tonight?" I asked, and she nodded in response. "Then let's get all of our stuff and go."

"That's not it, Taylor..." She mumbled. "They want us to destroy the campus, make it seem like some kind of disaster happened here so they can air it on the news and say there were no survivors. Make all of our families believe the lie, that we're supposedly dead, in case we actually do die in this war. They're covering their asses, making everyone lose hope of us and the others who actually did die coming home. We're going to become invisible to society."

My heart dropped in my chest. I was told that I could eventually go back and revisit my hometown, Ryan and even my father if he was sober enough to speak to. They already thought whatever lie a Mind had implanted into their head, but this will make it seem like I'm dead and never coming home again. If I did survive this war, I'd be coming back to nothing.

"Who's to say we have to do that?" I tried and Sophia just gave me a look.

"The director of the top-secret Supernatural division of the United States' government," she told me. "As appointed by the president." My eyes widened, not realizing just how serious we were taken over there. "Yeah, I know. Galen held in a lot of things from all of us."

We didn't say much after that and grabbed everything that Galen had left us before heading back to the common area. Everyone was now out, sporting bags full of personal belongings and supplies needed for our trip. Sophia gave them the rundown, earning nothing but blank, hurt stares from everyone around.

"Cole and Vanessa... You're going to need to burn everything down," she told them. "Make sure it looks natural, like some crazy forest fire happened but enough to erase the evidence of our kind being here. They're going to make this story seem like a normal school burned down and will be covering it, making it seem real." She gave out a fake laugh, "Who would've known... They do fake stories too," she finished sarcastically.

She then began sorting us into three different cars. Herself, Cole, and Colin, Mackenzie's instructors, became the designated drivers. Cole immediately grabbed me, Claire, and Alex to be with him while the others divided themselves out as well. The girl we had saved ended up being in Sophia's car, still unconscious.

"You'll be following me and we'll eventually stop for the night to get some rest. If you need breaks, switch with someone else in the car. There are at least two people capable of driving in each vehicle so take advantage of that." She then turned to Vanessa and Cole. "You two need to stop at various points while we exit and make sure everything is on fire. Demolish the arenas especially, those will tip people off that this isn't a normal school. Is everything else cleared out?"

Leona nodded, her face grim from everything that had gone these past twenty-four hours. For someone so joyful all the time, it was sad to see that even she was broken from this. "Everything that is important was taken. We grabbed all the food that wouldn't perish during the trip as well."

Sophia nodded. "Good..." She awkwardly rubbed the back of her neck, as if wasting time as she tried to come up with her next sentence. "I'm no Galen... but I'll try my best to make sure each and every single one of you guys is prepared. This is what she told us to do, and I trust her judgment more than mine. We'll make it through this."

We began quietly getting into the cars, Vanessa and Cole staying back. Claire and Alex climbed in the backseats, throwing all our bags into the trunk including the one that my roommate had packed for me with all my belongings. When Sophia gave them the go-ahead., we watched as the two Fires began incinerating our home, making everything catch fire and begin to burn. When Cole got back in the car, we began to drive, stopping every minute for him to climb out and set more sections of the land ablaze.

As we made our way out the gates of Supernatural Abilities, I looked back to see what had become my home for the past few months completely in flames. All traces of our kind, bodies, fighting, training, and all, were slowly being erased, as if we never even existed there.

———————————

And the last actual chapter of SA is finished! THERE WILL BE AN EPILOGUE POSTED NEXT WEEK. It will be posted on the same day I post the Prologue to book two, so keep an eye out for that! There won't be a wait time between books, so you'll be able to behind reading the second book, Catching the Catchers, next week :)

Question of the chapter: What was your favorite moment of Book one? What did you think about the secrets Galen hid and them all leaving SA?

Thank you all for the support and see you soon :)

Epilogue

- -

A bove is the cover to book two: Catching the Catchers! (Prologue now posted on my profile!)

———————————————

Dear Taylor,

I've written this letter every week since the day you received your Marking. While they all stay based around the same principles, each one must be revised to correlate with your ever-growing strength and power that you are achieving through your training. However, if you are reading this, then something terrible must have happened that has prevented me from being at Supernatural Abilities. That is why you have found this among the rest of the files.

While it is a travesty, please know that even if I am gone you are not at a disadvantage. Hopefully everyone in the Big Six is safe because without even a single one of you, we have already lost this great war. The importance of your safety reaches greater heights than anyone else's lives here. Without you, we will not survive ourselves.

In the weeks and months that you have been at SA, I've seen you grow much faster than any other Supernatural here. I know Sophia can be a rough instructor, but she has high expectations for you as she knows what Katherine is capable of. She has lived a hard life and is more similar to you than you know. Eventually, she will open up if she is still around following whatever event eliminated me from this situation.

You must continue training, even harder than ever before. Katherine is ruthless and unforgiving, but you're currently our closest link to her. You and Mackenzie are the ones with the upper hand in this battle and with time, you will discover why that is. With time, you will grow. And, with time, you will succeed.

This takes me to distractions. You're a young girl who had a bright future ahead of her and I'm sorry to have dragged you away from that. Leaving your entire life is hard, but you have to put that all behind in order to be successful. Your past should not affect you until you win. If Katherine is defeated, your life can go back to normal but until then, you need that separation.

The same goes with romantic relationships. I've watched you and Cole blossom since day one, forming a strong bond with each other rather quickly. However, distractions can cost you your life. In the battle, you must focus on your teammates and yourself, not solely on each other. The Big Six is a group effort and while you two make a great pair, any feelings will only hurt you eventually in battle. Katherine has a way of picking up on relationships like that, which is why she chose to hurt Sophia in the worst way she knew how.

You're too hard on yourself with your training, your past, and everything else. Even if you do not think so, Katherine and everyone else knows and believes that you're the strongest Mind out there. If she didn't, you wouldn't have been picked you and she wouldn't have to try to intimidate you by getting into your thoughts. While she plays tough, she is just as afraid of you as you are of her. She plays, but will not engage until she knows for sure that she has the advantage. You mustn't let her gain that and have her come to you.

You're very strong, Taylor, and I have stood by my judgment since the first moment you got here. Your placement exam was exquisite and I knew, right off the bat, that you were our Mind for the Big Six. You were a missing piece in the puzzle that I was trying to formulate prior to the Marking officially selecting you. I've held so much respect for you and your strength and hopefully you will eventually see yourself in the same way.

Supernatural Abilities, the Big Six, and everything else rely on you and the other five. You must train harder than before, be more confident, and focus or you will fail. I have the highest of admiration for you and I know that you will fill your shoes once you start believing in yourself. Even if you have nothing, know that you are so greatly admired.

Learn, fight, and win, my dear. I'll be rooting for you from wherever I am.

Sincerely,

Patricia Galen

Folding the letter back up, I returned it to its envelope and put it away so no one in this car would see it. They all received their own, but I wanted mine to remain just for me. Galen's words coursed through me, a wave of passion and anger hitting me like a rock. A few months ago I had been brought into Supernatural Abilities, starting a completely new and unexpected chapter in my life, but today marks the beginning of another.

I will train harder than ever before and take everything from Katherine just as she did to me. I was Marked into the Big Six as the Mind Supernatural for a reason and regardless of how many times she's degraded and weakened me, it was time for our enemy to see me as more than just some pawn.

I was ready to prove Katherine wrong and win this war.

―――――――――

And yes! Book one: Supernatural Abilities is completed! Book two, Catching the Catchers is also up with the prologue, so be sure to check it out and add it to your libraries so you can continue following Taylor's story :)

Question of the chapter... opinions on CTC's cover? Galen's letter? The book as a whole?

Thank you so much for your amazing support this book. I would LOVE if everyone could vote/comment, especially if you're a silent reader, so we can get this book even higher on the charts! I've worked very hard on this story and I'm so happy you all seem to like it :)

See you over at book two!

www.ingramcontent.com/pod-product-compliance
Lightning Source LLC
Chambersburg PA
CBHW071409200726
48294CB00002B/331